The Confessions Series ®
From Randall's Corner

Confessions Of A Fighter in Training©

Apryl Butler-Bennings

Prayer and Confessions Change Things

Confessions Of A Fighter In Training
Copyright © 2010 Apryl Butler-Bennings
Atlanta, GA

Library of Congress Control Number: 2016915518
Imagery Publishing, Atlanta, GA
ISBN-13: 978-1-940681-04-7
ISBN-10: 1-940681-04-9

Printed in the United States of America

"Never put a public face on a private fight."

Dr. Luke S. Hall
Lukeism

REFERENCES
The Holy Bible – King James Version, The Message Version
Pastor Andre' Landers – Higher Living Christian Church
Dr. Luke S. Hall – New Vision Christian Church

Special Thanks to the Confessions Team

Alice Alexander
Chris Quarles Branding & Design
Dream Publishing - Susan Blackmon
Irvin Productions
J. Z. Alex Editing - Juva Alexander
Lori Hanes
Maleka Watson
Raquel Pam Singleton
Scott Bennings
Sheneita Astin
Syreeta ShaNee
Weather Proof Designz
Willie M. Smith II

TABLE OF CONTENTS

Introduction

My name is Randall Washington. I am a fighter by profession; my fans call me Hooks. At Victory Church I am known as Deacon Washington, trusted head of security, my pastor's right-hand man, and his long-time friend. To my friends and family, I am Randy, RW, or Randall. My life overflows with what most people call success---a beautiful house, a showroom full of luxury cars, a closet filled with designer names, and all the other marks of fortune and fame. I am a faithful servant. Work and prayer are the twin pillars of my life. However, I feel empty. Something or someone important is missing. The question is, what or who? I pray someday God will lead me to the answer.

First Visit

Sunday

It is not yet light outside, and I have already sent Trevor Hunter, my pastor and my best friend, a text fortified with encouragement. I send a simpler text to my crew. Finally I blog an inspirational vitamin, before spending time with the Master.

You see, even though I am a fighter by profession—and not so long ago, a very good one at that—I choose to begin each day making sure I am in top spiritual shape. All the rest, I have learned, will follow.

As dawn is breaking outside, I take my time getting ready. Once dressed, I pull out of my driveway and head off slowly, collecting my thoughts. At church, I wait quietly in my office until my radio chirps, letting me know Pastor Hunter is pulling into the lot. Time slows the way it has of doing when something important is about to begin.

As I pace down the hall toward Pastor's Chambers, I know before even seeing my friend that he is ready--tie straight, teeth pearlized, hands parafinned and shoes gleaming. Together we have done this a thousand times, but somehow every Sunday seems like the first. My walk to his chambers, as always, reminds me of my walk from the locker room to the ring. My vision is tunneled, and my mind crystal clear. My heartbeat quickens. As I stride down the corridor, JJ, King and the rest of the crew stick close behind me. Behind the door, I hear Trevor praying softly.

The door opens. I step forward, hug my best friend and like always, I whisper in his ear, "You are on." He whispers those same words to me before each of my fights.

Just as we are all about to enter the sanctuary, my radio buzzes. Annoyed, I pause.

Whose idea was it to have these radios? Why do they always call me? There must be ten other deacons standing around and my radio is the only one calling.

I motion to Hunter to go ahead into the crowded sanctuary while I hold the radio close and speak quietly.

"Go ahead."

"Deac, we have an issue." It is the cheerful voice of Dexter Hall, who patrols the church's parking lot. "I am sending her your way. A first-time visitor. She doesn't want—or should I say, she absolutely refuses--to park on the grass."

"Send her through," I sigh, thinking to myself as I head outside, *Time to get my oils out. Hopefully, she will have gotten herself an attitude adjustment by the time Hunter finishes preaching.* I stand prepared for confrontation as I watch a six-series BMW pull around very slowly. *Great, I think, I get to deal with the problem visitors. I have to do everything around here.* I click the radio.

"Go ahead Deac," says Dex.

"Please tell me it is not the Beemer?"

"You got it. Just for you."

"And how did I get picked for this?"

Dex chuckles, "You are the fighter, right?"

"Please. I do my fighting in the ring."

"Well, this morning, consider the ring the parking lot. Try to stay off the pavement Deacon. I got my money on the honey in the BMW."

"Thanks," I shoot back. "I owe you. Believe me, there will be payback."

Why did I take this call? Technically, I was already in the sanctuary when my radio went off. I stand waiting to direct her. Granted, she does not look vicious; no, in fact she looks the exact opposite of vicious. Nevertheless, as I have come to learn the hard way, looks can be deceiving. When I have time, I will tell you about another woman in my life, a woman named…oh, never mind.

She maneuvers the car as I stand waiting patiently. She is either distracted or she is flat-out ignoring me. I decide abruptly that I simply do not have the energy today to deal with all of this attitude. I tap on the window. Instead of rolling it down, she opens the door.

I am thunderstruck. Her legs mesmerize me, given how close I am and how low the car sits. I cannot help but see her legs and thighs. I would have seen more—much more--had I not forced myself to redirect my gaze. Surely, she did not flash me on purpose. I just happened to be at the wrong place at the wrong time. On the other hand, the right place at the right time?

Washington, get your thoughts in order. The devil is a lie. Why would He put me on this mission? I swallow hard. I can feel my heat rising.

I touch her hand to help her exit the car. It is the softest hand I have ever felt. I pray mine are not sweating and that I will not stutter or say something stupid. Like an idiot I say, "Good morning beautiful, I am Deacon Randall Washington." *What a clown.* I escort her into the building while we continue to talk. She does not introduce herself to me. *What did that mean? Common courtesy requires introducing yourself back. Maybe she is vicious after all.*

I say politely, "Excuse me. I don't think I caught your name." She apologizes and introduces herself. *Did she say "Danielle Rose"?* I repeat to myself to make sure I remember it.

As she speaks, she extends her hand. For the second time this day, time slows to a standstill. I am surprised. Clearly, she is not accustomed to church, or she is unaware of the fact that here at church, we always embrace one another; then again, maybe she is such a business professional that she simply shakes hands.

Regardless, the hand she extends seems to confirm she is not interest in me. It says, *back off and stay in your place.* She is all about business, it says. Guys probably approach her all the time with weak lines. I am not about to humiliate myself by doing the same thing. As if I had game anyway, I think helplessly.

Even so, I feel the urge to step outside of my comfort zone. I look at that slender graceful hand. Shake it? That is so not my style. I actually feel the impulse to grab her hand and kiss it, but surely, she would slap me. I can tell from her body language that she is used to setting the rules. Therefore, I follow suit. After what seems like a too-long pause, I finally take her proffered hand and shake it. To my surprise, she squeezes my hand so hard it actually hurts. Without thinking, I start to shake the pain out. Finding myself engulfed in her presence, I cannot think clearly. My hand falls limply to my side.

What did she say when she introduced herself? Ms. or Mrs.? Neither, I decide. Now what? I see a ring on her left finger. Is it a wedding ring? Guys like me are not good at deciphering these things. Not that I have dated much anyway. However, I do have one hard and fast rule: Do not date, or approach a woman wearing a wedding ring.

I say, "Mrs. Rose," putting an emphasis on "Mrs." Most women, I find, will correct you if they are not married--more often than if you say it wrong the opposite way. I like the name Rose; it fits her. Sure enough, she corrects me.

"It's 'Ms.'," she says firmly. "But you may call me Danielle."

I am stumbling over my words. I need to say goodbye and walk away. Nevertheless, I continue to try to exchange pleasantries as I escort her to a seat in overflow. It is late, so the main sanctuary is packed. I decide that today, I will make a quick appearance in the sanctuary, then come back and sit in overflow. I desperately want to continue my conversation with Ms. Danielle Rose.

First, I steal outside to check her license plate. I need more information about this mysterious woman-- the one who shows up late Sunday morning at my church, demanding assistance in my parking lot.

I walk around to the back of her car and to my surprise; I see her license plate reads HUSTLIN. This has to be a guy's car. Maybe her boyfriend's. *Hustling. What does that mean?* Her ride is clean, sitting high, and chrome shining. The car is tricked out in a way not typical of girls. As I stare at the car, I realize it is not black, but rather deep purple. A man does not drive a purple BMW. Not unless he specifically orders it for his girl. She did not say whether she has a boyfriend. Nor did I ask. All she said was she is not a "Mrs."

How can I find out? What if I never see her again? What if she never comes back?

I reach for my cell phone. Not there–must have left it in my office. I race back inside. King stands like a sentry by the door, waiting. I motion for his phone. He hands it to me. Without a word, I walk back outside.

I quickly scan his contacts. I find my Vickie's name. As soon as she sleepily answers, I speak, "Vardo."

"Hooks, it is Sunday morning. One, I am asleep. Two, I am off duty."

"Okay, but get back with me in one hour tops, Vardo. I need you to run a tag number. Gather all the information you can get. How long she has been in Atlanta, how many kids, married, credit score, and background check. Whatever you can find."

"Who on earth is this mystery lady?"

"That is what I need to find out."

She laughs, "And why exactly should I care?"

"There are ten hundreds in it for you."

"Done!" Suddenly she sounds more awake.

"I need Facebook, Twitter, Instagram, the works. Who are her friends? Where does she hang out? When was the last time she flew, where and with whom? What is her blood type? When was her last cycle? Anything we can find. And Vickie--I need all this yesterday."

"You got it, boss," she says briskly, hangs up and rolls back over.

I call her right back.

"Hooks, I told you I'm on it. What now?"

"I am not playing, Vickie. This is urgent."

"Okay, okay. Why the big rush? On Sunday morning on the first day I've had off in a week?"

Because this is possibly my future wife, I feel like saying. "Because I said so."

I walked back in and hand King his phone. "Get on the horn," I tell him. "Call in a favor. I need to know who she is, every detail." I point out the door at the car. "I need you to have a tag number ran. No matter the cost."

With barely raised eyebrows King replies, "I have it covered."

"You are excused from the sanctuary until this is resolved," I add brusquely. "I will be back and forth between here and overflow. I'll have JJ and Keith with me."

This is not how I roll most Sundays, running around barking orders. However, I needed to know–I have to know--who this woman is. She intrigues me in a way I can neither explain nor deny.

I walk to the security room and switch the camera to overflow. I spot her at once, seated gracefully, her chin lifted, and eyes straight ahead. Feeling furtive, I snap several pictures of her, email them to myself, and head back to the sanctuary. As I pass, I steal a quick glance into the room. There she is, listening attentively. I quietly shut the door and call Vickie back.

"What now, Hooks?" I can tell from her voice that she still has not moved.

"Vardo. Get up now." I go back and sit through the rest of the service impatiently. After the prayer, Kings slips back to my side and discretely hands me a piece of paper. I unfold it and read:

D J Rose - HUSTLIN

Four other cars registered in this name

"And her address?" I whisper.

"A post office box," King replies. "I am working on the details."

It pleases me to see that the car is registered in her name. I need Trevor to preach a little longer. I have to get my courage up to ask her for her contact information.

I fidget with the paper. Fold it. Open it and fold it again. Finally, I put it in my jacket pocket. As the ushers pass around the offering plates, I hit on a plan–I will escort the money to security, then dash back to overflow and find her.

By the time I secure the offering and make it back to overflow, a quick check of the room confirms what I feared–she has left. That leaves a few moment before the benediction, at which point the whole place will empty out, and I will lose any chance of ever finding this woman.

I hurry back out into the hall and look right and left. No sign of her anywhere. I race to the door, which leads to the parking lot, and there she is, looking determined and composed in the deep-purple convertible, carefully pulling out of her spot. My first thought is to sprint out at top speed and catch her--but what then? What would I say? I stand there feeling helpless as I watch her drive away.

Upset, I reach reflexively for my phone, but just like before, it is not in my pocket. I hightail it back to the security room and summon the tape. Back outside, I catch up with King.

"The phone," I snap.

"You got it, Deac," he replies. Is that a smile playing on his lips?

I dial Vickie.

"Hooks," she says, sounding impatient, "What did I just tell you? This is my day off. Plus, I am in the middle of something. You need to chill. I'll send you what I have so far."

"Okay," I say fighting to keep my voice even. "Do it."

I run to my car to get my phone and stand like a fool staring at it as Vickie's email begins to download. How can a download take this long? I need to call my carrier and have a talk about the speed of this gadget. As I wait, another call comes to my radio. Thankfully, this time it is strictly routine; a little kid is separated from his mother. By the time I have gotten mom and child back together, I pull out my phone again and see that Vickie's email has finished downloading. The bad news is there is one listing after another for women named Danielle Rose. I will have to look at this again once I get home.

First, I return to my office and watch the tape I requested. There has to be more to her than this. So far, this is what Vickie has uncovered: Ms. Rose is an architect and engineer at a well-known firm—very impressive. Back in the parking lot, she made it clear she was not married--but what about divorced, a boyfriend, a baby daddy, or a balling boo? *What are my chances? I am a deacon and a retired boxer. Why would she be interested in me?*

I try hard to stay focused. I have never meet anyone who so demands my attention and astounds me. I confess, other parts of me are excited as well; but that is not the kind of thing I can express here on the church grounds, if you get my meaning.

I go home and without taking my suit off, I watch the security tape repeatedly. I try to wring out all I can from the blurred images. *What is the attraction?* Face it--from the moment she opened her car door, I was, for lack of a better word…hooked.

WEEK 1

I spend an incredibly long strange week just thinking of her. I feel like a stalker. I ride by every building Goggle says she designed. I ride by the building where she works and skim the parking deck looking for the deep-purple BMW. I cruise her neighborhood during the times of the day when I assume she is at work, although I cannot get past the security gate in front of the gated subdivision.

I cannot find enough information, no matter how much I search online for her or whom I offer to pay. I stayed cooped up in my office at the gym and at my house, stalking her via cyberspace. Except for my daily runs, I do nothing else all week.

I feel constantly hungry, but not hungry for food. More like desperate, to be truthful. A little more anxious this week than last. *God, please let her show up*, I pray. If not, I will be tempted to call her office. *Could I ask her on a date? What would I say? Do I invite her back to church?* I decide I have no other choice. I have to do what I have to do.

Sunday arrives, and I wait pacing the floor, looking from door to door, expecting her. No sign of her. Therefore, I do as I did the previous week, go back to the security room, where I scan every face. Clearly, she is not in the building. I feel miserable. A girl has stolen my heart with a simple, five-minute conversation, and I lost her. *Why didn't I talk to her more when I had the chance?*

After service, I radio Dexter Hall.

"Go ahead, Deacon."

"Dex, have you seen the lady who had the parking issue the other week?"

"Danielle?"

How does he know her name? "Yeah, Danielle."

"No, she wasn't here this week."

"Okay. If she happens to come back, you will let me know?"

"Hey, don't worry. She'll be back Sunday after next."

It is all I can do not to yell. "How do you know?"

"She told me she was travelling for the next two weeks, and promised she would be back in three weeks."

Here I have stressed myself out for nothing. You have not, Deacon, because you ask not. At least I know now there is a possibility she will show up again. This makes me smile. Suddenly, I feel relieved and happy. I have something to look forward to.

WEEK 2

The entire week I keep up my search to learn more about her. I have no idea what I am looking for. Finally, I call her office. I listen to her voice mail message for what seems like a hundred times. I am pitiful. It feels like what I am doing is illegal. *How did I let her slip by? What if I never see her again? How can I have been so dumb?*

This week, I prepare for Sunday service well in advance. I have a new suit made. My barber cuts my hair to perfection. I use my paraffin spa, and I work out hard every day to ensure my body is better than merely presentable.

At last, it is Sunday morning. After an early run, I send out today's inspirational text to my crew and the deacons. Then I send a different message Hunter. I don my new suit, and take my time driving to the church.

After we finish the Meeting of Preparation in Pastor's Quarters, I wait as usual with the other Ambassadors as Hunter finishes getting dressed. I catch his eye.

"Pastor, I need to talk to you."

Hunter looks up, surprised. "Is this business or personal?"

"Both," I say, and pause.

I see Trevor's eyebrows go up.

"Uh, mainly personal," I stammer. "Kind of business. Church business, but strictly personal."

Everyone in the room, including the crew, looks confused.

"So let's talk," Trevor says. "Here or somewhere else?"

"Here is good." I do not have the patience to wait while we debate about locations.

"My office or yours?"

"It does not matter."

"Then yours it is."

We proceed to my office. Hunter takes a seat. JJ, King, and the rest of the crew know me well enough not to intrude. Suddenly exhausted, I plop down in my chair. I feel out of breath. I do not know where to start. Hunter removes his spectacles and waits patiently.

"Tre," I say finally, "I am in a predicament."

I can tell by his expression that my pastor is praying for the best, but preparing himself for the worst. All he can see right now is that I am in a state. A state he has not seen me in for a long time. He knows I am human, and fully capable of falling, just like anyone else. Even so, I feel confident that whatever I say in this conversation, he will not force me to step down from my deaconship. He takes a deep breath. "Go ahead, beloved."

"Come on, Tre. Call me Hooks. It is not that serious."

"Okay," Hunter says, looking relieved.

"Do you believe in love at first sight?"

Hunter slides to the edge of his seat. "What?"

I ask the question again. I see him thinking, *Is this really what he wants to discuss?*

"Where are you going with this Hooks?"

"I met a girl."

I can tell Hunter is caught off guard.

"Oh, yeah?"

"For real."

"And?"

"And I cannot stop thinking about her. Night and day. Day and night. It is crazy."

"Why do you think it's crazy?"

"I am riding by her house. Her job. All the places I think she frequents. Like a stalker or something."

"That certainly does sound like stalking. How does she feel?"

"She does not know," I say.

"So why are you riding by?"

"Do you want me to just pop up at her front door?" I shoot back.

"Why can't you call her?" he asks.

"See, here is the deal. I have hardly even spoken to her."

"What are you saying?" Now Trevor looks truly concerned.

"I just met her. Here, at the church."

He cuts me off. "Oh, no you do not. Not in my church."

"What?" I frown.

"I will not. I do not. I won't condone it."

"You did not let me finish."

"There's no need," Trevor says, shutting me down.

"Give me one good reason why."

Trevor spins his wedding ring around his finger, indicating the reason.

"Minor technicality," I say.

"Minor?" Trevor yells.

"Yes," I say, wanting to believe it myself.

"The hell." Tre slips out.

"Watch your mouth," I snap, thinking, *now I will chasten you.*

"You need to rethink this nonsense, Hooks."

"You had no objection until I said I met her here."

"Oh, I had an objection, all right; you just didn't give me time to express it."

"Like what?"

"The same objection. It will never change." Trevor touches his ring. "Plus, I am not coming to bail you out of jail for stalking."

"Could someone really have me arrested for stalking?"

"Look at Mike Vick, TI, Wesley Snipes. Do you want to be the next example?"

"Come on, Tre. You are my best friend. Help me," I say. I know I am starting to sound desperate.

"Help you do what Hooks?" he says as if talking to a contrary child.

"Guide me. Tell me what to do. What to say? How do I approach her? How do I get her off my mind?"

"Easy. You say, *hi, my name is Randall Washington. I am married, and I have been stalking you.*"

"Trevor, for real. Do not be my pastor right now. Be my friend."

"Divorce your wife, and then I will tell you how to woo a love interest."

"God knows I have tried to settle this divorce. What do you want me to do?"

"Hooks, I'm staying completely out of this."

"I am sorry," I say. "I cannot let you do that."

"Hooks, you sure know how to make it hard to be your friend." Tre sighs and leans back in his chair. "Do you realize how many underage groupies I have fought off on your behalf over the years? Do you know how many female members we have in this church, just because you are a champion boxer? And how about fielding all those phone calls, all the mail, the gifts, the emails the church gets on account of you," he says, shaking his head. "Plus, who do you think checks your fake voicemail and email here?"

"What can I say? Being your friend ain't no cakewalk either, Tre. It has certainly crossed my mind to ditch you, too. Who in their right mind wants to be friends with a pastor? Except when they need a special prayer, a baby dedication, a wedding ceremony, or a funeral? Who wants to be judged all the time, for every word that comes out of their mouth? Believe me, you should take my friendship as the rare gift and compliment that it is."

Trevor looks like he's about to say something sarcastic. His face hardens. "If you were not a boxer, if we were not at church, and if I weren't a pastor, I would punch you right now."

"Now you know how I feel about you at this moment."

"Get a divorce. Then holler back at me," he snaps, getting up, walking out and slamming the door behind him.

I call after him to no avail. I get it; he wants no part of this.

After service, I drive to the house in silence. There, I do not make any calls or turn on the radio. Instead, I look at all of the stuff I printed out about Danielle Rose; finally, frustrated, I set the papers aside. I promise myself not to look at them anymore today. I lie on the bed trying to ease my aching head. Hunter and I do not fight often, but today we surely did.

Slowly, like the deep pain in my head, it hits me: *Tre is right, much as I hate to admit it. The fact that I am still married to Tameka is what is holding me back. I need to cut off all our remaining ties.*

I need to get this divorce, no matter the cost. It is time to move on, and be done with this heartbreaking chapter of my life. There is no way I can tell Danielle Rose I am still married, even though Tameka and I quit loving each other a long, long time ago. Danielle would run in the opposite direction as fast as she could. I need to resolve all of this, and soon.

***

Pastor Hunter was troubled. He went home and spoke to First Lady about the day's events. Next, he went to his prayer closet and prayed. His conversation with his friend lay so heavy on his mind that he could not concentrate.

As he prayed, he considered what Gabby said to him, seated on the sofa opposite him in their living room, gently holding his two hands in her own. He turned over in his mind what his friend Hooks confided. He understood both their perspectives. However, as a pastor, he was bound to counsel his friend to behave decently.

There had to be some way to discuss this firmly yet gently. As First Lady pointed out, Hooks needed a companion, a soul mate. Perhaps it was time to take the pastoral boots off, at least for a while, and put on the Air Force Ones. This was no dress-shoe situation.

"Hooks is like a force of nature lying dormant for years," Gabby had said. "The man is long overdue to start living his life again. Why, Hooks he has everything a man could ever want, dream of, or desire-- except for love." Moreover, just as Gabby said, love was the most important thing of all. Hooks asked him for help. Surely, it was his obligation, both as a pastor and as a friend, to provide it.

***

Lying in bed on cool Egyptian cotton sheets, Hooks tried without success to close his eyes. Over and over, he stared at the picture he downloaded of Danielle Rose. Surely he was nuts. Hunter was right. This was insane. He did not even know this woman.

Sleep loomed like a faraway planet. He lay wide-awake, his head aching, until at last, feeling defeated, he got up and forced himself to do a long, hard work out. Later, in the wee hours of the morning, he decided to ride by Danielle's house. He wrestled with himself, trying to resist the temptation. However, he felt as if he had to see if the lights were on, and if the cars in the driveway changed positions.

Did she have a gentleman caller? It was a Saturday night. Sitting in the dark in his car, he glanced around nervously—for all he knew, she could be coming in any moment from a date or a girls' night out. On the drive over, he decided to try to slip through the security gate behind another car. Once there, Hunter's stern warning—"I will not bail you out of jail."-- rang in his ears. Now, there could be no slipping inside tonight. What a wasted trip, he thought bitterly, turning his car around for home.

WEEK 3

Sunday

Hooks laid out his Sunday best neatly on the bed. Then, seated at the oversized, carved desk, he sent out the usual emails, texts, and blogs, after spending personal time with the Master. He dressed carefully and left earlier than normal. He felt oddly refreshed, even though he had not slept in days.

At the parking lot, he gave Dexter strict instructions. "When you see Danielle's car pull up notify me. Have her park on the pavement, even if that means in Hunter's spot--I will deal with him later if need be. Tell me which direction she is headed, so I can be at the door before she enters. Are we clear?"

"I am clear that my magic worked."

"Meaning what?"

"Meaning I will send her your way. Keep your radio on," Dexter replied cheerfully.

Next, Hooks instructed King and JJ: no disturbances today. He would entertain Danielle Rose alone. No one–neither man, woman, boy, nor girl—would be granted even a minute of his attention. He glanced at the clock on the wall; it was fifteen minutes before the hour. At five before the hour, he rose, and was walking toward the parking-lot door, nervously straightening his tie, when his radio buzzed.

"Go ahead," he said, working to keep his voice steady.

"Coming up on your left, Deac," said Dex.

"I owe you big time."

"I'll dance at your wedding."

"I will remind you of that when the time comes."

Hooks watched anxiously as Danielle approached the door where he stood waiting. The glass was tinted; he could see out, but she could not see in.

There at last was the woman he had been stalking. The woman who banished sleep from his nights. He felt uneasy and excited all at once. *Act the gentleman*, he told himself. He opened the door and, remembering their previous conversation, purposefully addressed her incorrectly. "Glad you could join us again, Mrs. Rose."

As before, she corrected him. "It's 'Ms.' But remember, I already said you can call me Danielle," she smiled. "It's nice to see you again as well, Deacon Washington."

We are obviously playing word games with each other, he thought. *What does this mean? Is she interested? Is she available?* Confused, he escorted her to a seat, and nervously sat down beside her. Her presence was overwhelming.

All through service, he sat fidgeting. He simply could not hold still. He drank in her fragrance. He did everything imaginable to avoid looking in her direction. He counted light bulbs. He counted rows, aisles, and people, anything to keep his mind occupied. He stole glimpses of her out of his peripheral vision when she was not looking in his direction. One time she caught him, all he could do was smile helplessly.

Focus, Randall. This is not what you are here for. Pay attention. This is the house of the Lord. He felt his chest tighten, his lips and hands begin to prickle and grow numb. *I am actually hyperventilating,* he thought frantically. *I have to get some air.* He touched King to let him know he would be right back. He exited through the side door, and stood gulping the hot summer air. He could not stay gone long. Someone would come looking for him. He had to regroup.

He re-entered. The offering was being collected. He took his place in front of the sanctuary, his back turned to her. His forehead and palms felt sweaty. He took the heavy offering plates back to the finance office to be counted. Never had he wished more to stay behind closed doors.

He returned to his seat just as Hunter began the benediction. To Hooks' dismay, pastor instructed his congregation to "hold your neighbor's hand." *I should have thought of this,* he thought in panic. *Of all the days for Trevor to pull this.* The benediction ended, but Hooks, having taken Danielle's hand, found he could not let go. He tried desperately to get his thoughts together. *I have to talk to her.* His mind halted. There was nothing to say.

Then Hunter's voice rang out. "Now, I want you all to hug your neighbors," boomed the pastor's voice. *I know he did that on purpose,* thought Hooks in confusion. *We have not hugged our neighbors after the benediction in a month of Sundays. Why is Hunter doing this? Is he trying to trap me? Surely, he knows this is her. Typically, I would be seated among my crew, with no need to hug anyone. This was taking me far out of my comfort zone.* I thought, *I should escape while she is hugging the person to her left.*

As he moved, he found King blocking him in. Hooks looked up. Tre was all smiles. *He knows exactly what he has done.* As soon as he shot an angry look at Hunter, he felt Danielle turn toward him. *Nothing to do now but hug her.*

Danielle gave him a true church hug, firm but modest, as if to make clear she was neither available nor interested. He was so nervous he did not care. All he wanted was to be free of this awkward situation.

However, as he moved again to escape, Danielle dropped her purse. Always the gentleman, without thinking Hooks reached down to retrieve the items at the same time as Danielle; suddenly they were face to face, their two heads almost touching below the seats. Close enough to kiss, he realized. Their eyes met. *God, what are you trying to tell me?*

Hooks looked away as he hastily scooped up her things. He could see clear down her top. He wrenched his eyes away, re-directing his stare to her beautiful feet, clad in expensive, peekaboo heels. Like an idiot, or like something Randall Junior would say, he heard himself say, "Nice toes." *That had to be the lamest line ever.* Immediately, he felt embarrassed.

JJ cleared his throat. Right on time to save me, thought Hooks gratefully. But this time when Hooks stood up, King shot him a suspicious look, as if it occurred to him this must be the Danielle Rose Hooks ordered him to research. "Everything all right down there?" King said, checking Hooks' face and protectively mean-mugging Danielle.

"Yes," Hooks snapped, willing his friend to shut up. He looked up at Tre; as Hunter's face was wreathed in smiles, as if to say, *Caught you! You are so busted, my friend!*

Excusing himself, Hooks exited the sanctuary and ran directly to the water fountain, then to the men's room. He unbuttoned his jacket, loosened his tie, and splashed his face with water. Composure restored, he exited the men's room.

Are you serious? Lo and behold, there in the hallway was Danielle Rose, coming straight at him. *Why was she over here? God, what are you trying to tell me? I am not getting it.* Not knowing what to do, he decided he had to do something. No way could he let this lovely creature walk past without speaking to her.

"Ms. Rose, you look lost."

She smiled. "Oh, not at all, Deacon Washington. I decided to buy a CD of last Sunday's sermon." *This too was odd. How did she miss the bookstore? She had to pass it. God, are you making this possible, or am I reading too much into this?*

"Well, Ms. Rose, you passed the bookstore."

"Thank you, Mr. Washington," she replied evenly. "Perhaps you could point me in the right direction." For some reason, this struck him as hilariously funny, although he was too anxious to laugh. *Right now,* he thought, *laughter is exactly what I need.*

Hooks walked her to the CD counter in the well-stocked church bookstore, debating on whether to break in line, or to stand with her at the back of the line, to make sure he could continue the conversation with her.

Other passers-by, most of them good-looking, well-dressed women, crowded around and acknowledged him. He prayed silently:

please do not let anyone call me Hooks. Thankfully, no one did. The looks the women were giving him--you would have thought he was sleeping with all of them. Mostly to get clear of them, he decided to break the line. Besides, it would be bad hospitality by making her wait. Better to beg forgiveness from those behind them later.

"What will it be, Ms. Rose, a tape or a CD?" he asked.

"A CD," she said softly, her breath warm in his ear. *She must never whisper to me ever again,* he thought. His body temperature rose. He knew King and Keith were close by, observing. Right now, he could not acknowledge them.

Still breathing into his ear, "No one buys tapes anymore."

At last, he let himself laugh, and felt himself able to speak--but this time with confidence instead of anxiety. "Beautiful *and* funny," he said aloud, as if to the room at large.

An older woman standing behind them smiled, while the woman behind the counter–the one who has tried for years to get his attention—shot Hooks an angry scowl.

"Eight dollars, Deacon," she said curtly. *Is she flirting with me, or sending a warning to Danielle?* Either way, he did not like it. He gave the counter woman an expression he hoped said, *stop it.*

Time to pull your hands out of your pockets and pay up, fool, he thought. That was the last thing he wanted to do. He could feel his hands were starting to shake and sweat. What's more, he did not want everyone around them to see how much cash he was holding in his money clip. Nor did he want Danielle to get the wrong idea, the notion that he was some kind of baller. He was not trying to impress her.

Still, given what he knew about her so far, he did not think she was the type to go after a man just because he had money. *But who knows? No one wants to fall victim to a gold digger.*

With the precision that comes of years of practice, he flipped a twenty off the stack in his pocket and handed it over, just as Danielle started to rummage in her purse. To his chagrin, he saw the bill in his hand was not a twenty, but a one-hundred dollar bill. Careful to turn so he was facing Danielle, he pulled the money clip out. Better to take his chances with her seeing his wad of cash than the others in line or the scowling woman behind the counter. He knew their motives all too well. Danielle, he decided, had none.

As he handed over the twenty, Danielle seized the moment to make a fuss.

"No, no, please, Deacon," she said. "I can get that."

"Beautiful, funny, and independent." he shot back, smiling at her.

What happened next was humiliating. Ignoring his attempts at gallantry, she proceeded to pull out her Black American Express Card, and presented it triumphantly to the cashier.

She probably thought that was cute. But it was all wrong, he thought angrily. *No way in hell, I am going to let a girl outdo me. She is not going to pay for her own CD, even if that means I have to buy a hundred of them. It would be a total disrespect to my manhood. Not to mention, I would be sending the wrong impression to the vultures, cougars, and pythons behind the counter and in the line.*

Be yourself, he thought. *Enough with the niceties.* He snatched her credit card and the CD, dropping them both in her bag, and escorting her out of the bookstore. For the second time that day, he thought to himself, *I will beg for forgiveness later.*

This was the moment to speak his mind, not let it slip away as he did the first time. "Enjoy," he said. "But please, do not insult me by offering to pay again. If I decide to give you a gift, please do not refuse. That will hurt my feelings."

"I can buy my own gifts, thank you," she said coolly. This woman is a piece of work, he thought--and still he had not gotten her telephone number. He motioned to the crew to stay back. He did not need them right now. *I get it. She can buy herself anything she wants.* Her job as an architect with the renowned Atlanta firm, her reputation as one of the best in the industry, even her rides--told the same story. Her proud carriage and posture confirmed it. The Centurion Card she flashed proved she spent over $250,000 annually.

So yes, she could raise the bacon, slaughter it, bring it home to the house she built, and fry it in a pan. *I do not eat bacon,* he told himself. *So none of this applies to me.* Sure, she had her own stacks. She did not need his. This also showed she was not someone looking to see what she could get from a guy. She had her own established career. She would not be out to get him. She was much too ambitious to be a balling baby mama.

Before he knew it, his anger cooled, and he was walking her to her car. He motioned again to the dogs to stay back, cease, and hold fire. This was all so out character, he thought. He keenly felt that all eyes were on him. *Believe me, I am cognizant of the fact that I am walking beside and talking to a beautiful woman. Is that completely unheard of for me?* He hoped all of them could read his mind, especially Trevor, whom he saw was now standing in the vestibule with JJ. *Since when does he do that? He should be in the sanctuary; my territory is the vestibule. Why is he there? Is he spying on me? Jerk!*

Hooks' attention snapped back to his surroundings. They were almost at Danielle's car. He had to delay her. This was not the time or place to ask for her phone number. He needed to keep her there to lead the conversation back to that point.

If they had been anywhere else, he would have had the courage to ask outright. But here at the church in the parking lot? It was not right to be so bold. *This is so far from my normal character*, he thought. *Who would have ever thought I would be scared to ask a girl for her phone number, much less be stalking her?*

In desperation, he said the first thing that came to mind.

"So, Ms. Rose, tell me about your car."

"Mr. Washington, I can honestly say I love this car," she said gaily.

That surprised him. He was not expecting the word "love." *Wow,* he thought, *she likes automobiles just as much as I do.* It was not every day that a chick rode like this. It was not a girlie ride by any means. Yes, it was purple, but so dark a purple you could hardly tell. He knew it was a custom color from the registration King researched.

There were more surprises.

"Do you want to know why I love this car?" she asked, smiling at him.

"Why?"

"Because of the speed." *A girl after my own heart*, he thought. *I knew nothing about her. Nothing more than what I paid people to find out. However, I love her. If I do not love her already, I will surely come to love her, someday very soon.*

"So, Miss Beautiful Lady with the fast car, are you going to take me for a spin?"

"Of course. It is a date. But only if you call me Danielle."

Any fool could see that this was my cue. *Get this girl's phone number! Make the date!*

For reasons he could not discern, once again his courage evaporated. He continued to make conversation, trying to find the right opportunity. He could see the crew watching him closely out of the corner of his eye. He ignored them as best as he could. The magic moment came and went. All he could think to say was, "Will I see you next week, Danielle?"

"Maybe," she replied, with a look he could not interpret.

He did not have a comeback; they said their goodbyes. He watched her pull off, unsure if he would ever see her again, furious with himself for having failed to get her phone number.

He turned and walked back to the church, determined at least to complete his duties as a deacon. With any luck, he could at least avoid his treacherous pastor, he thought. Then Trevor caught him as he was coming out of his office.

"Deac."

Hooks looked up wordlessly.

"So?" Trevor asked in a probing tone of voice.

"So what?" *Trevor, stop being a jerk.*

"Who was the lovely lady?"

"I think you are fully aware, that is Ms. Danielle Rose."

"Nice whip."

Hooks' head snapped around. *Why, had Trevor been sitting at a monitor watching them, as well as hanging out in the vestibule spying?* Even so, he decided that now was not the time to confront his friend. Not here in front of a crowd.

"It's a nice ride for sure," he answered.

"So what are you going to do?"

"Pray that she returns next week, that I am divorced by then, and I have the courage to ask her out."

"Good luck," Trevor said.

"Which part?"

"All of it."

Hooks finished up at the church and drove back to his house. That is how he always thought of it--a house, not a home. For it was not a home. True, it was immaculately clean and well furnished. It looked like the house of a successful man, a man with good taste and the means to live well. However, there was something missing.

All afternoon and through the night, he felt distracted. He pored over the downloaded documents, the ones listing Danielle's many accolades and honors. *Why didn't I get her number?* He berated himself all night. When he grew tired, he threw himself into another hard workout, thinking, *Beat yourself up mentally, then kill yourself working out.*

All he could think about was Danielle. Exhausted at last, he lay in the bed looking at the ceiling, his thoughts cloudy, filled with Danielle Rose.

WEEK 4

I try all week to avoid asking or paying anyone to gather any more information about her. I make it for seven days straight without stalking her. Instead, I agonize over our next conversation. What will I say? *Hi, I Googled you and found out where you live and work*. Or, *I paid my crew to locate you*.

Should I hire a private investigator to get her cell phone number? Surely, it will be easier to wait and ask her myself. Plus, hiring a PI seems like asking for trouble. It is a long, tough week. About the only thing I manage to do successfully is think of her.

By Saturday I am worn out, exhausted from my mind racing day and night. Not to mention, I have been working out as if I were preparing for a fight. My body feels sore and bruised. If by some miracle, Danielle should appear in my room and talk to me or touch me right now, I think to myself, I would be too exhausted and too sore even to appreciate it.

Hunter keeps after me all week, trying hard to make sure I stay sane and on the right track--two things I am not at all certain about myself. The truth is I feel stuck. I confide a lot in Trevor this week. No different from what best friends always do, but different for me, because I have never had such strong feelings to confide before. We hang out mostly at my house. Thus week Trevor put the cloth down, so to speak, and acts solely as my friend.

It is perverted and lustful, but I am also having dreams about this woman I still do not know. It feels as if I am fighting my own mind, my body, my soul, and my flesh, all at the same time.

One morning, Hunter rides out with me to go see my divorce lawyer. We spend several tedious hours waiting in the cool, air-conditioned law office waiting room, trying without success to arrange a meeting with Tameka's attorney. It is a frustrating way to spend a day. But I know in my heart Trevor will continue supporting, listening to all my feelings, thoughts, and emotions, as long as I keep trying to deal with this divorce baggage first. Whether I want to admit it or not, Trevor is doing and saying all the right things. Instructing me to be wise is not just the cloth talking; it is my true friend speaking. He would say the same thing even if he were not a pastor. Honestly, if the situation were reversed, I would, too.

One afternoon as we sit and talk, Tre makes an observation: "You know, Hooks, she doesn't appear to be the type who would holler at you even if she finds out you are married anyway." He is right. I do not think she would. For a moment, I actually contemplate telling her. Quickly I decide that surely this is the Enemy devising a plan.

How can she not already know? All she has to do is Google me. If she had, she would have instantly discovered as much about my life as I have about hers. In a way, it shows she is not interested. She would have Googled me after our first encounter, and found out I was a married man. So the truth may be that she neither knows nor cares who I am. To her, I am merely a deacon at the church.

Either way, I convince myself the right thing to do is to wait until this business is settled between me and Tameka. The last thing I want is to be involved in a scandal. I do not want anyone--especially Tameka's attorney--to think I am doing wrong. I am not trying to have my cake and eat it too. As much as I hate to admit it, I have to wait. If this is God's will, Danielle will still be around and available once the divorce with Tameka is settled.

Is she available now? I do not know the answer. As badly as I want to know, it is best I do not. I should stay away from her altogether. Out of sight, out of mind. Right now, I have bigger battles to fight.

WEEK 5

Sunday

I wake up early, feeling refreshed as I prepare for my run. The long, hard run kills my body but relaxes my mind. After I shower and cool down, I take my time looking at my suits and ties before making a decision. It is that time of year in Atlanta when it is so hot, so steamy and tropical, that Trevor does not require us to be suited and booted. Despite the allowed dress code, I normally stick with a suit and tie.

However, today I am thinking of wearing something more casual. I am halfway dressed when my gut tells me to change my clothes. I study my options carefully, then pull out my favorite suit and tie.

I steel my resolve: under any circumstance, will I initiate conversation with Ms. Rose today. If she happens to be in my vicinity—well, then I will be polite. Otherwise, it is in my best interest to stay away from her. I decide against hanging out in the vestibule. Best to stay in the back occupying myself.

I call Trevor and tell him I will be with him all morning, helping him get ready. That is something I have not done in a long time. As usual, King arrives promptly to pick me up, and we ride together in comfortable silence. Once we unlock the church, I head directly to my office, where I sit quietly, alone, reading the newspaper, answering my usual flood of emails, texts, and blog responses.

So far, so good. Then JJ calls to say Hunter is pulling up. I drop everything, and race to the door facing the parking lot, so I can be ready when Trevor pulls up to his spot. Lo and behold, to my shock, Danielle is standing at the door when I open it.

Are you serious? Really? Come on, God. What are you doing to me? I said I was going to stay away. Why is she here this early? This looks all wrong. It makes me look desperate. To be honest, that is exactly what I am — desperate.

I quickly run the 23rd Psalm in my mind. *The Lord is my shepherd. I shall not want. The Lord is my shepherd. The Lord is…* common courtesy dictates I address her. There is no way to avoid it.

"Ms. Rose," I say, "such a pleasure to see you this morning." Next, I do the only thing I can. I reach out to hug her. Somehow, that goes wrong. She does not reciprocate with the same church hug she gave me last week. This is a hug like no other. It is body to body. This one hug confirms all of my nocturnal emissions. This time there is no mistaking the message she is sending me, and my body answers back instantly, sending an urgent message that I am afraid she can feel through my trousers.

I can see Tre coming in the door, which distracts me from the physical problem which is quickly arising. Again, he is all mischievous smiles. *The jerk. What are friends for?* He gives me the man hug, and whispers, "I thought the plan was to avoid her. You may need to check yourself," he adds, in an acknowledgement of my all-too-visibly enhanced body part. At that moment, I am to powerless to respond. Of course, Hunter does not stop there. He puts on his best pastor face and turns to address Danielle.

"Good morning," he intones graciously. "I am Pastor Hunter."

"Good morning," she says smiling, introducing herself, and thankfully paying no attention to my compromised physical status.

Hunter extends his hand. "Danielle Rose. It is such a pleasure to make your acquaintance." Then he hugs her—to make a point, of that I am certain. However, Danielle does not seem to get the message; and of course, she does not hug him the way she hugged me. As far as I can see, she does not actually touch him. It is more like a hasty lean-in, lean-out kind of hug.

"I will be waiting for you in my chambers," he says to me. "Nice to meet you, Ms. Rose. I feel wonderful things are in store for you here," he adds as he walks away.

Trevor manages to escape without giving me eye contact. As he moves, JJ steps in behind him, and both men take off. I feel a little breeze on my face. I breathe in, and smell Danielle's perfume. It mesmerizes me. I am like a vampire to blood. This is going to be much more difficult than I imagined.

"That is a lovely fragrance you are wearing today," I say.

She responds warmly. "Why, thank you, Deacon."

I was leading her on, trying to keep her talking. However, my compliment is sincere. For some crazy reason, her simple reply makes me laugh hard. Whether she knows it or not, she is making my day.

We head for the sanctuary, jesting and bantering with one another. Her statements are non-committal, and could be taken either way. I take the bait, and start throwing out my best "come-on" lines. I remind myself that I am supposed to be avoiding her today; instead, here I am, delivering weak lines minutes before Sunday Morning Service. I am clearly beside myself.

Luckily, we are approaching the sanctuary doors. This saves me from making any more mischievous comments. I am supposed to be with Hunter this morning. The last thing I want to do is subject myself to his scolding. Therefore, I walk her to her seat and take a place next to her.

I watch her for the entire service, at times secretly, at times openly. It is impossible not to. During service, I feel myself getting the once-over by every member of my crew as well as by, of course, Hunter, looking down from the pulpit.

It hits me that not only did I completely fail to get with Hunter as planned before the service—worse, after the collection of tithes, I failed to go to the front of the sanctuary and take the money back to security. Who covered for me? I have no idea. Instead, I sit and whisper comments about the service in Danielle's ear. I smell her fragrance, so tantalizing. After the benediction, I turn to her and say softly, "Wait for me by the door to the parking lot."

As I leave the sanctuary, I think, *is this all a big mistake?* No matter. I race down the hall to security and check the cameras. To the surprised high-school kid whose job it is today to watch the screens, I point at Danielle's image and snap, "Keep this camera on her at all times. If she so much as picks her nose, I need to see it. Once you shut the cameras off, send me a copy from each. Plus, footage from the front parking lot all the way to the back lot." He nods, knowing enough not to ask questions.

I get myself together and head back out to look for her. She is not where I asked her to be. I go back to security to find her. I spot her on one of the cameras, close to the overflow. I cannot tell what she is doing. I race back down the hall towards overflow, and there she is. Before I know it, I am touching her hand. *Inappropriate,* I tell myself. *You are completely out of line, and you know it.*

She confirms my thoughts. "You certainly are being forward today, Deacon," she says with a smile.

"It's my nature. I have to be," I sputter, thinking, *being forward is required for my profession. It is who I am.*

Our conversation progresses rapidly. It is flirtatious on both of our parts. Actually, I am completely nervous. I laugh a lot to camouflage my nervousness. When I do not know what to say, I laugh. Honestly, she is funny; she makes me laugh. Yet beneath the kidding and the joking around, I feel she is sincere.

Somehow, we end up talking about the word "submissive." At this point, she says something that tells me all I need to know.

"I will not submit to anyone, ever," she tells me. "I am single and living a good life. Why would I submit my will to someone else's?"

I think to myself, *Single. That is the only thing I would change about you.*

What I say to her next sounds crazy, even to me. "Danielle, I believe you have met the man who is going to be your husband," I say. "You may not realize this yet, but I am telling you, marriage is in the works for you soon."

For a change, she is speechless. I know it was wrong for me to say something so bold aloud. It was not in the order of God. However, I said it anyway. I knew without any doubt that I would one day marry this woman. At that moment, I claimed her as Mrs. Randall DeWayne Washington.

I think I see a hint of fear in her eyes. The last thing I want is to frighten her away. Without meaning to, I have turned our conversation to high-intensity. Before Danielle can answer me, one of the members who speaks to me every week interrupts us. She is a lovely older woman in the group we call the Wise Saints.

"Good morning," she cries. "You and your wife both look beautiful. And you coordinate perfectly."

We both look at her, pleased but bewildered.

"The gray and pink looks so nice on both of you," she goes on.

We look down at ourselves and then at each other. It is true--we are dressed alike. I have not noticed until now. I am wearing a gray pinstriped suit with a pink shirt, and a pink and gray paisley tie. She is wearing a soft gray skirt and a beautifully tailored pink jacket.

I look her up and down and say, "See, they already think we are married. Let's do it. Then all your worry about submission will no longer be an issue."

She does not reply. Instead, she catches me off guard with what seems like a random question--one I would have preferred not to answer.

"Randall, there's something I need to know. Are you a Deacon, or are you part of the church security?"

No need to lie, I decide. "I am a Deacon," I tell her, "but I also head up the church's security." She does not ask, nor do I tell her, that I work security for the church chiefly because I am a professional fighter. Feeling a little lame, I start going into details about the security system. Anything to avoid the uncomfortable topic she seems not to want to address.

We start exchanging flirty looks again, and I feel as if our conversation is back onto another track. Another older woman walks by and congratulates us, as if we were young newlyweds.

"My, you two look perfect together," she says. "Fresh off a magazine cover."

I smile at Danielle. "See, that makes two people saying the same thing in the same ten-minute period," I tell her.

I cannot stop smiling at her. Now all I need to do is make it happen, I think. Of course, there is still one huge dilemma, the one Tre keeps needling me about. Suddenly, I feel more determined than ever to handle it. Now I have a reason to finalize. I have to get my game plan in motion.

We continue walking, our hands barely touching. I escort her to her car. I know the crew is watching me. I do not know if the call is legit, or if they think they are rescuing me, but my earpiece buzzes. I make my apologies to Danielle and take off. This time, the timing is not good. I prefer to keep talking to her.

I decide I have to go back and entertain the crew. They all demand to know why we were laughing so much. I can be honest with the guys, so I confess. We discussed some hard questions, I tell them—a woman's place, a man's duty, and even our future as a couple together.

Seeing the astonished looks on my crew's faces makes me stop and think about where my life is about to go, and about what I have to do now.

I finish church business and ride home feeling massively confused. I have all of this information, and this feeling, but none of it fits together yet. I think hard and long for most of the night. If I am waiting on Tameka, I decide, this divorce stuff may take a lot more time than I originally bargained for.

WEEK 6

I struggled all week. I wanted to see Danielle; I needed to see her. I hardly knew her, and yet I adored her. It made no sense. My behavior worried everyone around me as well--Trevor, King, JJ, my attorney, Tameka, Vickie, and everyone else. Nobody wanted to bother with the love-struck fool, which was I.

Sunday

I decided I was going to do what I did not do last week, namely, lay low and try to stay out of sight. I did an excellent job. For better or worse, I successfully avoided Danielle, and had no idea whether she arrived or not. I refrained from calling Dex, my man in the parking lot. I did allow myself to request a tape of the service, thinking I would watch it during the week. As Tre gave the benediction, I was feeling proud of myself. I knew I could do it.

By the second service, I felt full of energy, not nervous like at the start of the first service, or for that matter all week. *I have to let Tre know,* I thought proudly, especially after the way he has been ragging me lately. I was back to the old Deacon Washington. No one could stop me, not even the devil himself.

There we were, all the deacons lined up outside like we always do for the second service, greeting, shaking hands, and giving hugs. It was a beautiful Atlanta morning, clear blue sky with a soft breeze. When all of a sudden…you guessed it. The Devil jumped out. What was the movie starring Denzel? *Devil in a blue dress.*

I watched as she approached. What was she doing here now? She has never attended the second service before. Why was this happening today?

To be honest, I was overjoyed, but my heart was racing. There was no way I could turn and walk away. I clicked my earpiece and directed some desperate whispers. Surely, somebody around here must need me. My whispers went ignored.

My radio remained silent. Danielle was quickly coming down the sidewalk with her heels clicking and her face hidden under an oversized hat with a beautiful satin bow. To run away at this point without acknowledging her would be unspeakably rude.

I did the only thing possible. I stepped out in front of the line. I could hear the door behind me open as King and Keith's feet hit the pavement, both of them finally responding to my distress calls. *Too late, guys.* I motioned both of them to stay back. King sized up things at once, and let out a big laugh. I was afraid Danielle would notice and feel insulted, but she seemed unaware.

"Inside voice, please," I whispered in my earpiece, praying the crew would refrain from embarrassing me even more. Not that I needed their help. I was embarrassing myself just fine on my own.

"Ms. Rose," I said breathlessly as she approached.

I could not read her expression. She did not speak, but instead shook my hand—one of those hard handshakes I took to mean, *Stay in your lane.* I had the urge to arm-wrestle her right then and there. *These are the strongest hands in the state of Georgia*, I thought, *hands that are lethal and licensed to kill.* And here comes some girl named Danielle Rose who thinks she can put a vice grip on my right hand, which happens to be insured for more money than Iron Mike's hands used to be. *Nothing about a rose should be deadly*, I thought. *Everything about her is dangerous.* Just think how toxic, destructive, and disastrous a spell she placed on me all week. As if crushing my hand was not bad enough, she then proceeded to crush my feelings.

"Good morning, Deacons," she purred, pointedly including everyone but me in her glance.

"Are you clowning me?" I ask.

"Enjoy the service," she replied, again seeming to address everyone except me.

I was appalled. One of the other Deacons, a stout fellow who probably did not get noticed very often by beautiful women, managed to gulp: "Now *that* is what I call a beautiful hat."

Danielle, smiling, threw up her hand as if to say, *what, this old thing?* I could not think of a single comeback, and before I knew it, I heard the click of her heels as she strutted away. I spun around, took a step, and grabbed her around her slender waist. Without thinking what I was doing, I spun her around and in the same motion, I hugged her hard, the same way she hugged me last week, body to body.

"You look beautiful as always," I said softly as I embraced her. "Why are you late?"

"What are you saying? I am not by any means late." She spoke carefully, stressing each word. "I am actually early."

"I was expecting you at the first service. This is not your hour," I explained, letting her go and trying to organize my thoughts. It was true—just when I finally thought I escaped temptation, she caught me with my guard completely down. I could see she took my words to mean something else altogether.

"Oh, now I see, Mr. Washington. So I take it this is the hour for your wife to attend services, or maybe your girlfriend?" Her voice was cold as ice.

To recap thus far: she started with the Kung Fu Grip, and then went dead into the jab punch. This was one fight where I could not respond with my hook, if you know what I mean. I was still trying to get to know her better and coming back with a hook would erase any chance of that happening. Much better to be honest and go with the truth. I decided to tell the whole truth, and nothing but the truth.

"You don't ever have to worry about that," I told her. "What's more, you are the one who looks like my wife."

At that, I had to laugh. Maybe more like smile. Either way, I showed all thirty-two, then went back in for what I hoped would be a sweet knockout punch.

"Since we managed to dress alike again, why not call me next week and give me your color scheme? That way I can stop racking my brain trying to figure out what to wear."

To my relief, she smiled. "Oh, I believe I can do something for you that's even better than that," she said.

This was getting to be too much. I felt blindsided. Wow, could this woman flirt. "Too many ears," I whispered, looking around. "We need to go."

I walked her into the sanctuary. With each step, her fragrance filled my nostrils. It was unbearable, but in a good way. I placed my bible in the chair next to hers and stepped away, headed back to where I normally station myself--not because I was actually planning to sit there, but because I needed to put space between us and gather my wits, at least for a moment.

The service began. I sat back listening to the praise and worship team, waiting for Tre to come out, when it hit me how weak I was being, and how suspicious this must look to everyone. For the past few weeks, I led the same female into the sanctuary. Today I did it again. I did not want people thinking the wrong thing. Worse, it was far from clear to me if I would be able to control myself physically.

Although people filled the sanctuary, Danielle continued to fill my vision. The more I smelled her intoxicating perfume, the more my hands wanted to touch her.

I quietly stepped back to where she was seated and told her I had to leave for the remainder of the service. Then, a bit hesitantly, I asked her to meet me afterwards.

But at that moment, it seemed she was either suddenly filled with the spirit, or something lay heavy on her mind, for her body grew stiff, immobile, and she neither spoke nor looked at me.

I felt confused, but decided not to try to figure it out right now. All I knew was I needed to leave.

Outside the sanctuary, I paced the vestibule, walked back and forth, up and down the hall. You would have thought I was an expectant father. After what felt like hours, I went back inside, and stood in the back of the room.

At first, I could not see her, so I moved around until I could. I decided I better stay in the back of the sanctuary until the offering was collected. It was for the best. After all, I needed to be able to live with myself next week.

So why did you tell her to wait after service, fool? I should not have said that. I wanted to disappear, but instead I moved outside the vestibule door. I could see her coming through the crack without her being able to see me. As soon as she stepped across the threshold, I spoke.

"Hey, babe."

That was not what I intended to say. Sure, it was how I felt, but it was exactly the wrong words to use. I was mortified. For whatever reason, she smiled and handed me her Bible looking completely at peace. Outside, as we headed toward her car, the same two Wise Saints from last week spotted us and hurried over.

"My, you two are looking nice again this week," the first woman, said.

"And don't they look so happy," added the second. The two stood there nodding to one another as if they discovered a wonderful secret. Danielle and I stared at each other in surprise. Yes, somehow we did it again—matching suits, right out of Central Casting.

"Oh, and such beautiful shoes," cried the first, this time addressing Danielle. Of course, at that point, I could not stop myself from checking out her feet—stilettos with ankle straps. The exact kind of woman's shoe I never have been able to resist.

Lord help me, I thought. There was no one to help me but myself.

As soon as Danielle opened her car door, I grabbed her and hugged her again. I am not going to lie--there was not an ounce of godliness in my hug. It was full of passion, which consumed me. I brushed her ear with my lips, forcing my need for her to grow even stronger.

"Six more days until I see you again," I said softly. "Take care, my love."

What did I just say? Before I knew it, I spoke aloud what I felt, and what I spent weeks wanting to say, only this time without hesitation. Just as quickly, my joy turned to shame. I felt vulnerable as never before. Without waiting for her reply, I turned and walked away as fast as I could toward my own car.

The rest of the day, I spent feeling angry with myself. I could not believe what I did, leaving myself so open and unguarded. If I analyzed the day's events according to my professional training, I thought to myself, maybe I could figure this out.

In the language of the sport, I set her up with a cross punch she did not see coming. Now, the cross is a straight punch, and one I train on regularly, unlike what many other boxers do. I prefer it because it is the most powerful punch of all.

True, I got my name from my lightning-fast, fierce hook; but my cross is how I get most of my knockouts. I have actually thought about changing my professional name—probably not a good strategy at this point in my career. Besides, I like the name my fans gave me.

Here is what is so shocking--that most of my opponents were never prepared for my cross punch. I would attack them with my cross, and then would serve it up with the hook--so the cross, you could say, was like the appetizer, and the hook was dessert. There was, needless to say, no option for the main course. I am in, and I am out.

Only this time, with Ms. Danielle Rose, I slipped. I laid my best cross out there, but I did not follow up with my hook. I mean, this was the perfect opportunity to ask if I could I call her—but I failed. *Who does that? A married man.* As bad as I want to, I cannot start this. I have to stick with my original plan.

The rest of the evening, all I could think about was how pissed I was with Tameka. Not only her, but with myself as well. Why have I let this divorce drag on this long? Why have I not nipped this in the bud? Am I waiting for something to change? Do I think anything will change? Do I really want things to change? It took me all night to confess the truth to myself. The answer to all of those questions must be no. No, I did not want things to change.

The truth is I did not, and I still do not, want to admit this marriage to Tameka failed. From the start, everyone warned both of us this would happen--my family, her family, Trevor, Gabby, our friends, Trevor's family, and everyone else in between. We did not listen. We were young, and full of ourselves.

Neither did I listen when people I trusted told me they suspected Tameka's pregnancy was a lie. Sorry, but we soon had proof that much was true. Then people said the baby was not mine—wrong again. All you have to do is look at Randall Junior—the kid is living proof of my paternity.

Therefore, Tameka and I stuck it out, choosing not to pay attention to all the naysayers and doubters. We were stubborn and did not want to admit what a disaster it was, and our marriage was a big mistake.

The result? Here we are unhappily married. Out of fifteen years, I will admit two of those years we were happy. That was before we were married and RJ was born. Once he came, everything changed. On the other hand, should I say, Tameka changed. Maybe after fatherhood, I began to grow up. Tameka did not.

So yes, I should have bailed out long ago. Then I started having success as a fighter; I officially became known as Hooks. Except for my relationship with my wife, I have never failed at anything in my entire life. As my professional triumphs began to pile up, one after another, it grew even harder to admit to the failure of my marriage.

I know what you are thinking. It is insane to choose pride above life and happiness. Millions of people do just that, settle for the sake of settling. Up until now, there has never been a good enough reason for me *not* to settle. It sure was not about money. I could have cared less if Tameka took everything. That has not changed.

Now, I thought, lying there in the dark, all I want is for that woman to be out of my life. After all these empty years of *settling*, I want this marriage to be finished. The money ain't a thing. I could make the money back in the ring a hundred times over.

Tameka never made the slightest contribution to my boxing career. When it came to boxing, she wanted no part of it. She never wanted anything to do with it. Not because she had some big career of her own, but due to a complete lack of interest in what I was doing, or even the slightest desire to learn more about it.

Tameka never attended any of my fights, neither amateur nor professional. Looking back, I suppose that alone should have told me it was over between us. She never supported me, but boy, did I ever support her. Her debit card continues to work. What a fool I was and am.

Suddenly, everything about the Tameka situation felt crystal clear. My pride, my reluctance to admit to failure was what was hanging me up. Pride has been the big roadblock to my future. *This has to end.*

In my frustration, it was all I could not to call Tre, even though by that hour it must have been three o'clock in the morning. I felt like this was his entire fault. He should have helped me to admit the truth; he should have urged me to get the divorce. Now here I sat at a complete standstill in my life, all because of a single, dumb, childhood mistake.

I will never fornicate again, I thought. *Fornication is what caused me fifteen years of pain. If I ever get out of this mess, I will not make the same mistake twice; no matter how fine the woman is, even if the woman is Ms. Danielle Rose. That is my vow, and I will stick to it. Not just because of Tameka, not just because of Trevor, but more than anything, because of my God.*

I forced my mind to shut down. Exhausted, I lay awake and prostrate until the sun rose.

WEEK 7

It took me all week to shake myself loose. Then I made up my mind not to let this new love turn my life upside down. I knew what I needed to do; in the meantime, it was important to stick to the old routines at church, and to keep being myself. I was not going to hide from a girl who built buildings. She was no mind reader, nor was she a therapist. Even if my palms were sweaty and my heart seemed as if it would burst out of my chest, I was still going to be me.

On Friday afternoon, I called my lawyer and told him I needed to reach a final settlement with Tameka quickly, no matter her terms.

Sunday

By bedtime Saturday night, I knew I was obsessed, fixated, whatever you call it.

Where did this all come from? For years, I have not looked at a woman with this intensity and magnitude. Why her? Why Danielle? It was as if I had suddenly become weak. As if I had grown weak for her. Such a strange feeling. I have no other weaknesses in my life, not even one—well, unless you count my weakness for cars, music, shoes, and gadgets. Other than that, I truly have no weaknesses or obsessions. Not for food, not for partying, not for television, not for anything else. Now not only do I have a weakness, but I also have a serious problem.

Once at the church, I headed straight for security, thinking I would watch the monitors until she surfaced. If that meant I had to watch all morning long, no problem. I radioed Dex in the parking lot.

"Go ahead, Deac."

"You know what time it is."

"Deacon Washington, do I sense a little attraction on your part to a certain Ms. Rose?"

Attraction is an understatement. Danielle is, quite literally, what my dreams are made of. This was nothing I could ever say aloud, of course, least of all to Dexter, but I loved the way I was feeling.

"If you have to stop and search every car, Dex, do it. I have to know when her tires make contact with the parking lot."

"Gotcha, Boss."

"By the way, this so-called 'little attraction' you just mentioned? Nothing little about it, my friend," I said.

He laughed. "I can see why."

As fate would have it, today she pulled up in a different car. So despite my orders, Dexter failed to recognize her, sitting behind the wheel of a full-sized BMW with tinted windows. Plus, she was wearing sunglasses.

Not until the car finished gliding to a halt into the tight parking space and kicked those long, beautiful legs out did it dawn on Dex who she was.

Meanwhile, I was sitting at my post in security, watching the front entrance and the single parking spot normally reserved for her. I failed to recognize her until she removed her shades and was steps away from the door.

My radio buzzed frantically with Dex desperately trying to signal me, but by then I was already in high gear, racing down the corridor. I snatched the headset off my waistband and tossed it to Keith, standing watch by the entrance. "Tell Mr. Hall I got it," I snapped.

I could see her as she swept through the doorway. She checked her watch. The glitter of diamonds momentarily blinded me. I stifled a gasp; I knew that brand even from afar. She drew close, and the scent of her perfume enveloped me. My heart was pounding, though not from running. It was as if I was sliding into home plate after a grand slam in the final inning of the World Series.

"Good morning, beautiful," I said, pulling to an abrupt halt, trying to make it seem like I had been standing there all morning long, not racing to the door like Usain Bolt.

"Good morning, Deacon," she smiled.

The next words out of my mouth surprised me, a sensation I was beginning to get used to. "Where is your hat?" She looked momentarily puzzled. *Just go for it, fool,* I thought. *Say something. Something about the hat.* "What I mean is, you really know how to rock a beautiful lid," I said. "Why no hat today?" *Plus,* I was thinking, *you are in a different car and you had on shades, so how was I supposed to know it was you?*

Not knowing what else to do, I decided to play the manly card. "You should wear a hat to church every Sunday from now on," I said decisively. Her look let me know this was one an order she might decide not to take.

"Had a long week?" I asked, trying a different approach, thinking to myself, *because it surely has been a long week for me. It seems like forever since I have seen you.* Oh, lame again. Hooks, where did that line come from?

I kept talking, and thus kept right on embarrassing myself. "The past six days have been torture for me," I threw out, knowing beyond a doubt that at least this was the truth.

I could tell from her eyes that for once, she got what I was saying. I was suffering a kind of torture, and all because of her. Therefore, I proceeded to unload my pain and confess how I thought of her every minute of every day. How I dreamed of her every night. And how I stalked her every day.

I could not take her presence any longer. I turned away and dropped her gaze. I took her arm gently. We walked together, in silence, the rest of the way to the sanctuary.

I left her there, and headed back to Hunter's office, knowing more or less what awaited me there. Sure enough, Tre began ragging me before I even had a chance to sit down.

"Have you no self-control?" he half-shouted. "I saw what happened between you two outside. I know exactly what you are up to, my friend." I ignored his accusation, and instead leveled one of my own back at him.

"I believe it is high time to disable these monitors in here," I said, pointing at the screens. "It makes me sick to think of you sitting in here, spying on me."

This was going to be the last time I would let him see me making a fool of myself, I thought. *Truth is I am making a fool of myself just fine on my own. The last thing I need is my best friend spying on me.*

I left Tre's office and headed quickly back to the sanctuary. Later, during praise and worship, I watched Danielle. She was fidgety, as if something was going on. I tried not to stare, but it became increasingly clear that something was wrong.

She seemed to be frantically clasping her legs and rubbing them. I crept close. To my shock, her face was a mask of sheer agony. She rubbed her legs, then stomped her feet, trying to shake out what seemed to be an enormous pain.

It dawned on me: *A cramp. She is having a bad muscle cramp.* I know from experience how much that can hurt.

"King, switch with me," I whispered.

"No," he snapped.

"*Move*," I hissed.

He sat stone-faced, refusing to give ground or even look at me. "Not your problem."

"*King. Now.*"

The last thing I wanted to do was to make a big scene. Instead, I carefully stepped over King as if he were a big boulder or some other impediment to stand beside Danielle. She noticed none of the commotion. By now she was bent over double in what looked like excruciating pain, frantically rubbing her calf muscle with both hands.

"Is everything okay?" I asked softly. "Have you been overdoing your exercise routine or something?"

I knew the feeling all too well. Every day that week, I pushed myself to the limit in my workouts, trying to get her off my mind. Therefore, I knew the discomfort she was having.

Some folks call it leg cramps; my grandma used to call it a "Charley horse," whatever that means. No matter what you call it, it is a painful spasm or cramp in the foot or leg muscle, lasting anywhere from seconds to hours.

I also happen to know the cause. It could be from strenuous exercise, hormone imbalance, dehydration, low levels of potassium or calcium, along with a few other conditions, pregnancy among them— although from the look I got of Danielle's figure earlier today, I decided I could safely rule out that last reason.

"You're right on target," she moaned. "All week I've been doing a lot of leg extensions and squats."

If I had to guess, she has probably been doing too many reps, and using too much weight. Unless she is preparing for a fitness event, there is no reason for her to be pushing herself so hard. What is going on here?

"It sounds as if you have been training too hard, as if for a marathon, and not just working out," I said quietly. "First off, we need to get you on the right work-out schedule. Not that you even need a workout regimen at all. I mean, you are already perfect."

She groaned. Trevor eyed us with concern. His expression asked what was I doing to this poor woman. With a jolt, I realized this might not be the time or place for a lecture on physical education. Still, it does happen to be my line of expertise. As most people know, being healthy and feeling good are what you get from regularly scheduled exercise. In addition, there was my career—in boxing, if you wanted to survive; there was no choice but to stay in top shape.

For now, what this woman needed was not a lecture; she needed to walk, to rehydrate, and to get a good rubdown from an experienced set of hands.

"Can you walk?" I asked quietly.

"No. I don't think so."

I wanted to pick her up right then and carry her to my office, lay her down on my desk and do whatever it took to eliminate her pain. *Calm down, Deacon.* That would raise huge red flags. Tre would jump down from the pulpit and choke me.

Instead, I asked her to sit up. Once she extended her leg, I could see the knotted muscles. I knelt down and rubbed her leg hard, using as much force as I thought she could stand. It was crazy for me to be touching her like that; but there was no other choice.

As I embraced her lower half with my hands, she placed her arms around my neck and lay her head on my shoulder. I could hear her breathing and panting from the pain. As I continued to massage and rub, I began to feel the knots in the muscles dissolving. Her breathing slowed, and she sat back, letting go of my neck.

"You are a lifesaver," she murmured gratefully.

Suddenly, I was a lifesaver. God only knows how long I have waited to hear something like that. It was just what I needed to hear. And all I had to do was to rub out a Charley horse.

At that moment, I needed Danielle so much, and suddenly it seemed possible that she needed me as well. I thought to myself, this all proved there was no other man in her life, at least not an athlete. Otherwise, he would told her about the proper exercise regimen, or at least worked out with her. For once, I was as honest as I could be. It was not the right place, but my heart was not to be denied.

"I want to be your permanent life-saver," I told her, keeping my voice just loud enough that she could hear me above the choir. "As in, for the rest of our natural lives. Also, Ms. Rose, I am hereby counseling you to ease up on the leg extensions. Did you say you are lifting two hundred pounds? That is way too much for you."

She smiled. "Deacon, I really think I can handle this myself."

"Oh, of course you can," I shot back. "And here I was moments ago, down on my knees, rubbing your legs so hard that sweat was popping out on my forehead. I guess I am not remembering this correctly."

She laughed, and all at once, we were flirting like mad, oblivious to Trevor, the congregation, the choir, and even to King, who at that moment was smiling at me like an angry demon. Smiling was something King never did, and when he did smile, you knew you needed to beware.

"Now remember, Ms. Rose," I added, standing up and stepping back over King. "We are going to talk more about your workout routine, and especially your weights. Your legs cannot handle it. You probably also need to get more potassium in your diet," I said before stepping back to my seat. *Dr. Washington was in the house.*

Without skipping a beat, King proceeded to publically chasten me right there in the sanctuary. Thankfully, no one but me could hear his words. He kept his voice low, but anyone could tell from his body language he was laying on the mother of all tongue-lashings.

"King, I think you have made your point," I quietly spoke looking straight ahead. "You are my trainer. You are my friend. Nevertheless, you are not going to make a fool of us both. Save it for later."

King turned his back ending the discussion. As soon as I started to relax, Trevor summoned me to the pulpit. I did not need this right now. My intentions were to ignore him. King nudged my ribcage as hard as he could. Against my will, I stood and approached the altar and leaned my face up against Pastor Hunter's face. *Here we go again.*

"Not now, Tre," I begged. "Deal with me later. My apologies, but she was in severe pain. I had to do something."

"My house will not become a den for your nonsense. Don't make me tell you again," Tre snapped.

Strangely, I found I was not angry, not with Tre nor King. Tre's response was to be expected. Neither was I regretful. Danielle's lips moved soundlessly: *Thank you.* It was confirmation that every crazy thing I did because of her not in vain. I smiled and nodded back, acknowledging her.

I knew I received only the prologue to all the lectures I was about to receive. I smiled although I was aware I would probably obtain a few broken ribs by the end of the day, compliments of King.

On the way back to the finance office with the offering I spoke. "Sol, a favor?"

"Sure, champ. What will it be?"

"Grab me a banana and a bottle of water from my office. Then meet me in the vestibule."

I reentered the sanctuary from the back. Immediately after Hunter gave the final blessing I stepped next to her. I asked if she could walk. She assured me she could. "Meet me in the lobby in a few minutes," I told her.

I exited the sanctuary with Trevor and made sure he was in his office before I made my way back to the vestibule.

There I found Danielle waiting for me, leaning gracefully against a wall, looking slightly amused. "Can you walk okay now?" I asked.

She nodded yes. I held my hands behind my back so she could not see them; sure enough, Sol walked past and discretely handed me the water and the piece of fruit, just as I had asked.

"Here," I said, holding out my hands. "This will help. Potassium and hydration. You should be fine."

"Why, thank you, Dr. Washington," she said, receiving my gifts like a happy child.

"I do not want to be your doctor, Danielle. But I surely do want to take care of you."

We strolled outside and sat beside the fountain in the courtyard. "Now, I'm curious. Why do you feel you have to push your body so hard?" I asked.

"Oh, you know. To combat stress and stay in shape."

Stress—the word actually made me flinch. All my life, I have battled against that terrible curse, vowed never to give in to it. No way, the woman who has stolen my heart will ever feel that awful emotion.

Give me all your stress, I felt like telling her. *I will never let worry touch you again.*

I asked her where she worked out.

"The neighborhood gym. And I run at the high school track." Then she said something which caught my attention. She mentioned boxing.

I could not tell if she was pulling my leg. I had to know. "You like boxing?"

"I sure do."

This practically about knocked me over. "Who do you like best?" I queried, figuring she would come up empty-handed.

"Past or present?"

Now I was impressed. She reeled off the names of some of the greats and near-greats, old ones as well as new. Much to my disappointment, she did not include me among the new guys. *She has to be playing me. Was I being punked? Had I been set up? Was she for real?*

"Of course, there are quite a few more with lots of potential," she added sweetly. *"Potential"? Did I have potential?* Was she being nice or just naïve? I had no idea. I was crushed that she did not seem to know me, but at the same time humbled.

One thing seemed certain: she was not chasing me because I was a headliner, a man known to have made big money in the ring. A man who quit, they said, at the peak of his powers, only because of what happened in the match when he. . .I shook the thought out of my head, and changed the subject.

"What track do you use?" *Bad move, Hooks,* I thought. *Now she'll think you just want another place to stalk her.* No matter; she obliged me with details about what days and times she ran, as well as where and when she worked out at the gym.

Curiosity got the best of me. "So, are you training for something in particular?"

"Yeah. A wedding dress."

Once again, this girl totally knocked me off balance.

"I see you are wearing a ring," I said, taking her hand. With relief, I realized it did not look like a wedding ring or an engagement ring.

"Oh, this? The person who gave it to me is . . ."

Before she managed to get the words out, King's voice rang urgently through my earpiece. "Hunter wants you," he said. "Now."

I ignored him and continued the conversation, "Do you have any prospects or date?" I asked.

"LL Cool J and TI are about all for right now," she laughed.

"Oh, next round." I cried. "If those are the guys that I have to fight for you, then I have my hands full." *Better than Furquan,* I thought.

Her answer made me feel happy. Now I felt ready for Trevor, King, and anyone else who had it in for me. There was hope for Danielle Rose and me, and there was nothing anyone could say. No amount of chastening, would upset me right now. The girl of my dreams was free and available.

As I stood reluctantly to take my leave, who should approach us one more time but our two old friends, the Wise Saints. Spotting us seated beside the fountain, one called out, "Deacon, you and your wife look so nice together in your black and ivory."

Danielle and I covered our smiles with our hands. We did it again. *Come on, what are the chances two people could randomly choose the same colors three weeks in a row? Unbelievable.*

"Hey, what's the rush?" said Danielle, tugging at my sleeve as I rose. I sighed, and sat back down. We talked for a while longer, the compliments flying like a tennis ball we kept giddily hitting back and forth. I tried hard not to start pressing her with more workout advice, but I could not resist.

"Drink your water, lovely lady, and as soon as you get in the car, eat that banana. And please remember to have some protein for dinner."

"Yes, Daddy," she squeaked in a tiny voice, looking up at me like a disobedient child. "Speaking of dinner, my dinner is cooked. All I have to do is make cornbread," she said with a twinkle.

That sure would be something different. Tameka used to complain that I never ate. Maybe because she never cooked for me. I could not resist making a fuss about this welcome announcement. "Girl, you cannot cook," I yelled.

She clapped her hand over my mouth.

"Oh yes I can," she rolled her neck. "I didn't get this thick eating bananas, Monkey Man."

That was all I could take. Between her calling me "Daddy," and her putting her hand over my mouth, I felt I was two steps shy of completely losing control. For the last time, I stood up, pulled her to me, and gathered her in my arms for a long hug. We said goodbye, and just like that, we went our separate ways.

That night, thoughts raced through my mind. Tameka and I never made the scene together as a couple, so it was weird having people refer to Danielle as my wife. To be honest, I liked it. I also liked the person they were referring too.

Only one problem remained: I already had a wife. A wife I did not like. One I married because I had been caught in my sin and wanted to make it right. A wife who did not want to deal with fighting. The one I was given authority to divorce by the Old and New Testament law. The same wife who refused to sign the divorce papers. The wife who refused to tell me what price I would have to pay her to walk away. I needed to get this divorce. Money was no object. Some things, like my freedom, were priceless.

Barring all else, I could just say the word, and have Tameka just… disappear. My guys and I would have a watertight alibi. An accident is what it would look like.

Thank God, I was not in that frame of mind. Hence, no need to worry about an alibi. All this waiting on Tameka to sign the divorce papers suddenly seemed like a burden I could bear.

 Danielle Rose mentioned stress. All I wanted was for her to set all her cares aside, to give them all to me. I still did not know what was the cause or the nature of her stress—was it health, work, family, finances, a relationship, or some other issue?

All I knew was that I wanted to be her knight in shining armor. That was my mission, to make sure she would always be happy and living a life free of stress.

Even if I myself was never allowed to love her. Even if Tameka held me in bondage for the rest of my life, I would still do everything in my power for Danielle. Why? I did not know. I had an unnatural attraction for her. No doubt about it. It was love at first sight.

WEEK 8

Tre summoned me to his office first thing Monday morning. I sensed my summons came from the man of God, even though Tre said it was 'just a friendly get-together'. If that was the case, why were we meeting in his chambers? I felt like I was headed for the principal's office. I have been blessed not to spend a lot of time on the other side of the wood, getting the finger pointed at me; but today I sensed things might be different.

I soon discovered my instincts were right. I could not determine if he was ministering to me, counseling me, or lecturing me. However, I listened with my ears and my heart open, and my mouth shut. I did not say a word of rebuttal to him; how could I? Everything he said was true.

"You do not know this young lady. She does not know you. You are not in any position to make a commitment to her. For all you know, the same may be true for her."

I kept quiet and nodded my head. Once he was done, I asked him the question that had been burning a hole in my brain since last Sunday.

"Trevor, why have you not insisted I get my situation with Tameka resolved long before now? If so, I would not have found myself in this predicament. I mean, did not we know this day was coming? Didn't we know I would eventually get tired of being in bondage? Why didn't you help me?"

I have never before gotten emotional about the subject of Tameka and me. Now, I felt full. I felt I was about one sentence away from a meltdown. I was fighting to hold it in, but honestly, at that moment I felt no shame.

Here sat Tre, my best friend. The person I got whippings with as a kid. The one who was the lookout on the night Tameka conceived. The man who told me I could be a fighter, who said he believed in me. The person who travelled with me in a smoking car to all the hole-in-the-wall dives, most of them surely illegal, where I got my start as a fighter. The friend who would lend me his last dollar for the gas to get there, and later on, the friend with whom I shared my winnings. The one who wore the ribbon, the medal, and the belt as we rode home together. The one who had my back. The brother who has always, and I mean *always*, been there for me.

So, yes, I was paying close attention, although my mind was made up. Not even he could change it.

"Trevor, I hear what you are saying. Yes, you are right. I do not know her from Adam's house cat, but I know how I feel. I cannot stop thinking of her. My heart pounds when I see her. I can smell her two days later. I hear her voice all week.

"You are right, she may not be the one for me; she may not even be interested. But Tre, she has brought me back to life. I mean, when have you heard me mention a woman?" I laughed. "Okay, other than Halle Berry, Janet Jackson, or Beyoncé? Never! You have never heard me talk like this about a real woman, someone I can literally put my hands on."

Tre smiled and shook his head. "I beg to differ. You can have your pick--Gabrielle Union, Paula Patton, anyone else for that matter."

"But that's the point, Tre. I am not interested in them. I am interested in the girl who would not park on the grass."

"By the way, be prepared, Hooks," he added, with a twinkle in his eye. "I am going to preach on that very subject someday soon—the love that sneaks up behind us and takes us by surprise."

"What? Never mind. Explain to me why I would be interested in any of those other women you named."

Tre leaned over and spoke as if he were knocking me on the head with the obvious. "Because, fool, they are hot!"

I grinned. "No way. Those types require attention."

"Do you know any woman who does not?"

Now we were almost talking like the old friends we were.

"Tre, come on. Be real. Why are you so against her?"

"I am not against her at all. I am against you doing something inappropriate with her."

"Do you believe in love at first sight?"

He laughed.

"Come on, Tre. I remember how you and Gabe met. Do not give me that. Try it on someone who does not know your history."

He let out a shout of laughter, knowing I was right. That is how it went for the rest of the morning. After I left his office, I still felt confused.

Tuesday

Today started bad and got worse by afternoon. I received a call from my attorney, advising me that Tameka was dragging her heels, and not committing to a meeting to draw up the divorce agreement. When I heard this, I punched a hole in the sheetrock in the wall in my office. *This is ridiculous. I have had enough of her.*

I was on my face all night. I need answers. I need help.

Wednesday

Today, for the sake of my sanity, I tried hard to stay occupied. I busted my tail working out. King aided in my torture. Once I had taken all I could physically take, I drove home trying to ignore the pain. I wanted to get back to the house, jump in the hot tub, and soothe my aching muscles.

I soaked until time for bible study. I toweled off, dressed, and soon enough took up my post in the vestibule, leaning against the wall, talking with the other Deacons about how terrible I felt. Not going into details, of course, just passing the time. One of the Deacons was clowning me, forcing me to burst into laughter, when suddenly I look up and see Danielle.

I was unprepared, caught off guard, and momentarily speechless. I had no idea she was coming to bible study. As I stood there more or less paralyzed, she walked up and gave me a big hug. Then she whispered a command in my ear.

"I will see you immediately following service, are we clear?"

Did she not know I did not take commands from anyone other than King and JJ? How was I going to explain to the guys what just happened?

"Yes, ma'am," I said humbly watching her walk away. A dozen pairs of eyes, mine included, were riveted to her retreating figure. As soon as she was out of hearing range, they jumped all over me with questions, and would not take any of my lame attempts to respond. I had to get myself back together, mentally and physically. I called my parking lot guy Dex.

"Man, could you not have given me some kind of warning?"

"Hooks, I called! You didn't answer!"

I guess I had been too busy talking about my bruised muscles and aching ribs, which only felt worse in the wake of what just went down. I did something I normally do not do—taking my time, I slowly and painfully walked back to my office, where I rummaged through a desk drawer, and pulled out a bottle of Tylenol. I popped two.

Next, I headed back to the sanctuary, the pain still making me take my time. I wanted to locate her. She was not in the seat where I normally direct her. Did this mean another trip to security? Carefully I turned my body sideways, bracing my aching ribs, just to make sure I was not missing her.

There! Almost right behind me. Seeing her made me forget all about the pain. I was smiling from ear to ear, unable to stop myself. I winked and nodded; she did the same, and then lowered her head, blushing. *Was she embarrassed, or was she delighted to see me too?*

This was going to be tough. I was going to have to sit in front of her for an entire service, and not turn around and stare. Now it looked as if I would have to start preparing myself to see her not just Sunday, but Wednesday as well.

I could hear mumbling behind me. I wanted to turn around and tell the two stoogers to hush. Unable to turn all the way around because of the pain, and not wanting her to think I was flirting, I sat sideways in my chair.

Someone touched my shoulder. The person sitting next to her asked me my name. Of course, I replied, "Deacon Washington." Right then, I knew I was busted. They knew who I was. Not that I cared, but I wanted to tell her who I am myself. The young lady asked for a Kleenex. I was not sure if that was a real request or not.

Danielle sneezed—one of those cute little sneezes girls do where they literally say the words, "ah-choo!"—so naturally, I had to turn all the way around and speak.

"God bless you, Ms. Rose," I said smiling.

At that point, the collection plates finished going around, and I realized I needed to get up and take the money back. Not because it was my duty this week—today the task fell to one of the other Deacons--but frankly, I needed a breather. As I passed her row, I turned and told her, "Don't leave."

I met back up with her and her guest to speak briefly before I lost my nerve and like a coward raced off. Shortly afterwards, I fled the building, heading home. I think I was exhausted, in every way possible. I punished myself mentally and physically all night for being a coward.

Thursday

Today I took it easy. I had to--my body needed to recover. I worked quietly in my office all day. I tried not to think of Danielle, Tameka, or the divorce. It cleared my mind to catch up on other important business.

Later, I returned to the church for the Women's Conference. As a Deacon, I had a lot to do, no matter how tired and sore I felt. I arrived early, and figured I would probably be staying most of the night. Part of my duties would include driving Gabby home. Gabby decided Trevor was not allowed to attend the Women's Conference. That left me in charge of everything, including parking-lot duty.

This was always a big night for Lady Gabe, but to be honest, I would have liked to have been excused tonight also. In settings like this, I never knew if the women were coming out to hear the Word, or if they were here to annoy the famous boxer. The other guys always found this particular situation hilarious, for some reason. They know the cougars, the wolves, and anything in between will be out in full force, and all over me. Funny for them, yeah, but sheer torture for me.

As I stood there at my post in the vestibule, dreading what was about to happen and trying to figure out a way to escape, who but Danielle Rose should walk in the door? To be honest, I am very impressed she came two nights in a row. Surely, this is a sign. I stepped away from my fellow Deacons, and decide that I have hugged enough of the crowds of women pouring into the hallway. There is enough lipstick, makeup, and perfume on my shirt that I will probably need to trash it. Despite that, Danielle's beautiful scent stood out above everyone else's.

She approached me and before I knew it, she gave me yet another order: "Let's walk."

This was a new Danielle, a version I had not met until recently. This was the same fierce woman the parking lot attendant warned me about. No matter, I was ready. I followed her outside, to a secluded spot where we were alone.

"What on earth was up with last night's antics?" she asked.

This definitely did not seem like the right time to bring up the fact I was married, and having a hard time getting a divorce. I could not say, *You have no idea how nervous I get around you. Yesterday I was not expecting you, so I freaked. Neither was I expecting you today. Right now, I am close to having a full-blown anxiety attack.* Instead, I apologized.

She stared at me, a little smile playing on her lips.

"Do you think you can manage to walk me to my seat, Deacon?"

I stirred the strength to do so, and stood nearby for a few moments, just so I could avoid all the other women in the room. Then I went back and escorted Lady Gabe in the sanctuary. I returned briefly to Danielle's side, and explained I was on duty outside the sanctuary, but I would be watching for her.

After service, as bad luck would have it, I had parking-lot duty being one of the few guys here tonight. There was no way out of it. I was going to miss her leaving. Or so I feared.

Instead, she pulled up next to me, right there in the lot, but this time in a totally different car. As soon as I recognized her, I apologized for not being where I said I would be after the program.

"Danielle," I said, "I know you must be wondering what is going on. We will talk outside of church. Be safe. Good night."

Friday

Tonight was another night for the cougar convention—sorry, I should say the Women's Conference. Danielle attended two nights in a row. I was not expecting her again tonight—surely, she was as worn out as I was.

However, just in case, I decided to be prepared. She was easy, I told myself—it was all the others I dreaded. One day those women were going to gang up and take me out. Last night, for example, I really thought they were going to kidnap me. Thankfully, Danielle arrived too late to see all the commotion; I have no idea what I would have told her.

To prevent the same drama from happening again tonight, I instructed the crew not to leave my side. I did not want to be hugged, kissed, whispered to, or flirted with tonight. No more autographs, no more cell phone pictures. Besides, I was not about to trash another good shirt.

If Danielle did show up, it would be fine, I decided. Maybe she could save me from being suffocated by all these clucking hens; I could use her as my excuse to get away. Therefore, not to miss her, I stood directly in front of the door, and gave Dex strict instructions to let me know if she showed up.

Just when I begin to relax, my radio buzzed.

"Boss! It's her!"

Sure enough, she was approaching the door. She stopped. I stepped forward and held the door. She did not move. Did she stop to allow me to be a gentleman, or was it something else?

No, she was on the phone. We exchanged quick smiles, then she continued with her conversation. I could not tell for sure whom she was speaking with on the phone. Her sentences were crisp and firing rapidly as if they were about a business deal. She turned to face me as her call was seemingly ending.

"No electronic devices," I said, a little stiffly. I must admit, I was feeling jealous. Who was it commanding all her attention, when it was me who needed her attention? She gave me the one-finger sign which means, "Give me a minute". *All right, beautiful Ms. Rose,* I thought, *but now you are on my clock.*

How could I be annoyed? Truly, she was just in time to save me. If I heard one more female voice whine, Deacon? Can you speak with me over here? Deacon? I was going to bolt for the door and run. Sure, most men would have thought all this female attention was heaven, but after so many years of contending with demanding, older female fans and underage, jailbait groupies, I was sick of it; it was all pure torture for me.

Using the glass doors as a shield against the crowd, I gave Danielle five minutes to finish her call. As I drew near, ready to shut her down,

I could not believe my eyes. She was talking on the first phone, texting frantically on a second, and holding a third one in her hand.

Was this what her life was like? No wonder she was stressed. Tending to three calls at once was enough to stress anybody. I started to say something, but she held up her hand.

"Please, Deacon. Just five more minutes," she whispered.

Suddenly, I was furious. "Countdown," I snapped. After all, she was at church. Her phones should have been left in the car. I shut the door and walked away, leaving her outside alone, thinking I probably needed to cool off and calm down.

She was behaving badly, and it irritated me; but for some strange reason, I found I also liked it. I loved watching her through the glass. I appreciate a woman who is all about business. It made a profound statement about who she is, motivated and disciplined.

However, I could not stay in the vestibule much longer. Seeing I was alone again, the vultures were on me like white on rice. Every year it is the same thing at this conference; *I am not going to do this next year,* I thought to myself. I excused myself, walked to the back of the hallway, and tried to hide, more or less, watching the time closely.

In exactly five minutes, I was back at the door. Danielle spotted me and like an obedient child, she handed over all her electronic devices and car-keys. In spite of myself, I was delighted.

"Is this all the contraband you are carrying tonight, young lady?" I asked. Too late—she raced off. *This was getting weird,* I thought. *Can I really handle this woman?*

I yelled after her. "Where are you going?"

"Ladies' room," she replied, walking swiftly. I followed her, of course, like a desperate dork. I stood outside the bathroom door waiting for her. She raced out so quickly she walked right past me. I caught up to her, and we headed for the sanctuary. She was suddenly firing questions at me so fast I could hardly think what to say. She did not hesitate when she asked me if I was married.

I knew all along that I would have to answer this question. Currently, I was not ready; this was not the right situation. No matter. All I could do was to answer truthfully.

"Yes, I am."

It took no more than five minutes to tell her the whole story.

I could tell from her look she wanted to believe me, but did not entirely understand what I meant. I hardly knew myself.

Later that night, after escorting Gabby home, I reflected on what I did. I finally told Danielle the truth. Not all the truth, not the part about what I did for a living, and how I built a career. For now, I was finally meeting Danielle as the person I was. Even better, I was meeting her as the person I wanted to be.

Saturday

I woke up this morning thinking: *I am so obsessed, I cannot think straight.* I surely did a lot of talking and confessing last night, so how can it be that I still failed to get her phone number? Granted, I did have her work number. I also had plenty of sources I could pay to find her home or cell phone numbers. However, I did not want to do it that way; I wanted her to give me her numbers herself.

I reflected on the last few nights. How does a lady show up at church one day, and make all those long, empty years of my life seem like a brief few days of hell? Right now, the way I was feeling, it had been worth all the hell, to find myself finally here at this heavenly place.

I kept to myself all day. Other than going for a long run this morning, I had a quiet day. A peaceful day was so not my normal pattern.

Sunday

The end of an awesome week. A week where I got to see Danielle five times in seven days, three days in a row. It felt good. To top it all off, I saw her again this morning at church. She showed up looking beautiful as ever. Her presence lit up my soul.

It was First Sunday, and as I specifically explained to her earlier this week, we traditionally wore black on this day. Nonetheless, Danielle shocked me. She arrived wearing cream colors from head to toe.

When I questioned her, she informed me she is always rebellious. I loved it. She added an additional challenge to the situation, one I was sure to enjoy. How dare she do the exact opposite of what I instructed her to do?

I felt everyone's eyes on us as I hugged her. "I am always on display," I told her. "The eyes in the sky are watching." I am sure I was being observed from the moment she approached. "Ms. Danielle, you look beautiful as always. I appreciate you wearing the hat. Promise me one thing."

"What is that?"

"That you will wear a hat every week." Now it was her turn to look shocked.

"I beg your pardon, Deacon. Before you can make that request, I will need you to buy me some hats, and pay for the cleaning fees, not to mention extra hair appointments."

I reached into my pocket and pulled out two hundreds. "Here," I said, slipping her the bills. "This is to ensure you always wear a hat." Then I gave her a hug—a body-to-body kind of hug—as I spoke into her left ear. "We have an audience. But you know what? I do not care. You look beautiful when you are rebellious."

"And you look as handsome and sexy as always. Deacon Randall."

That sent me right over the top. I could not think the entire service. All I could do was smile. If someone thought they were playing some kind of a game by sending Danielle Rose my way, why, all I could say was they were winning.

WEEK 9

All week the skies were overcast and filled with heat and high humidity. Strangers to Atlanta feel as if they cannot catch their breath because the air is so thick and heavy. Natives are so accustomed to it they do not even notice.

Although my mind was occluded, I still felt I could not breathe. In conversations with Trevor, I kept telling him all the complications and delays in this divorce would be worth the wait. When in actuality, I was convincing myself. I begin to see there was a reason why the situation with Tameka was stalled for so long. It was a part of God's plan for her to hold out, I told Tre excitedly. If she had given in and signed the divorce papers before now, I might have been involved in yet another failed relationship. I would not have been called on this assignment. For I was convinced that it was no accident or coincidence that I was called.

I felt increasingly sure of this. I was at the right place at the right time. There was no such thing as coincidence. Our lives were purposed and ordained. Everything happened according to His will in decency and in order.

I could not admit it to anyone except Trevor and myself, but right now, I was honestly grateful Tameka held out. Little did she know, her stubborn attitude spared my life. She taught me a valuable, hard-won lesson in patience.

Currently, I have a lot of problems. The biggest one, for right now, was I still did not know Danielle's phone number. All I knew about her is what I researched. I did not know her family, friends, what her dreams were, or her goals. I desperately needed to find out more about her. I wanted to spend as much time with her as I could. Here I was, looking forward to a lifelong relationship with this woman, and she knew even less about me than I did about her. All I revealed about myself so far was that I was married, so to her, I was off limits. *Not for long, Miss Danielle Rose,* I thought. *My current marital status is temporary and very much subject to change.*

For two days, I considered these thoughts in my mind, and thanked God for the way things had gone down. Yes, I was stuck between a rock and a hard place. Nevertheless, things were so much better than few weeks ago. Back then, I was stuck. Now, things were not great, but they were finally looking up. All because of a grassy parking spot.

I had to be patient, I told myself, and why not? I had been patient for so long already; why not continue waiting? *Because, fool, while you sit there being so patient, you may lose your only chance at loving her. What makes you think she is waiting just as patiently for you?*

Suddenly, I remembered that day at church when she gave me her workout schedule, right down to the exact times and the place. I spent a few minutes debating with myself before I decided on a plan. I jumped up, pulled on some clean sweats, hopped in the car, and set my GPS for the address of the track she mentioned.

Sure enough, she was there, walking at a fast pace around the quarter-mile track, not paying the slightest bit of attention to her fellow walkers and runners, but with her eyes glued to her cell phone, texting and talking non-stop. I watched her for a few minutes saying nothing, hanging back at the side of the track, under the shadows of some big trees, jumping my rope.

Each time she passed by me, she failed to look up. Finally, her third time around the track, I tried to get her attention. She gave me an annoyed glance, which seemed to say, *not now; can't you see how busy I am?*

I did not know what to make of that. Was I flat-out being ignored? Was she handling important business? Was she trying to be rude? Or, worst of all, did she decide she was no longer interested in me? *No, you fool. She does not know it is you.*

I decided to chill and see what would happen. I shadowboxed, jumped rope, and finally ran. She paid as much attention to me as she did an ant crawling across the pavement. I had no idea if it was on purpose, or because she was that deep into whatever was going down in cell-phone land.

Wednesday

Here it was bible-study day and I had no idea if she was coming or not. Who knows? It may have been a rough week for her. I did not want to get my hopes up. At the same time, I did want to be prepared, just in case. I showered, shaved, put on a nice linen sports jacket and some lightweight summer trousers. I popped a breath mint and hopped in the car, driving slowly and carefully to church.

Sure enough, she showed up a few minutes after I had taken up my post in the vestibule. *If I could be certain of seeing her coming toward me like this every Wednesday for the rest of my life, that is all I would ever ask, Heavenly Father; I would be a happy man.*

"Good evening, Ms. Danielle. How was your day?"

"Excellent, especially now that I'm here; and yours?"

"The same. You look wonderful."

"I would have thought I looked tired."

"Yeah, you should," I said, pitching my voice lower, so no one could hear me but her.

"Why do you say that?" she asked in surprise.

"You worked long and hard last night. You should be tired."

"Says who?"

"Say I."

"And how would you know, Deacon Washington?"

"I saw you."

"You saw me where?" Now there was a touch of fear in her eyes.

Better explain myself; otherwise, she will think I am up to no good. "Let's just say I am your protector. Kind of like a guardian angel--except I'm a little rough around the edges."

She looked puzzled. I confessed I was at the track the night before watching her.

"Are you telling me that you're stalking me again?" she asked.

She wanted to know why I was at the track.

I answered with a question of my own.

"Here is what I want to know, Danielle," I said. "Why is it that you are so stressed that you cannot even have a workout without being glued to your cell phone? Not looking up for even a minute? Not long enough to notice that I was there?"

"All my stress is work-related."

This struck me as the right moment to ask about her job. Knowing the answer full well already, I asked innocently, "So what kind of job do you have that is so stressful?"

"I build buildings. I'm an architect and an engineer."

That was it—she offered no further details. She did not have to, of course, I already knew the details. She was one of the best-known female architects in the world, in a totally male-dominated profession, and she was revered by aspiring young female architects everywhere. She attended Georgia Institute of Technology, known around here as Georgia Tech, and completed her graduate degree there. I found she was also working on her doctorate.

To keep the conversation going, and to see how she would react, I pretended not to know any of this. Instead, I made jokes and intentionally sexist remarks about her career.

"So you are the receptionist for a contractor and order materials?" I said, fully expecting an angry retort. "You are the pretty lady they hired to sit at the front desk?"

To my surprise, she did not bother to correct me. Apparently, she wanted to keep the rest of her story secret, at least for the time being.

In the same way, she does not seem to be very curious about the details of my life. Once she told me she liked boxing and followed the sport. I always tried to drop some reference to it in our conversations. She never followed up, in fact seemed oblivious, and posed no questions nor asked for more details. I was positive she had no clue about who I am. How was I supposed to feel about that? Was I that bad of a boxer? Had I been gone from the scene that long? The whole thing made me nervous.

Of course, I could have told her my entire history. I had been as honest with her as I felt like I could for now. She was keeping her guard up, so I kept mine up as well.

I was preoccupied the remainder of the week. Mostly with her, but also with making travel arrangements to Vegas. There was going to be a big fight this week, with Floyd Mayweather matched against a promising young guy the odds-makers seemed to like. There was no way I would miss this. Okay--maybe if I had a date with her I would. *How I would love to ask her on a date. However, both legal and biblical law forbid it.*

My crew and I planned to fly to Vegas and hang out with Floyd during the week. We were going to train with him and his team—that was the plan. Every day I trained with King, I would find myself thinking of her. It was only when I was being hit that I could totally concentrate. Then I would think of my Rose, do a cross hook, and the fight would be over.

As the week wore on, strange stuff started to happen. It seemed that when I thought of Danielle, my punches were most powerful. When I closed her out of my thoughts, my punches were just average. The same thing was happening round after round, with one guy after another.

I was on to something. Where had Danielle been my entire career? She could be the third man in the ring. Or shall I say, woman. This unseen, invisible source of strength was proving brutal to my opponents. Maybe I was just imagining it. As the days went by, I decided I better try as best I could to contain my thoughts of her – mainly to avoid hurting one of my sparring partners too badly. For whatever reason, by the end of the week, I was more than ready to take on the world.

Saturday arrived, and I had to get my act together for the flight to Vegas. For a fighter, it always feels like the closer you get to the date, the further away it is until fight time. Then, once the fight starts, it is usually over almost before it begins. Those twelve rounds feel like thirty seconds in real life.

This week was no different. Saturday, fight day, was the longest day I had in years. The fight seemed even longer. Of course, Floyd won. I never had any doubts about the outcome, no matter what the odd-makers said. Floyd wanted me to hang with him afterwards, even though (as I already explained to him) there was only so much celebrating in which I could partake.

For the interviews and post-fight TV events, I mostly sat on the sidelines and watched. I broke loose once he went to his nightlife appearances. Clubbing is not my thing--never has been, probably never will be. I went back to the room and gave King, JJ and the rest of the guys the night off. Just because nightlife was not my thing did not mean the crew could not enjoy themselves.

Back at the hotel, I decided I had to break free. I needed some time to recapture myself. My mind was on overload, totally consumed with a woman I barely knew. Before I knew it, I was calling Vardo, asking her to change my travel arrangements, and to book me onto any available red-eye into Atlanta. It was time to go home.

Sunday

The next time my eyes opened, I was hearing, "Welcome to Hartsfield-Jackson International Airport." It was music to my ears. I was home. I had not been gone for twenty-four hours but every time I left Atlanta, I was always more than ready to come back. This time I was extremely anxious to be back home and "in the house".

Vardo picked us up from the airport, just the three of us—King, JJ, and myself. I did not need the whole crew back on my account. The celebration was still going on back in Vegas. I abruptly made the decision to return home to make Sunday-morning service. There was no way I would miss an opportunity to see her.

I was jumping out of the car at my front door before Vardo put the car in park. The guys, knowing my motives full well, started calling me all kinds of names, but I paid them no attention. I was on track to map out the rest of my life.

In my bedroom, I stood in my closet deciding what to wear. Until this moment, I always thought of my closet as just that – a room that held my clothes. Standing there blinking in the light, I realized it was not just a closet; it was an entire clothing store. The shoes, the jeans, the shirts, the suits—the sheer numbers were ridiculous. I did not even bother to look at all the sweats and clothes I trained in daily. I laughed aloud. Where did all of this come from? Was I obsessed with my appearance? In my loneliness did I pick up a compulsion? Either way, I was staring at all of these threads at a total loss as to what to wear. I did not like any of the options--none of them seemed good enough for what I was trying to do.

No matter, I had to get moving. The clock was ticking. I picked out a suit, showered, and dressed. I drove myself to the church. Vardo, at my instruction, called my barber the night before with orders to meet me in my office at the church, no matter the cost.

All this for a girl I did not really know, whom I was nowhere near dating--already she was costing me a fortune. Vickie was on quadruple time. Do not even ask about the cost of this last-minute flight. I sat in my chair at my desk, draped in a sheet, waiting for my barber to shape me up, even though I probably didn't need it. Earlier I decided I needed to order, at minimum, a dozen new suits. I would be lying if I said I was not buying them for her. I told myself I needed them. I knew I did not. To be honest, I really like nice clothes. Honestly, all of this was for her.

I was finally lined up in my usual spot in the vestibule. Hair trimmed, cuff links in place, cologne fresh, suit hanging right, shoes polished, and waiting on her to arrive.

Right on time, she pulled into the parking lot and parked neatly in the space I let everyone know was hers. She opened the door and gracefully swung out her legs—those beautiful, long legs seemed to go on forever—and stood there arranging herself. To my delight, she was wearing a beautiful new hat, per my request. I went with my first impulse and flew back to Atlanta, although there were a thousand reasons why I should not have. Right now, I was glad I did. At the door, much to my surprise, she asked about last night's fight.

"By the way, who won the fight last night?"

This was unbelievable. What were the chances of this? Did she know I was there? The fight was televised on pay-per-view. Could she have watched it, and spotted me ringside? What should I make of this question? I had no other choice but to answer. "Floyd won, of course."

"Dang. I hate I missed it."

I started to panic. She knew about the fight but did not bother to watch it? This told me she was either truly interested in fighting or current enough to know there was a fight last night.

"Long night last night? Hot date?" I said, trying to sound casual.

She did not answer, so I asked again, this time in a different way.

"What were you doing last night that made you miss the fight?"

"Oh, the same old thing. I worked late."

"At eleven o'clock on a Saturday night?" I thought for a moment.

"Yeah. I know. Pathetic, right? Just think how exciting it would have been, to be sitting there on the front row."

"No different than seeing it on the big screen, really," I said.

"How would you know, Deacon?"

Why lie about it, I decided. "I was right there on the front row," I told her.

"No, you were not," she laughed, shaking her head.

I pulled out my money clip and showed her the boarding pass from the fight home last night. In the midst of the gesture, I suddenly sensed this was going to be a bad idea. It was going to require an explanation. After all, Danielle was not your average girl, and I was going to have to explain exactly why I was ringside in Vegas.

Luckily, the clock saved me. Before she could reply, I glanced at my watch. "Wow, we should have been in the sanctuary two minutes ago," I said. Quickly I walked her to the row, which was now permanently reserved as her seat. The ushers had been informed no one else was to sit there, even if Danielle were a no-show.

Trevor was getting through his introduction, and I could see Danielle out of the corner of my eye, bent over her bag, reaching for something inside. Before I knew it, she was in motion. I tried to sit still. *Let her go*, I thought. *This is not the time to run after her and try to explain your long-term goals include her being a part of your life.*

I could not help myself. I spoke softly into the device on my wrist. "I'm moving," I said, as I left the sanctuary. I could sense Tre spotted me leaving, but I did not look back.

Out in the hallway, she was nowhere in sight. If she were not in the corridor, the only two places she could be were back outside, or in the ladies' room. I checked the bathroom first. Sure enough, she was there with her phone in her hand. As I was starting to push the door open, she stormed past me like a tsunami. I caught up to her and grabbed her arm.

"Danielle, wait."

"Who the hell are you, Randall Washington?" she snapped.

Right then, I knew the game changed. I wanted to tell her everything, but at the same time, I was afraid of how she would react. To be honest, I was not ready. It felt like neither the time nor the place to have this discussion.

"Please, do not be upset," I begged.

"Who said I was upset?" Her voice was low but tight with anger. "Why did you travel to Las Vegas and back in less than twenty-four hours?" It was a statement more than a question.

I had to reply, "It's my job." It is my duty to support other fighters. It is training for me. I could learn something or maybe offer something. It was work for me. The same way she said she was working last night.

"I'll ask you one more time. Who the hell are you?"

"I flew back because I wanted to see you."

She looked down in disgust at my hand touching her arm. I got the hint and let her arm go all while praying the monitor was not capturing this. The last thing I needed was an assault case. Therefore, I let her arm go and watched her flee back to the sanctuary. Right after the benediction, she made a quick escape in the midst of the crowd. By the time I caught up to her car in the parking lot, she was pulling off. I stood there half-blocking her way, and asked her to please stop. She either did not hear me or did not care. Either way she did not stop.

I stood there feeling like a fool. Here I had gone to so much trouble, spent so much money, purely to get back home so I could see her. How could I explain this so she would understand? I finished my Deacon duties although I was technically off duty today. I got in my car and started for the house, feeling about as low as a man can feel.

Halfway there, an idea struck me. I turned around and headed to the track. It was during the hours she had told me she was normally there. *Maybe we could try to run this scene all over again.*

I felt like a high-school boy standing there in my suit under the hot afternoon sun, waiting for her. Sure enough, she was there, dressed smartly in expensive sweats and what looked to be brand-new shoes. I raised my hand in greeting.

She walked right past me without saying a word. I could not believe it. This was going to be even tougher than I imagined. I did not know what to say, so I said nothing, watching her walk away. *Where was all this anger coming from?*

As she rounded the track a second time, I stepped in her way and said, as politely as I could, "Excuse me Danielle, but I knew I would find you here. May I please have a minute with you?"

She removed her ear buds, and replied, "Go ahead, Randall--or should I say, Randy 'Hooks' Washington. Whoever you are, you have exactly one minute."

Her words were like a knife to my heart. I wanted to be the one to tell her who I was, not Wikipedia or Google. I found myself explaining and apologizing at the same time, the words tumbling out in a rush.

She stared impatiently at the face of her watch. "I'm so sorry, Danielle. My intentions were never to hurt you. I hope you can understand. I am doing what I believe in my heart is best—best for you, first and foremost, but also best for me."

She still was not looking at me. I hoped she was at least listening. Praying silently that this was the case, I kept going.

"Danielle, I didn't want you to meet the man called 'Hooks' first. I want you to know me, Randall Washington. Hooks is my job. It is not a job I plan to have my whole life. I will be Randall forever. When the day finally comes when Hooks passes on the torch to some other fighter, I want you still to be happy with the real me, and not just the person I am now. My work is not my life, Danielle—God comes first. Then the family I hope to have someday comes second. Hooks is how I make a living. Some say I am good at it. Some say I have done great things. Others may disagree. Some may even think my job is barbaric and unworthy of the benefits I receive."

I stopped, took a breath, and like a drowning man, plunged back in. "But I work hard. I hit hard. Sometimes I get hit, and when I do, I get hit hard. Furthermore, I fall hard. In case you have not noticed, Danielle, I have fallen in love with you. I want nothing on this earth more than to make you happy. I am so sorry I didn't tell you all of this sooner."

I kept talking, though by now my minute was long up. I explained how people either really like my job, or else they hate it. How many people, women especially, hate boxing, but that does not mean they will not stick around to reap the financial rewards that come with success.

"My wife hates it, for example," I went on quietly. "Hates it so much you would think she's the one taking the hits, not me. But all these years, she has been more than willing to reap the benefits." I explained how Tameka and I have been going through an ugly divorce for years, and how she continues to prolong it. Then I got to the hard part.

"The truth is, Danielle, I have not fought in four years, but since meeting you, I feel like the old spirit is back inside me again. I have made it known to those around me that I am ready to start preparing, mentally and spiritually, for my next fight. I think Tameka is waiting for the next fight so she can claim half of the prize money." I thought bitterly, *I would gladly give her the entire purse if only she would walk away.*

"I have not been mentally prepared up until now," I continued. "I swear I was going to tell you when I felt the time was right. I wanted to tell you everything at once—all about my wife, my son, and my job. I did tell you about my wife, because I needed you to understand it was not you keeping us apart, but me.

"You must know I am attracted to you--hell, Danielle, I'm in love with you. I have never known someone as smart, intelligent, beautiful, God-fearing, and hard-working as you. I promise I only want to do things in decency and in order. Please do not lose faith in me, Danielle. Please trust me. All I ask is to be able to spend time with you before my divorce is final."

Standing there on the track, under the blazing summer sun, I confessed my heart to her. Then I waited for her to say something.

I feel the same way Randall, would have been nice. *I am not interested. I am sorry you were misled. I am in a committed relationship.* I would have even taken an *'I hate you. You are a jerk. I never want to see you again. You are a selfish bastard'*—it would have been something.

Instead, we had a stare-off. I took her hands and kissed them. That was all of her I was allowed to touch, much less kiss. It was so distressing—here I had the woman of my dreams before me, and I could not hug her, touch her, or kiss her the way I wanted too. It was extremely painful.

Finally, she turned and walked away, putting her buds back in her ears, resuming her run without saying a word. I stood still and waited patiently. *I have already waited thirty years. What was another afternoon going to do?* I sat there waiting, sweating in my suit and tie, feeling dizzy in the sweltering heat, for two hours, while she kept up a routine of sprints, jogs, and walks. I would have gladly waited for two days.

Then all at once, she headed to her car. I jumped to catch up to her. This was no time for silence. I had to think. What was I going to say? I raced down the track, catching up as she drew close to my car. I reached over my seat, and pulled out a banana and a bottle of water. It was the breakfast I did not eat. I placed these unlikely gifts gently in her hands, feeling foolish but not knowing what else to do.

She took the banana and the water without a word. I sensed now might be the time for a hug. Stiffly, she allowed it. Again, I apologized, and, letting her go, tried once more to tell her how I felt. Still not speaking a word, she turned, walked to her car, got in, and drove off.

For a moment, the pain I felt was so deep I could not move. At last, I got into my own car covering my face with my hands as I lay my head on the steering wheel. I called Trevor. Like the good friend he was, he quietly listened as I sobbed and wept, trying to explain to him what happened.

Back home, sitting in my driveway, I decided it was time to call in a favor. Being Hooks Washington had its privileges at times, and this was going to be one of those times. I phoned my florist, and explained I needed the shop to make a rush delivery, of as many long-stemmed roses as could be rounded up. As a rule, this was the kind of thing I would have called Vickie about, but for some reason I wanted to handle this myself.

I explained to the flustered woman on the other end of the line that I did not care how much it was going to cost. I knew in my heart that it was a long shot. Danielle Rose probably had guys sending her roses all the time. Roses—how lame can you get.

Then there was the issue of what color. From experience, I knew different colors of roses suggested different meanings. I for sure did not want to send the wrong color. I have already messed up enough. So I did what any desperate man would do, and chose them all. I ordered a mix of red, yellow, pink, orange, lavender, and white. I did not ask the cost. I did not care. I would have roses delivered to her every day until she spoke to me again.

That done, I stomped into the house, feeling worn out, hopeless and frustrated. I literally rent my clothes, not even bothering with buttons, but tearing the sweat-soaked shirt off my body, ripping the coat at its seams, tearing off the new trousers, and slinging my perfectly good Italian-made shoes across the floor.

I showered and toweled off, drew the curtains, and turned off the lights. I lay on the floor for hours, dead to the world. I woke once, feeling numb and exhausted. I did not move for the rest of the day and long into the night. My phone rang incessantly, it seemed, but I ignored it. When at last I got up, the sky was starting to darken. I decided to blog.

> I failed her. I disappointed her. I hurt her. Therefore, I hurt too. Until she heals I remain in pain. Please forgive me, my beautiful Rose.

It was the first time I ever blogged something so personal. My blogs normally consisted of scripture, proverbs, wisdom, thoughts, quotes, news and headlines. Tonight, it was me blogging, not Hooks nor Deacon Washington. It was Randall. The Randall who was in pain. The Randall who had been in pain for years.

WEEK 10

Monday

I rose early and, counter to my usual routine, I blogged again—my second post in three hours.

> I am not myself. I will be incomplete until my Rose blooms again.

I had a short, hard work-out. I was impatient for the day to begin. I needed to make some more phone calls first—punk-style, this time. Once the sun rose and the city was up and moving, I called Taste and See Catering and ordered a hundred chocolate roses. They must be delivered today. I knew I was being unreasonable, I patiently explained to the woman on the phone. I had no other choice. It was urgent.

I dressed and went over to the shop to hand-write a card to go with the chocolate roses. It was the least I could do, I figured. I would have delivered the chocolate myself, but that would be weird. Shoot, I did not even know if she *liked* chocolate. Whatever; maybe someone in her office did. An expensive apology, yes, but it was not as if I could call—I still did not have her number. I needed it all done before I saw her at church again on Wednesday. That is, if she ever came back.

I messed up several cards, even though I practiced what to write on the way to the shop. Everything I wrote sounded stupid. Too embarrassed to ask for yet another card, I left the last one as it was. The others, I wadded up and stuffed into my pocket, and paid without even looking at the bill. The card read:

Roses for my Rose
Loving you,
Randall

Back home, I did nothing for the rest of the day, not even taking phone calls. I finally responded by text to one of Tre's voice messages. I felt horrible that I hurt her, but too bad to talk about it, even to my best friend. How did I let myself get into this situation?

Around midnight, I decided I had to man up. I left three messages on Danielle's office phone, all of them apologies in some form or fashion.

Tuesday

I could not recall what time she told me she got to her office. I think she said "early". Was her early my early? Was anyone's early as soon as mine was? I waited until eight to call. Every office in the time zone would surely be open by then. Naturally, I was placed on hold. My heart raced; the blood jumped in my veins. Finally, a voice in my ear blandly announced, "Sorry, Ms. Rose is unavailable. May I take a message?"

"No thanks. I will call back."

I knew where this was headed—this was my game. I screened calls on a daily basis. How could Danielle know how many times my girl Mimi fed the exact same line to all the love-struck ladies, the TV reporters, gossip magazines, and all the other vultures who called me? Even the ones who actually made it through to Vardo, my human firewall, got the exact same line.

I was not to be ignored. I got dressed, hopped in the car, and within the hour, I was standing in the lobby of the gleaming Buckhead skyscraper where Danielle's firm had its headquarters. I was alone, without my crew. The building security guard, a young man dressed in a smart black suit, escorted me up to her floor.

"Wow, what an honor, Mr. Washington," the awestruck kid said, holding the elevator door. "You have a great day."

You see, I did not have to grease any palms to get into her office; just being Hooks Washington was all it took. I was here today as Randall, trying my best to defend Hooks.

The minute I walked into the place, I was mauled. It seemed like everyone in the building somehow already knew I was there. Time for shrieks, selfies, pleas for autographs, hugs, kisses--the usual. Did a message go out over the building intercom? I was not in the mood for this today. I was here for one reason--to apologize for being the person I apparently was, Hooks Washington. No wonder Danielle was angry.

A polished-looking young woman who might have been fresh out of Spellman College greeted me in the lobby of the firm with a polite but knowing smile. "Good morning, Mr. Washington. I am sorry, but Ms. Rose is unavailable. Was she expecting you?"

Ouch. That was cold. I was expecting freezing temperatures from Danielle, but not from everyone else. I recognized the voice from my phone call earlier.

"No, she is not expecting me, and I can understand if she is not available. I do not intend to bother her, but I am prepared to wait. Shall I sit here?" My question was not really a question.

"Yes, of course. If you like."

Did I have a choice? I would wait until Danielle came out and spoke to me. As for Miss Spellman College, whom I figured must be Danielle's personal assistant, I knew I put her in a bad situation. She sat there shuffling papers, making a point of not letting Danielle know I was waiting. Obviously, the two plotted beforehand—Danielle made it clear that she was not speaking to me. Barring an alternate escape route, like stairs leading down for fifteen stories, I felt certain Danielle would have to come out eventually. I certainly had nothing else to do. Sad, right?

On the other hand, everywhere you looked there were little vases of roses. Evidently, my gift was shared among all the employees. The place smelled as fragrant as the Atlanta Botanical Gardens on a hot day in June. So at least she accepted my gift. Now if only she would accept my heart.

Meanwhile, the fans and groupies kept up with their infernal racket. Trying to be polite, I kept waving them away. Louder than I intended, I finally announced, "Sorry, everyone, but I am not signing autographs today—though if one of you can get Ms. Rose to speak to me, I'd be more than happy to give you all the memorabilia you want."

The fuss must have disturbed Danielle. She peeked through a door I could see directly behind the reception desk, spotted me just long enough to make eye contact, and slammed the door. I looked around at the crowd. "There--that's the lady I'm here to see," I said. "Help make that happen and everybody gets what they want."

I sat there for most of the morning. After an hour or so, the autograph-hounds and selfie-snappers gave up and, I guess, went back to whatever it was they were supposed to be doing.

I did not move. I did not check an email, send a text, or take a call. All I did was to pick up some heavy book I found sitting on the coffee table, loaded with photographs of buildings, and idly flipped through it.

Around noon, the door to Danielle's office opened again. There she was, her hands full of bound documents, her face a tight mask of concentration. I quickly set the book down and stood up. Danielle, looking at me as if I were just another piece of furniture, took off down a hall that led off the reception area. I shot a questioning look at the assistant, who shrugged.

I took off after Danielle. By the time I caught up, she stopped in front of the ladies' room. Not saying a word, she handed me the stack of documents. I estimated that whatever she needed to do in the ladies' room would happen fast. I had to get my thoughts together in a hurry. Once she emerged, all I could offer was, "Good morning, Ms. Rose. It's a pleasure to see you."

"Thank you," she said curtly, taking the papers back. Not, I decided, thanks for the chocolate or the flowers—just thanks for holding her stuff.

Soon we arrived at a large conference room, lit by tall windows and with framed art prints on the walls, set with a long glass table surrounded by padded leather chairs. Danielle, having laid a folder before every chair, began fiddling with her computer. About this time, Miss Spellman came racing in, looking apologetic.

"What can I do, Ms. Rose?" she asked.

"It's okay, Leigh," Danielle replied. "Just show our uninvited guest over there to a seat in the hall, and see that he is comfortable."

I took the hint, and sat down in a chair outside the room, my hands folded in my lap, waiting to see what would happen next.

People began to arrive, slowly and then in a rush. Most of them recognized me and greeted me by name. They all looked surprised and thrilled, but no one pestered me for autographs—this was the executive group. I discerned.

Shortly after almost every chair was taken, Danielle peered through the doorway, as if looking for latecomers. She spotted me sitting against the wall. "Hi," I said, feeling a bit foolish. "Ready to hold more stuff, anytime you need it."

For the second time today, she shut the door. I could not decide if I felt like crying or laughing. How long was this going to go on? Tameka has played this game with me for years, and I have been okay with it—after all, I am a fighter, and I can take blows. The problem was I did not want to get beat up anymore.

"Let's get started," I heard Danielle say. "This is a big project, and I think you all know that a lot is riding on it." A few minutes into her presentation, an older gentleman approached me, his phone to his ear, laughing as at some joke.

Seeing me, he spoke. "You locked out on account of tardiness, too, friend?"

"Locked out, yes. But not for tardiness."

I saw the change come over his face as he realized who I was. "Look," he said quickly, speaking into his cell, "I'm at Danielle's meeting, and I better run. The last thing I need is to arrive late and talking on my phone." Of course, that reminded me of Danielle showing up late at church, still on her phone. *Probably best not to bring that up right now.*

The old fellow eagerly stuck out his hand. "Henry Sanders," he said. "An honor to meet you in person, Mr. Hooks."

I stood up.

"Why are you sitting here outside, champ? Do not tell me you are late, too. That Danielle despises tardiness."

"No, Mr. Sanders, I am not here for the meeting. However, thanks for letting me know she hates lateness. To be honest, right now, I think she hates me, too."

"Hates you? Hell, champ, nobody in the whole country hates you! Why, you are an all-American hero! The top fighter in the entire U.S. of A!"

"Thanks, Henry, but honestly, I think that may be precisely the problem."

"Never mind, champ," the old guy went on. "The lady is a tyrant, a real stickler. You have your work cut out for you, sure enough. But I have seen you in the ring, and I know you can handle her." He lowered his voice to a loud whisper. "Do not tell her I said this, but deep-down, she is just a lonely little girl. She acts as if she is hard as steel, as if she can fly and walk on water. How about we interrupt this august assembly, and you just watch—she'll get upset with me, not you."

"Okay, sir. I am right here with you," I said, reluctantly but happy for the help.

 Sanders flung open the door as if he owned it—which, as I was soon to find out, he actually did. "Excuse me, Danielle," he bellowed cheerfully. Turning and seeing both of us, she stopped dead in her tracks.

"Why, Mr. Sanders." Her voice was brash yet cool. "So delighted you could be with us today."

Sanders pulled me into the room. "Dani, I know I am late again, and I know how much you despise tardiness. But I wanted to introduce you all to someone I ran into sitting right outside this room—the great Hooks Washington."

He tugged at me triumphantly.

"Get on in here, Hooks."

If looks could kill, I would have been dead at that moment. "His name is *Deacon* Washington, as far as I'm concerned," I heard Danielle mutter.

Luckily, Sanders did not hear her sidebar remark. "I'm sorry to barge in, Ms. Rose," I said, feeling all the eyes in the room on me. "Please forgive my interruption. I'll be leaving now."

"You'll do no such a thing," Sanders shot back. "You are our honored guest. Besides, someday you may need Sanders, Carmichael, Morrison, Schwartz and one day Rose to facilitate a venture for you. A boxing arena, perhaps—what a boon that would be for our fair city."

Then the old guy spun back around, facing Danielle. "I'm sure our talented, rising young star here would love to add that to her long and impressive resume, right, Dani? You two should check out the idea over lunch."

Danielle rolled her eyes. "It would be my honor to add more accomplishments to Ms. Rose's list of accolades," I said. "In fact, I do have a few proposals in mind. But I'm not sure Ms. Rose will accept my first proposal, which is to take her to lunch."

Danielle picked up her cell phone; her thumbs tapped the keyboard furiously. Somewhere, a phone pinged. "Leigh, I believe that's you," she snapped.

Out of the corner of my eye, I saw Leigh tap her phone screen. I wondered what her text read. Did she just text a person in the room and openly say she was receiving a text from her? Wow, could this woman play hardball. She was not giving in, and I was not giving up. This was good for me, I decided. I was getting the chance to see another side of Danielle. The results were surprising. Gone was the sweetly flirtatious young woman from church; here, she was tough as nails, all about business. I winked at her once, just to see what would happen. She gave me the death stare. Whew. I could see what old Henry meant. She was relentless.

The meeting went on as before, with her giving everyone in the room hell about one thing or another. I felt happy it was not just me. One fellow, the kind of guy who used to play football in high school but has gone to fat, leaned over and whispered, "This is nothing. Can you come more often, dude? She's going easy on us today."

Easy? That scared me. The silent treatment I was getting could go on for months at this rate. As I pondered all this, it seemed the meeting ended. Danielle stood up.

"That's it for now," she said crisply. "Let's make sure all the kinks get ironed out of this before we meet next week. Now, if you'll excuse me, I have an appointment I can't miss." With that, she was gone.

Everyone in the room looked at me as if it was my duty to go after her. Therefore, I got up and followed her. Without looking back, she asked, "No crew? No bodyguards today, Mr. Washington?"

"Call me Randall. And yes, I kind of think I can handle this on my own."

In no time, we were back at her office. "Good day, Mr. Washington," she said briskly, and slammed the door. I had to laugh—not because I found it funny to have the door slammed in my face three times in one day, but because we were back where we started. Nothing changed.

I took my seat back on the sofa as before. Leigh appeared at my side, offering me a bottle of cold water. I picked up the big book I was paging through earlier. This time, I noticed the title: *A Decade of Great Buildings, by Noted Architect Danielle Rose*. A thought occurred to me.

"Leigh, I would like to purchase a copy of this book," I said. "In fact, I'll buy as many copies as you have available to sell."

She looked up, surprised but pleased. "I'd be glad to inquire about that, Mr. Hooks," she replied. "Let me speak to Ms. Rose for a moment." Behind the door, I heard the two women's voices, low at first, then louder.

Leigh stepped back into the reception area and looked at me with something close to embarrassment.

"Um, Ms. Rose says it will cost you one thousand dollars a book," she said.

"That's perfectly fine," I replied. "Give me as many copies as you have. She is selling herself short." I pulled my money clip out, peeled off ten bills, and handed them to her.

Next, I knew, Danielle's door flew open. She charged out and snatched the bills from her astonished assistant's hand, and threw them at me. "Take your book, Mr. Washington," she snapped. "There won't be a charge."

In shock, I bent down and began to pick up the bills. Among them was what I took to be a business card—dainty, ivory-colored, with embossed lettering. I picked it up, puzzled. There, beneath her name and title, all in prim, flowing script, were two numbers—her cell phone and a home phone. The Holy Grail. I felt like my smile was threatening to split my face in two.

"Thank you for the book, Ms. Rose. Thank you for allowing me to observe your work. I really appreciate it." I handed Leigh two hundred-dollar bills. "Young lady, this is for all the trouble I caused you today," I said. "Please treat yourself and Ms. Rose to a nice lunch and dinner."

I turned to Danielle. "Ms. Rose, I hope to see you at the track tonight. I won't be late." I took her hand, and daringly, kissed it. Then, like a man in a dream, I took the elevator down to the busy street below.

As I walked to my car, I considered the day's events. I did not get what I went for, but as far as I was concerned, I totally won. It seemed I had managed to annoy Danielle enough for her to at least speak to me—and even to hand over her precious contact information. Maybe she was not as tough as she thought she was.

On the drive home, thunderheads loomed in the sky. All of a sudden, a huge squall of rain swept through. There would be no track tonight, I thought to myself. Hopefully, she would show up at church tomorrow night. Plus, I officially had her contact information. At last, I had permission to call her.

Back home, I undressed and sat on the edge of my bed, thinking. The real issue between us remained the same. I could not change who I was. All I could do was show her who I wanted to be—namely, the man in her life. I needed her, and from what I could tell, I think she needed me too.

We were both disciplined, yet both our lives were lacking order. Of course, we had God's order, divine order, spiritual order--but no emotional logic in our lives at all. It was evident in the way we responded to events, and in how seriously we took our careers. It was as if we were trying to find that inner order by controlling all other aspects of our lives.

What if I was all wrong? What if I was a nobody to her? Would she have felt differently if I were a stockbroker, an educator, or an attorney? She never once asked me where I worked, even though I questioned her eagerly about what she did.

Being a first-class architect and engineer was her job. After today, I could see she took it seriously, not to mention she was good at it. As for me, fighting was my job. At the end of the day, the guy they call "Hooks" does not really exist--he is just a character, a role that I play.

One thing was true; we each poured ourselves into our work and fought through the pain. She may not have agreed, but it looked to me as if we were exactly alike. She worked hard, and she played hard. The proof was there, in the rides she pushed, the house she lived in, and the clothes she wore. It was the same for me. Our work was not enough for either of us—we both wanted to be loved.

As CEO of Hooks Incorporated, I decided right then and there to make an executive decision: the time for love was now.

Then, I blogged.

Today, I learned what it means to turn the other cheek. In my world, you cannot, or you will take a jab. After today, I see that I may not always come out the winner. As in boxing, you have to pick and choose your battles. You do not take on an opponent you know is bigger and better than you. Nor go into a fight unprepared. You weigh the pros and cons; you strategize. Most of the time I have someone else doing this for me, so all I do is throw punches. But today, I had plenty of time to sit back and strategize. There was never the right time to jump in the ring. So I sat back and watched my opponent. And at the end of the day, I walked away, like the song about the Gambler. *You have to know when to hold 'em; them; know when to fold 'em; know when to walk away, know when to run.* I walked away. Tomorrow I will get up and try again. It's the fighter in me. I pray the God in her will give her the strength to forgive me. I will be waiting and watering my Rose until she blooms again. I am fasting and praying that tomorrow, I will receive her forgiveness.

With all my love,

Randall

Wednesday

I woke up feeling just as comatose today as I did two days ago. I was certain this would wear off, and I would feel better. I felt so sure Danielle would have contacted me by now. Honestly, though, I cannot say *I* would talk to me either. I do not like being the center of attention, so why would she want to thrust herself into my crazy life? From the books and framed awards, I saw at her office yesterday, I do not think she is by any means shy nor do I think she would ever pursue me for the money or the fame, as she herself has plenty of both?

Nor is she the impressionable type. Which means all the gifts I sent her may have been useless. The same goes for what I have planned for today. Too bad--it is too late to cancel. Chatting with Leigh yesterday, I managed to discover some of her boss's favorite foods and restaurants. I am sure giving me the information was against Leigh's better judgment. Although I can be quite pleasant on the surface, I can be also extremely peremptory. It is one way I get things done. I am not militant, but I have a lot of military thoughts and behaviors in me. It is part of my discipline. The mindset keeps me and those around me focused.

In any event, after I got the information I needed, I called my favorite chef, and ordered a beautiful platter of tasty victuals and culinary delights to be delivered to Danielle's office at lunchtime today. I went by the restaurant and hand-wrote another note to be delivered with the food.

Trying not to think about what this latest stunt was going to cost me, I was praying maybe this time, my efforts would trigger her to call me. Even if she did not, maybe she would at least come to service tonight. I desperately needed to see her, to talk to her. I could not possibly humiliate myself by showing up and sitting in her lobby for yet another day--although I would do it if I thought it would help. Judging by her disposition yesterday, I suspect I would have to sit there for weeks.

What a woman she was--tenacious, feisty, resilient and flat-out stubborn. I laughed at the thought. For some reason, I loved it—it challenged me. Danielle was so polarizing—so frustrating, and yet I fed off her energy. She stimulated my mind and body, in ways I had best not describe. The sad part was it could be weeks before she spoke to me again, and I knew it.

I wanted to call Tre. I wanted to call my Dad. I needed to talk to King. Somehow, I had to make sense of everything I was feeling. What could I do? What should I do? Finally, I did what any confused and inexperienced kid would do. I called my father – and not just one, but all of them.

First, I lay prostrate before my heavenly father. I told Him what I needed, what I wanted. I asked, I pleaded, and I begged. *"Father in heaven, let the words of my mouth and the meditation of my heart be acceptable in your sight; oh Lord, my strength and my redeemer."* After my tears ran dry, I finished up and then I called my natural father, my dad.

"Hello, son. What a pleasure to hear from you."

I immediately broke into sobs.

"Son, what on earth is wrong?" I could hear the alarm in his voice.

"Dad, I am hurting."

Being the father of a professional fighter, he misunderstood. "Where are you, son?" he asked. "What hurts?"

I heard Mom yelling in the background. "Where is Randy? What is going on? Let me speak to him!"

"Dad, this is guy stuff."

"Hold on honey," he yelled. "He's okay. Randy and I need to have a man-to-man talk." I heard the sound of a door closing. "Okay, what is going on, Randy?"

"Dad, I have messed up my life."

"What do you mean? Randall, are you in some kind of trouble?"

"No, Dad, calm down, nothing like that. I should have listened to you. Here I am, thirty years old. A grown man married to a woman whom I do not like, and whom I no longer know. I have not known Tameka for years--not physically, mentally, or spiritually. She has totally wrecked my life."

"Son, I think you can take some of the blame too."

That hurt, but I knew my father was right. "I know. I should never have gotten myself into this mess. Once I did, I should have gotten out years ago. Here I am, a talented athlete, scared to face the public. Scared to live outside of my own walls, because I do not want others to see the mess, the total failure my personal life has become."

I drew a deep breath, trying to compose myself. "I feel like I am living a lie. I have everything, yet I have nothing. My hands are tied. I am so tired of this fight. I cannot go after what I want, because I still have this dead weight, this ball and chain around my ankle. This marriage is dead. It is killing me from the inside out, like an infection. I have to do something. I need you to help me get out of this. I need you to make it go away."

Now I was sounding like the little kid I felt myself to be at that moment.

"Randall, exactly what is this all about?" His father sounded confused.

"Dad, I have met a woman."

"*Umm hmm.* Okay--now this is all starting to make a little sense."

"I do not know her as well I would like to. All I know about her is what I have read, seen, or been told. I have tried to be open with her. At first, I did not tell her who I was, but she found out anyway. Not that I am ashamed of what I do--I wanted to make sure she knows me first as Randall, not Hooks. I finally told her I was married, which is why I cannot be as close to her as I want to. Now she will not talk to me. Tameka still will not give me a divorce. I feel my whole world is crumbling around me. I found the person of my dreams, while the person of my nightmares is holding me back. What can I do?"

"Well, now, RW. I am shocked, impressed, happy, and hurt."

"What do you mean?"

"You have a son of your own--one day you'll understand. What I am saying is, I am shocked you finally stepped out and found someone to love. Your mom and I almost gave up hope that you would ever love again. I am impressed at how you feel--how emotional you are, and not afraid to express it. I mean, a big, strong guy like you, spilling his heart out to his father—well son that takes guts. Guts we all know you have, and this conversation confirmed it on a whole new level."

"I'm happy you have found someone to love you, for who you are, the good man you always have been and will always be. Not for the guy you are in the ring. I am impressed that you finally acknowledge the difference between Randall and Hooks. I am proud you want to do things correctly, and in the right order.

"But son, anytime your child hurts, so do you. This is a pain I cannot fix, which hurts me. There is one thing I do know. Just like I hurt for you, so does our father in heaven. You are my child, Randall, but you are His child first. The last thing He wants is for you is hurt. Talk to Him, son. Trust Him. Lie down and labor before Him. If it is in His will for you to find happiness, He will bring it to pass. Your latter days will be better than your first. Believe, stay focused, and continue to pray--you know what to do. He sees you. He knows your pain. He can take it away in the blink of an eye. He is faithful. I am proud of you, son. I love you, and I will pray for you diligently."

"Thanks, Dad." It felt as if a big weight on my spirit had been lightened.

"Oh, and one more thing, RW," he sounded like he was smiling.

"Yes, sir."

"Your mother and I cannot wait to meet her."

He said this as if I had never brought home a girl to meet my parents. Which happened to be true.

"Thanks." I hung up and got ready to make the next call, this time to my pastor, my spiritual father.

Tre picked up the call on the first ring. "Pastor Hunter, how can I help you?"

I could not speak.

"Good morning, Washington."

All I could do was sniffle.

"I knew this was coming. Your morning inspiration led me to believe today would be the day. Do you want to talk about it?"

"I do, Pastor, but I can't." Tre knew whenever I called him Pastor; it was not going to be one of our normal friendly conversations. As a rule, we had an unspoken agreement—he did not call me Champ, and I did not call him Pastor. It was not out of disrespect. I revered Trevor as a man of God. However, we both treasured our friendship. Today, I needed him both ways.

"You want to talk, but you say you can't. Tell me why."

"Because you do not like what I am doing, and I know you will disagree."

"Humph. Do not worry about what *I* like. You need to worry about what your Father likes. I am not your judge or redeemer, RW. Believe me, I feel your pain. I feel it in your life, your conversation, even your body language. I want you to be whole and holy. God gave us all the help we need, including His only son. So call on Him."

This all sounded familiar. Dad and Tre were on the same wavelength for sure.

"Of course, keep your attorneys and accountants involved, they will do the work--but you need to ask God to give them the wisdom to speak the right things on your behalf, and to have your interest at heart."

Good point, I thought.

"Now go, and do things in decency and in order. I want only the best for you, my friend. It has already been written--God is the author and the finisher of your story. All you need to do is pray about it. Walk in faith."

I listened saying nothing.

"It's no coincidence you two met, and I don't think we have seen the end of this story. This is only the beginning. Eyes have not seen nor have ears heard what you two will accomplish."

My Pastor declared and prophesied the Word to me. His words breathed life into my dry bones.

"He is a faithful and just God," Tre went on. "Trust Him now as you have always done. He is not a man that He should lie. Nor is He the son of man that He should repent. Whatever He promised will come to pass. Speak his Word back to him."

"I love you, Pastor."

"I love you, Champ. Get up, shake the dusk off, handle your business first, and then do what you need to do. Go get the girl of your dreams. I plan to dance at your wedding. It is all in His plan."

"Thanks. I will see you at church. I do not know about a wedding, but if there is one, you will be pronouncing us husband and wife."

"Oh, no. I'll be the best man."

"Call it what you want. And for the record, I am proposing in your sanctuary."

"You will do no such thing!"

"Watch me."

"*Champ*," he said in a threatening tone.

"Yes."

"Don't wear the carpet out today." He was insinuating I would be at the altar all day long.

"I will not. I will lie down in one place."

"You can do this."

"Thanks for believing in me," I told him. My heart was overflowing.

"Anytime. I will be so happy when I can marry you two, even though I will probably lose half of my female congregation, as well as all the men who follow that half. Oh well."

"Good-bye, Pastor. And thanks." I was not ready to make the last call. This time, to the man who is my head trainer, and my strong right hand—King. I knew this last call was going to be the most excruciating.

King answered right away. "Boss, what's up?"

"I need to skip training today."

"I can't let you do that."

"I have to."

"Not an option."

"I did not ask your permission."

"Nor was it granted."

"I will be at the church if you want to talk more."

"Don't start this, Hooks," he sounded angry.

"Start what?"

"Getting weak on me."

I paused. Honestly, I was beyond weak. I prided myself on my meekness, but this was beyond meek. It was pathetic. It was heartbreaking and embarrassing all at once.

"King, I am not up to it. I have to do this. I have to have a life outside boxing. It has taken me so long to discover it. I am sorry I have held you all hostage for the past ten years. I should have released you all from bondage. I have worked so hard, and I have worked you guys just as hard. We have accomplished a lot--but we have failed in many ways. Look at us, King, a bunch of single, lonely men. All of us avoiding love because we have no clue what to do with it. Here I am hurt, twisted up inside, and destroyed, all over a person I know nothing about. All I know is that I love her. I have spent my whole life fighting, when I should have spent more time loving. I am starting over from scratch. I need your help, King. I need to learn to love. I need to learn to be intimate and emotional. I need more than fighting, and you do too. We all do. King, we cannot fight forever. We need to think about this now, or it will be too late. What about the future? What happens if I never fight again? Does that mean our lives amount to nothing? I mean it--we all need someone to love."

Once I started, I could not stop. The words came pouring out. I asked King to trust me. We cannot do this forever, I told him. Then I sprang the news—I decided I want to fight again. I am ready to be back in the ring. At the same time, I wanted to love again.

"I hope and pray you will support me on this journey. The same way I need you to help train to fight, I need you to let me learn to love. The truth is I am desperate."

Not to my surprise, King did not get it at all. Why should he? Fighting covered all his needs. King could hear the desperation in his fighter's voice. He did not agree. He could not teach him to love if he did agree. Had Hooks not seen his track record of love? Evidently not. He did not want to love. It was too much work and too much emotion involved. He liked the way he was. Fighting covered his needs and thoughts of love. Now here his only fighter was proposing a change, one he did not see coming.

"This Rose girl is ruining your life," he snapped. "She will pay for this. She is destroying you, Hooks. Me as well. I will meet you at the church," he added dryly and hung up the line without offering any other words.

I thought about my conversation with King. I was not disappointed. I knew King would be the toughest of anyone in the crew—not like JJ, who was always easygoing. A guy who gave you his opinion and that was that. Or Keith, a hard, disciplined man, but always fair. Or Sol, for that matter—all about business, his eye on the bottom line.

What if King was right? What if instead of a new start, this would be the end of my career. Was I asking too much to want someone to love? Someone to touch. Someone to trust. Someone to know and hold. I need arms other than His to love me. Why couldn't King understand?

I thought about the conversation all the way to the church. Once I arrived, I was not exactly delighted to spot Melissa.

I do not believe I have told you about Melissa yet. She is what you might call the church's German Shepherd, the first one you see when you come in, always stationed at that front desk. Does she ever go home? If it were not for Trevor, I would call the Department of Labor myself. I mean, the girl must work twenty-four hours a day. People swear she goes home, but I do not believe it. Any time and every time I arrive, she is here.

To make matters worse, Melissa comes close to being a stalker. She is completely infatuated with me, and she does not try to hide it. Even though she is by no means ugly, she is the last person on earth I would think of in that way. Today was not the day for her silly innuendos and flirty teasing. So I snuck in a back door to avoid her. Thank God, I had the keys to the kingdom, so to speak.

I went straight to my office before I realized the folly of my strategy. Melissa had cameras at her desk; she could see everything that was going on. No way could I sneak in. Sure enough, in no time at all, I heard her footsteps approaching. Hastily, I closed the door. Once she was gone, I raced to the sanctuary. I threw myself down, and there I lay, laboring hard before the Lord.

Next thing I knew, JJ was lifting me. "Get up, son. The congregation is arriving. Go get dressed."

"No way," I groaned. "It cannot be that late." JJ pointed to the clock on the wall—a quarter to six. I had been there all day. A few rows behind me I spotted King, sitting off to one side, on guard but minding his own business. I never heard him come in. Outside, I saw flashes of lightning and sheets of rain pouring down.

"Hooks, what did you do to get King so upset?" hissed JJ. It was apparent King told him we were at odds. I understood King's position, but I needed him to understand mine. I started to fill JJ in, but I was interrupted by Tre's voice. That was unusual--Hunter was never here this early on a Wednesday night. Someone must have summoned him. Let me guess—the stalker-poodle Melissa on the front desk? No way was I feeling her. That girl could call down Jesus Himself, and I still would not be interested. I only had eyes for Danielle Rose. Could Melissa get Danielle to talk to me? Not likely, but if so, she would be my friend for life.

As I realized what a huge storm was raging outside, I decided Danielle would probably not show. If she was on the road right now, I was worried about her safety. You see, her driving record was given to me, and it proved beyond a doubt that she was not afraid of speed, and putting the pedal to the metal. In that case, she needed to stay home. However, if she decided to come anyway, surely I should send someone to greet her in the parking lot. On the other hand, would that be acting like a stalker again? Either way, it might be too late now. I pulled out my phone, spotted King glaring at me, and had second thoughts.

Instead, I radioed Dex, hoping he brought his rain gear, given how flooded it must be in the parking lot. "Dex, if she shows, will you instruct Ms. Danielle to the back?" I asked him. "I will have someone park her car to avoid her getting drenched."

"Sure enough, Deac," replied Dexter, cheerful as always. "But hey, I didn't know we offered valet service. Is that for everyone, or only people whose last name Rose?"

"Her last name is Rose for now, my friend, but it will soon be Washington. Mark my words."

"Confident, are you?"

"I sure am."

"Deacon, I'd like to see you take that confidence back into the ring someday."

"Hold on. I am working on that too."

"All right, Deac, if I see her, I promise to send her back nice and dry."

I was sitting watch at my monitor when she arrived. I saw a group of guys with umbrellas approach her all at once, each trying to be the one to escort her out of her car and into the building. She entered the building looking completely composed. She took her usual seat, not seeming to notice I was nowhere in sight.

I watched her during the entire service. Afterward, I did not have the balls to face her. I did not want my feelings hurt any more. Especially not in front of all these people. My pride was involved. At the track, or sitting in her office, was one thing; but this was my zone. I watched her leave, escorted by one of the deacons, who was walking at top speed trying to keep up with her. She got into her car and pulled out of the lot. The deacon approached me shaking drops of water from his umbrella.

"Miss Danielle asked where you were," he said. "She didn't seem very happy to hear you were somewhere inside." I hated to admit it, but hearing that made me happy.

Just then, Trevor walked by my office, looking in and shaking his head. "Coward."

There was nothing I could say to respond. Hiding in the back of the church, not speaking to her—yes, that was cowardly. On the other hand, if I had hidden at the very start of all this, I would not be in this jacked-up situation.

I drove home slowly in the rain, feeling chastened. Once inside, I went straight to my study and blogged. I wanted to get some things off my chest. Who knew whether she even read my blogs? I took a chance and posted anyway.

> Today has been a painful day, full of misery. My will to fight is gone. I am in a losing battle. I could not face my opponent. I was a coward. I hid in the shadows and let someone else have the victory. This is my first real defeat, and I hope the last. I am glad for the rain today; it matched the feelings in my heart. May God comfort, keep, and strengthen me to continue this battle. Be blessed until we meet again. Missing your presence,
> Randall

Thursday

Today I got up and started getting ready to meet King at the gym. I took my time. Before I left, I arranged for gift cards from the spa in Danielle's building to be delivered to her office. I hope she uses them, but who knows? It was still dark, five past the hour when I arrived.

King, seated in a chair with an unfolded newspaper, spoke without looking up. "Why are you late to my training?"

"I am here, aren't I?"

He glanced at me furiously. "That was not the question."

"But that was my answer."

King grunted and threw the paper down.

"You got a problem?" I asked.

"No. But you do," he snapped.

"You want to take it to the ring?" Now I was being a smarty. King stood up. I was shocked to see the fury in his eyes. I raised my hands, ready for whatever he had in mind.

The next thing I knew, I was flat on my back on the floor. I could hear, but not see. Was I even alive? *I cannot die now. I just found love.* Did he really hit me? *If I ever get up off this floor,* I decided groggily, *I will kill King with my bare hands.*

I must have passed out again, because when I opened my eyes, I was lying in a bed. White lights glared in my face. I heard the sound of beeping.

"Mr. Washington, how do you feel?"

I tried to open my eyes. No way could I be in a hospital. I felt a surge of anger; I sat up, looking around for King. Bad idea--my head started to spin, whether from blows or from anger, I do not know. With a moan, I flopped back down.

I heard a faraway voice ask weakly, "Can I have a Tylenol?" *Surely, that was not me,* I thought. Then a second thought: *King will die. As soon as I can stop my head from hurting.*

A short, cheerful lady dressed in a pink uniform brought me a tiny cup with a pill. She helped me sit up, so I could swallow.

Gathered around my bed, looking anxiously at me, were Trevor, his wife Gabby, most of my fellow deacons, the crew, including King, Keith, Nate, and JJ. My head throbbed; I could barely open my eyes. *Is this how my opponent usually feels? I have been fighting a long time, and I have never felt like this before.*

"Gabe, what time is it?"

"Hi, sweetie," she said mildly, as if it were normal for me to be laid up in the hospital. "How do you feel?"

"My head is killing me. What time is it?"

"Eight o'clock."

"What? Like, eight o'clock at night?"

"That's right," Gabe answered, being the civilized spokesperson of the bunch.

"What day?"

"Thursday," Trevor interjected. He stood over me wiping his hands. Had he put oil and unguent on my forehead?

"Thanks, Tre. I'm good." Everyone seemed to sigh all at once, and there was a hum of relieved-sounding murmuring. Squinting against the pain, I looked around.

"How long are they going to keep me?"

"A few more hours and then the doctor may let you go home," Gabe said.

"Where is my phone?"

JJ handed it to me. I was still dressed, except for my shirt and shoes. I desperately needed to make a call in private, but there was no way I could get up. Squinting against the bright lights, I checked my messages. I shielded my face with one hand, to block the glare and, I hoped, to disguise my anger. There was no message from Danielle.

"Did anyone call my parents?"

"Yes, they left a little while ago with my parents. You should call them," Trevor advised.

"Has Danielle called? Did anyone call her?"

"She called the gym last night, and numerous times today. It got pretty annoying," said JJ.

"So she knows I am here?"

No one answered. I was relieved to know she called me. Her numbers are in my phone, but I am in no condition to call her yet.

"What did you want us to say to the esteemed Ms. Rose?" King asked sarcastically.

"Nothing, man. I got it."

The nurse returned to check my vital signs. I told her I needed to use the restroom.

"Okay," she said, her accent lilting with the sound of the islands. "The doctor is on his way. But before you stand up, Mr. Washington, let's do a quick neurological check." She held up fingers for me to count, then gave me permission to move. Trevor and Keith helped me. King sat off to one side, hunkered down in a chair, staring at the floor.

The second I was back on my feet, I felt all my rage at King return. I jumped around the room with my fists flying. Gabe and the rest of them stared at me in shock. *I know I said let us take it to the ring.* I am the fighter. There is a logical reason why we fight in a cushioned ring. This was the reason why. Here it is: the trainer I pay questions me why I am late to my gym, and then lands me a full day in the hospital. He was going to pay for this. I walked over to King and snuck him while he was sitting in a chair. "That is for hitting me." Then I flipped the entire chair. "That is for GP." I leaned over, my head reeling with pain, and punched him again. "And that is for me spending the day laid up."

Finally, I made it to the bathroom, still mad as hell, not caring a damn about all the ruckus I just caused. The room was a complete mess when the doctors and nurses arrived. By the time I finished my business, two uniformed officers surfaced, and were standing at the foot of my bed. Washing my hands at the sink, I cracked the door and beckoned to Gabe.

"Gentlemen, it's cool," I said. "You can stand down. I promise I will behave," I said to the officers as Gabby closed the restroom door. "Sorry you had to see that. Can you take me home?" Suddenly I felt exhausted.

"Sure, as soon as they release you. Assuming you can control yourself." She was smiling, but I could tell she was dead serious.

It was after midnight before they released me. No one left the room. My parents were back, so things were starting to get a bit cramped. My mother had taken up a post beside King, by now back in his chair, and she was chastening him royally.

"I do *not* expect my child to end up with a serious head injury inflicted by his own trainer, his employee, and the person I *thought* was his friend," she scolded. "This needs to be the last time we do this. I hope everyone in the room understands, and passes my message along to anyone who isn't here."

She shook her head disbelievingly. "It's bad enough I have to worry day and night about some punk trying to make his rep by attacking my son, just so he can brag about it," she snapped. "Not to mention when my baby is in the ring—then *you know* I am worried to death. But I surely do not expect to get a call saying Mr. King here has gone and knocked him out."

She bent down so she was face to face with King. "My son is a world champion. There is no way you all are going to insist this was a fair fight. I might have been born at night, but not tomorrow night! You take that and feed it to the birds!"

Whew. Mom was just getting started. When she got this wound up, well, everybody watch out, is all I can say.

"Do you know why most of you in this room even have a job?" she yelled. "I didn't think so! 'Cause I worry like crazy about my child in those streets running, driving nice cars, wearing flashy jewels, carrying unthinkable amounts of cash, living in that museum or mausoleum or whatever you call that house. Cause it surely ain't no proper house or home. I told him when he was twenty-three years old, and his bank account reached double-digit millions, the only way I would be at peace was if he hired someone to be with him at all times. I told him to hire you all. Do you really think he wants you all hanging around him all day? Do you honestly think he could not kick someone's butt by himself? Safety is better in numbers, right? When we grew up, you didn't fight each other; you fought the ones that were *against* you, not those *on your team.* Ain't that right?"

"Uh huh. Yes indeed. You know that's right." Everybody in the room, including my dad, Hunter and Gabby, were nodding their heads and saying amen, even the two cops. Mom, of course, was far from done.

"This is absurd. I *knew* something was going on yesterday when my baby called, keeping secrets from his momma. Then today I have to worry, is he is going to come through? Is he in a coma? Is he in his right mind? Will he ever be the same? So now not only must I fear every opponent he has fought deciding to get revenge--now I got to worry whether he's gonna get hurt by the same guys paid to train and protect him!"

"Mom, it's okay," I said. I was lying. My head was splitting. I knew what they meant when they said "seeing stars". Man, could my Mom ever lay it down. This was going to warrant a team meeting. It was going to be bad. After all, I thought, *I am the boss. I make the rules. What I say goes. Period. The end.*

My personal doctor picked this somewhat awkward moment to show up assuring, me he had been by earlier. "Doc," I said, "all I want from you is to tell these folks to let me go home."

"To the mausoleum, as your mother calls it," Tre's mother piped up, as if to affirm what Mom said. Hold it, I thought; I was already laid up. It was probably not in my best interest to dispute my mother's word or her best friends.

I kept trying to look at my phone. My son called a few times. I was ready to go, close to getting belligerent, which is completely unlike me. It must have been anger and spite driving my emotions.

Finally, the hospital quack—sorry, I mean the doctor—came back. He was doing his job, I told myself--imagine the lawsuit he would face if he let me go with a serious head injury. He checked my eyes, and asked me on a scale of one to ten how bad did my head hurt. Fifty would have been about right, but I said seven, a total lie, thinking to myself, *Father, forgive me.*

"It will hurt for a few hours, maybe even days, since we can't give you anything stronger than Tylenol," the doctor was saying. "No running, boxing, fighting, or any strenuous exercise for seventy-two hours. And I need you back in my office in three days for another MRI, and then we need to see you once a week for thirty days to monitor for head injury."

I mean-mugged King. "I am going to kill you," I growled

Doc interrupted me. "How many fingers am I holding up?"

I saw twelve; that could not possibly be correct, so I guessed six. I must have been right.

It was way after midnight when at last they released me. Had I known the paparazzi, ATL pics, the gossip columnists, groupies, and radio stations would all be waiting outside in the hallway, I might have stayed put. Sleeping here was probably better than being alone in my museum, as my mother called it; but tonight was definitely a time I wished I had someone to come home to. I yearned to call Danielle, to ask her to come over and nurse me back to health.

I stood shakily in the doorway of my hospital room, the flash of cameras blinding me. I had to make a decision--either stay here all night, or trample this crowd to get home. I was still seeing stars, and my head was spinning, so option number two was did sound great. Plus, I would have to rely on King to get me through the crowd. "King, I can't see," I whispered. "I need your help." Much as I hated to admit it.

King gave me his baseball cap. I placed it on my head and pulled it as far down over my eyes as I could. I pulled my hoodie over the cap, and stuck my phone in my back pocket. I ducked down as low as I could, and King covered me with his right arm, like an eagle covering its prey. No doubt, I will get a big bill for all the equipment we collectively demolished, and people we knocked down, trying to get out of the building and back to our cars. Once we made it safely to the parking deck, we stopped to talk logistics.

"I am riding with Gabby," I said, shooting King a look to let him know I wanted nothing more to do with him. Tre, understanding, jumped in the car with King. The rest of the crew started to argue.

"It is done, guys," I said quietly. "Follow us, or don't. Your choice." So there we were, in a half-dozen or more cars, pulling out of the hospital parking deck, trailed by what seemed like hundreds of noisy, yelling, honking paparazzi. My twenty-minute ride turned into a leisurely, two-hour cruise of the delights of I-285. It was all good, though--Gabe and I rode and talked while the others eluded the vultures trailing behind.

"Gabe, what is going on here?"

"I was hoping you would tell me."

"Can I be honest with you? I have no idea. I am clueless, Gabe. Today is a blur. I walked into my gym and got the life knocked out of me. I don't know if I threw the first punch, or even if I swung at all."

"What is this about?"

"King is mad because I was late. But truthfully, all of this is over a girl."

"Oh--the infamous Ms. Rose," she side eyed me.

"*Infamous?*"

"Well, that was the description I heard a few hours ago."

"But she is not a bad person, Gabe. Right now, she will not talk to me, and I have gotten my tail kicked over her. Nevertheless, she is a nice person. She is angry with me right now for two reasons—first, because I told her I was married; and second, because I *did not* tell her I was a fighter. I am not sure anyone will believe it now that I have this big black eye. My question, Gabe, is why everyone is so against her?"

"Pastor wants you to follow order. The guys? They are behaving like guys. It has been all of you for so many years, Randy. This is a big change for them. Is she going to push them out? Are you still going to need them? Will you continue to fight? They are worried. I don't care, but these are the kind of questions they have."

That was all it took. I broke down and sobbed like a baby, my head buried against the headrest. Why was this happening to me? I needed answers, but I did not know the right questions, much less who to ask.

"Whatever you do, RW, promise me this—you won't change," said Gabe tenderly. "Be the same good person you always are."

She dropped me off at my house. Somehow, we managed to lose the caravan, leaving King and the rest of the crew, who walked me inside, JJ and Keith both supporting me. I headed straight to the kitchen, where I found two icepacks, one for my eye and the other for my head.

"See you all tomorrow," I said to the crew.

"Be on time," King said, in an ominous tone.

"You, my friend, had better not speak another word to me," I snapped at him. I went to my bedroom and lay down. The pain did not

> I will not grow weary in well-doing. I will press on. This is nothing. I have handled worse storms and larger battles. This too shall pass.

hinder me from wanting to blog, so I got back up.

I am sure some of you will think I was referring to her. Right then, I was referring to King. We do battle daily. However, this was one battle I was not going to engage in. Something was going to have to give. King had to choose. He was either with me, or against me.

Friday

With some difficulty, I got up and dressed. It was a stretch. I felt like I had been hit by a Peterbilt 379. In a word, I felt awful. Once I made it to the gym, I sat in my truck, unable to move, my head throbbing. After a few minutes, JJ walked out and opened the truck door.

Inside, I tried to act as if I was fine. "Meeting in one hour in the conference room," I told the guys. "Whoever cannot make it in person, get them on the phone."

The hour passed quickly. I walked into the conference room exerting all the power, determination, and authority I could muster, even though every bone in my body felt broken, and my heart ached.

"In case you all have not noticed, or maybe forgot, this is *my* gym. I sign every check," I said. I paused, looking everyone in the face, starting with King. I spoke quietly. "I want to thank you all for your hard work. Thanks for keeping me rooted, grounded, and focused."

Then I yelled at the top of my lungs, *"Remember! I am the boss! What I say goes! Period, the end."* I lowered my voice to a conversational level again. "Any questions, gentlemen?"

There was stunned silence. I got up and walked briskly back to my office. I shut the door, and lay down on the sofa for what seemed like hours. At one point, I hauled myself up, made some calls, sent a few emails, and issued directives for the remainder of the day and the weekend. I could not take my head spinning like this any longer. One thing was for sure, I would never lose a fight again. I would do all I could to win. I never wanted to feel this way again, ever.

At dark, I left for the house, and crashed for the night. I turned off all my phones the night I got back from the hospital. I called RJ from my home phone, and silenced the ringer again once I ended the call. I wanted to ignore the entire world. The only person I wanted to speak to would not be calling me.

Saturday

I kept it low-key all day. King stopped by—probably at the urging of the others, not because he wanted to. I was a zombie from thinking of her than from the headache, which was finally getting better. I missed being injured--at least I had a reason to be pitiful. Whether King knew it or not, his visit helped.

After he left, I called RJ, and joked with him for a long time. I dared not tell my son I had been in the hospital--Tameka would eat it up. *Caveman,* she would say. Even though the money I made from fighting accommodated her slothfulness for years--and from the looks of it, there were still years to go.

Then I did something I had not done in a long time--I rested. My thoughts were finally at peace. This woman was changing my life already. After the sun went down, I got in my car, let the top down, pumped my music, and rode around I-285, until I noticed the same signs a few times. Time to go home.

Sunday

I could not decide if I should go to church or not. She might not show up. I replayed Gabby's words in my head: "Whatever you do, don't change." I got up and dressed, startled at my face in the mirror. Either I did not pay much attention before, or the bruises had gotten worse overnight. I surely did not look this bad yesterday.

Did I even want to go? She was already upset that I was a fighter, and now I was going to show up all battered and bruised. This will not be good. There was no way I could say, *I was hit because I was late to training because I was thinking of you.*

It was storming out as I drove to the church. I did make security arrangements for the day. So either the crew would all show up, or none of them would. Right now, it really did not matter at all.

Since it was raining, I arranged again for Danielle to drive around to the back. She might not be speaking to me, but I still did not want her to get soaked. Normally, all of us would be out in the rain with umbrellas, helping the women and children get inside. Today I hung back again, waiting inside with Hunter, watching as she arrived.

I watched the men carry out my instructions, escorting her into the sanctuary. I walked Hunter to the sanctuary door, like always, but decided at the last moment not to show my face.

Hunter's sermon felt customized specifically to me. It was as if he knew I would not show. He has been my friend long enough to know what to expect from me.

He began, "Just like John, never let your Isle of Patmos steal your praise. Trials and trouble will come, not only when you are doing wrong, but also when you are doing right. Remember this in the midst of the storm. The battle is not yours. It's the Lord's."

After the service, I could see Danielle at the door badgering one of the deacons. I wanted to rescue the poor guy. It was not he she was upset with. He was not the one being a coward, hiding. Was I being cowardly, or was I doing the right thing by staying back? I did not want to get too involved; I did not want anyone's feelings to get hurt again. I surely did not want to disappoint or let down my God. This was all so complicated. It hurt to sit back and watch her, while I faintheartedly tried to decid how to proceed.

WEEK 11

Monday

I awoke thinking: *there is no reward or benefit in lying around.* It was time to return to my normal routine. Therefore, I met King, and together we ran. Then we both headed back to the gym for training, neither of us saying a word the entire time.

"Hooks, Ms. Rose wants to know how long you will be today," King said.

"Huh?" Did he just say Danielle was on the phone? *Better brace yourself,* I thought nervously, eyeing King, *or you will be back down on the mat.*

"Ms. Rose asks how long?" he repeated.

"How long for what?" I said, looking at the clock. Had she tracked me down at my gym? Was she here? I surely did not want her to see me sweaty and bruised.

"How long are you going to be in the ring? By the way, she called you on Saturday as well."

She called Saturday. Why didn't someone tell me? Didn't they know I sat around for an entire week waiting on her to call--and now he casually tells me I missed her call? I wanted to kill everyone in sight. "Ask her if she is in her office."

"Yeah, she is at work."

"Tell her I will call her when I am done."

Still holding the phone to his ear, King listened for a moment. "She says you didn't answer her question."

"What?" I felt myself blushing. *That woman had a rocket for a mouth. She was like a time bomb--always ready to do battle.* I was still perplexed as to how to handle this situation. She surely had a way of consuming my mind, all day, every day.

It was late when I finally left the gym. I was hyped from knowing she called. So hyped that it was after eleven before I left the ring. Now, there was no way I was going to call her, not this time of night. It would be disrespectful. But which was worse? Not calling, or calling too late? I went with the first option, not calling. I will ask for forgiveness later. Instead, I blogged.

> Life is funny. Things change from day to day. You find yourself
> up one day, and down the next. I am not sure where I was
> recently, but I am not there anymore. Something has changed in
> me; yet there are still events and people keeping me in the same
> holding pattern. I have to break free. I want to be free. I need to
> be free. Free to live. Free to love. Free to be me.

Tuesday

Hunter's message on Sunday resonated in my spirit, uplifting yet disturbing me. I decided to call a meeting with him. We sat and talked for a good hour. He did not back down, nor did he try to soothe my pain. His tongue-lashings were always like this. I concentrated on his words. Did his chastising me like this mean he liked Danielle? Did he approve of her? Sitting with him in his office, I felt like one of the disciples when Jesus spoke in parables. I did not understand a word he was saying.

Wednesday

Just as I could not understand Hunter, I could not understand what God was trying to tell me. Outside, it was pouring down rain again. This made three church services in a row that it stormed. Was this a reflection of the storms in my life, or was I reading too much into the weather?

At church, I stayed back again, this time taking refuge in the security room. I sent no instructions to her today. Or rather, I did, but then I called off the guys at the last minute. It was not raining as hard as it was when I arrived.

Sitting there alone was starting to feel like a mistake. I could tell the spirit of the Lord was powerful in the sanctuary. Maybe I should have been present. There seemed to be a sweet presence in the room, from the moment Hunter walked in, until his sermon ended. Finally, he called for the doors of the church to open. I sat there in my office, kicked back, feet up, watching, when suddenly, I saw her get up. *Or was it her?* I rolled back the images. Yes—and now, she was headed toward the altar.

What was going on? I needed to be there. I could not get my phone logged in quick enough as I ran down the hall. I raced through the back door. Hunter looked up, acknowledging me with surprise. She was on her knees.

All the eyes in the church--my guys', the deacons', and Hunter's-- were on me. I was paralyzed, not knowing what to do. Hunter was beside her. I crept down the aisle to see more clearly. She was not exposing skin or anything inappropriate, but one of the ushers covered her anyway. I knew right then she needed me just as much as I needed her. I made my way to the altar and knelt beside her.

My emotions crushed me and lifted me all at once. *She was so filled with the spirit.* I helped her up, handing her things to one of the ministers, and escorted her out the door. Once outside, I gave her my handkerchief from my jacket pocket. I gestured to an usher for a bottle of water. It seems as if she was close to hyperventilating. This was a day she would remember the rest of her life. It will be ingrained in her memory forever. I was so glad to be here to share it with her.

As strong as she normally acted, right now she seemed weak and helpless like a flower wilting in my arms. Ordinarily in this kind of situation, I would have summoned one of the guys to help me carry her. Instead, I swept her up in my arms, easily. Once I placed her gently into a chair, she spoke words that thrilled my heart abundantly.

"Hi. I have missed you."

At that moment, it did not matter that she had been angry with me, or we had not spoken, or King landed me in the hospital.

"Are you okay?" I asked gently.

"Yes," she said, smiling. She sipped some of the water as she sat up. She was beginning to look herself again with the color back in her face.

"You scared a few minutes ago," I admitted.

She said nothing. She smiled, reaching out to touch my hand. Once she was fully alert, I took my leave. I wanted to stay with her; I think she wanted me to stay with her. It all felt so right... yet it was wrong. I could not stay. No one asked me to leave; I could have stayed by her side, partaking of this sweet salvation forever--but it would be wrong, at least for now. I had to do the morally correct thing. *Stay in the spiritual realm, not the natural.* I left the room. Truthfully, I knew she would be all right.

I tried to wait for her. I went to the parking lot to check if her car was still there. Sure enough it was. My radio buzzed--I was being called to my deacon duties. I ached to speak to Danielle before she left, if only to congratulate her and officially welcome her home to Victory Church. I took my keys out of my pocket, and used my truck to block hers in. This way, she had no other choice but to wait for me.

My duties took longer than normal. When there is something urgent you need to do, it always happens this way, right? I was moving as fast as I could, almost finished, when who but Trevor should hinder me? He wanted to have a conversation with me, he said, leading me into his office.

He told me he was going to request Danielle's contact information, and personally call her to welcome her himself. He wanted to meet with her. That struck me as a bad idea, since Danielle did not yet know Trevor was my best friend. I surely did not need another week facing her fury because I failed to disclose pertinent information.

As we talked, I was checking the video monitors from my phone. I spotted her in the parking lot, waiting. Little did she know, her parking spot was photo-enforced. Soon, my radio chirped.

"Deacon Washington, what is your location?"

I spoke directly to Danielle. I could see the two of them on camera, so I knew she could hear me. "I will be done in fifteen minutes," I said. "Please wait for me."

Then, not knowing why, I sat back down and watched her on camera for a few more minutes. Again, I was surprised—she patiently sat down, waiting. *Hold on,* I thought. She knew I was watching. As if to prove it, she looked directly at the camera. If she could spot my devices so easily, they needed to be moved to a more inconspicuous location, I thought to myself.

A couple of deacons passed her and spoke courteously. No one seemed to question her being there, or ask if she needed help. I wished they had--I wanted to hear what she would say. Of course, everyone knew exactly why she was there. She was waiting for me. Not like one of my groupies--no one could ever mistake her for a groupie. She looked more like my lawyer, publicist, or accountant. She was beautifully dressed. Her makeup was lightly applied, her hair perfectly in place. Her hands rested delicately in her lap, a cell phone clutched in each of them.

I admit it: I savored the moment. It made me happy to know someone was waiting on me, even though technically, she had little choice, seeing how my truck was blocking car. She could easily have demanded I move my truck. But she did not.

I decided it meant she wanted to wait—she wanted to talk to me as much as I wanted to talk to her. She was a busy woman--I knew. I have seen her in action, with bells ringing, phones chiming, texts alerting, emails popping, and everything in between. Right now, she looked as peaceful as a little angel.

I kicked back, taking in the view. I wanted to sit there and watch her as long as she sat still. Finally, she anxiously checked the time on her phone. That was my cue—better move fast. To my surprise, she did not seem to hear me coming as I raced toward her. I touched her shoulder. My jacket was unbuttoned, my tie loose, and my shirttail hanging outside my pants.

"Dude, did you get into a fight?"

I was hoping she would not notice my general disarray and the swollen contusions on my face. No such luck; of course, she saw everything.

I wanted to yell, *have I been in a fight? Yes, I have. I have been fighting with my trainer, my pastor, my best friend, and myself for weeks now. On account of you.* Instead, I took her hand. In a way, I had been fighting mostly with myself and with God, and my fight was nowhere near over. Technically, it had not even begun. I answered her this way:

"Yes. I've been fighting with you."

"Oh, really."

"It has been a tough week."

She thanked me for the things I sent to her. "No need to thank me," I told her. All I needed was for her to talk to me. *And praise God, I got so much more than what I asked for, so much more than what I prayed for.* Not only did she show up at church, she laid it at the altar. I did not know what it all meant. Was it repentance, salvation or a church home? Either way, she came forward.

It was all so unexpected after the week of hell I endured. She accused me of being a stalker, but then assured me she will use the spa gift cards. Calling me a stalker should have been an insult; but coming from her, it somehow felt like a compliment. She informed me she got some rest earlier in day. "Oh," I said joking, maybe all this kindness and sweetness was because she needed some rest. We sat there cracking jokes about it.

Then I could resist no longer. I took her in my arms and held her tightly, trying to absorb all of her through my skin and pores. It was as if I had taken all of her into all of me. I felt something I have never felt, something I could not describe. I knew without any doubt that this was the woman for me. Everything about me changed in the blink of an eye.

I was a new person. She made me emotional. I had feelings once again. I could breathe. We were sand in an hourglass. She poured life into me, as I poured life back into her. When I was around her, all I could do was express my truest, deepest feelings.

"You are turning me into a punk," I confessed, laughing. "You make me weak." No wonder King landed me in a hospital bed. If anyone so much as touched me right now, I would collapse in a heap.

I felt as if Cupid hit me in the tail, and hearts were flying around my head. I decided I better cut this conversation short before I do something dumb. We said good night and went our separate ways.

Back home, I was useless. Her fragrance suffused my soul. I smelled her scent on my hands, my skin, and my clothes. I could not focus. She drained away every part of my life, except for training-- mentally, spiritually, and emotionally. In addition, if I kept spending as I was, I would be drained financially, no doubt about that.

I tried to blog. I could not concentrate long enough to complete a sentence. I was completely empty, yet so full.

I called her office phone, which went straight to voicemail as expected.

"Hi, Danielle, I am sorry—I know it is early," I said. "This is the time of day I work out. I hope this call does not bother you. Yes, I admit, I am stalking you. I want my voice to be the first one you heard today—and every day. I also wanted to ask permission to buy you a present. I will see you soon." Shortly afterwards, I called back and left a second message. That was probably lame, asking permission, but I wanted to make sure I was not out of bounds by doing so.

Thursday

She did not respond to either of my calls. I did not worry—after all, everyone was pissed off with me these days. They would eventually get over it. If this relationship went nowhere, it was cool. If it went somewhere, I would be blessed.

It was the first time in over ten years I incorporated anything other than worship into my morning routine. I hoped these early-morning messages could be the beginning of two lives tied together.

The guys picked me up and talked trash the entire way to the gym. I blasted my Beats, ignoring them. I could not hear them even if I wanted to. All I could hear was my music and my own thoughts. I could feel my heart beating fast. It never raced this fast, even when I was preparing to fight. What was going on? I checked my phone to check my levels. I thought about taking the monitor off, but decided that would be too obvious. I closed my eyes and tried to calm myself. Finally, King snatched my headphones off my head.

"Take it down," he snapped.

I could hear my heart monitor beeping. My rate must be elevated for it to beep. I do not think I have ever heard it make noise before today. When we got out of the truck, King was all in my face, raising hell.

"If you can't get your levels down, we're leaving. I'm not doing this with you." I could see he was annoyed. "You're putting your health in danger," he roared. I did not see how that was possible, but I was not in the mood to argue.

"Remember my meeting," I said evenly, as I took off on my run. King huffed and puffed behind me. *Now whose levels need to be monitored?* He let me go the first lap without him. When he slowly rolled up on me, I knew what was about to happen next. He was planning to dust me off, overwork me, and embarrass the you-know-what out of me.

I tried not to be anxious. I checked my watch, wondering where Danielle was. I tried to remember what days and times she said she would be here. I decided I was on point--she was the one running late.

I could smell her before I saw her. The breeze wafted her perfume in my direction. I got calm and excited all at the same time. The first lap, I ran past her so fast she did not notice me. The second time I ran past, she was too busy with her phone to pay me any attention. *You cannot work out and work at the same time*, I thought.

I did not say anything. It was not as if she asked my advice. The third time around, she was still texting, and I made up my mind to badger her. Once I rolled up on her, I slowed and matched my pace to her walk. King blew past us, then realized I was not beside him, and slowed down. Keith stayed at a respectful distance behind, while Sol ran sideline on the grass.

She was so busy, she did not notice she was surrounded. It drove me bananas. She *had* to be more observant. Watching her told me a few things--she was either comfortable walking here, or she was ignoring me again. She would never accomplish any of her fitness goals if she walked like this every day. Either way, there was a problem. I was determined to be the problem-solver. I spoke to her.

"You are late."

"Says who?"

"My clock," I said, sprinting off before she could respond. I suddenly felt better. I looked at my heart rate; it was settling down. Something about the anticipation of seeing her was just like the anticipation of... I quickly diverted my mind. *Try to remain calm and not get excited,* I thought. Otherwise, I would have to explain an incriminating bulge in my pants.

My team and I worked out as if we were at the gym. Today was core training, which technically could take place outside. King was in his military mode, yelling and shouting like a drill sergeant. We were doing pull-ups, pushups, karate squats, and tossing the medicine ball.

After an hour, Keith handed me a rope. "Jump," he commanded. After three minutes, he switched, the way we always did in our daily routine. "Double under," he called. Three more minutes. "Side." Again, the timer ran out. "Criss-cross. Time. Skip."

Every three minutes we repeated this, for twelve rounds. Finally, I was allowed a sip of water. I ran two laps, and then started right back with the same drill. Another sip of water, and then I ran three more laps.

Keith pushed me harder. "Run." After what seemed like hours, he still had not called time. I realized he was running me the entire twelve rounds, which came to thirty-six minutes.

"Stop," he yelled at last. He gave me a three-minute break. "Double under."

Six minutes later, he called time again. I had three minutes to catch up with Danielle, but I decided not to try--if I went over, Keith would surely jump me until the sun rose tomorrow.

"Combination," he called out. I did thirty-six minutes; at the other end of the track, Danielle was still ambling along, preoccupied on her phone. Not surprisingly, she did not look very tired yet.

There was a difference in doing this inside, as opposed to outdoors in the middle of summer. "Time," hollered Keith. "Cool your legs off." I had only a few minutes. I jogged around the track. Once I met up with her, I matched my pace to hers. It was actually a little too slow to cool down, given all I had been doing.

I continued to check my monitor, not wanting my heart rate to go down too fast. That was just as bad as increasing too quickly. I had no choice but to take off jogging. I made my way back to the team to allow them to finish the routine, and un-tape my hands. I wiped my face with a towel, peeled off my dripping shirt, and put on a dry, clean one. I could train outside in the heat like this sometimes, but not every day.

I did like the way my lungs felt from the fresh air. As if they were revived. It was as if I was a fast car being pushed to the limit to blow the dust out of the exhaust.

At last, Sol stopped for the day, and we wrapped it up. To my delight, Danielle was waiting for me, just as we agreed. I offered her dinner— my personal dinner of champions, a high-protein shake. I could tell by the look on her face she was not impressed; but she obliged, and we sat on a bench beside the track, sipping our shakes together.

To Trevor, I thought, this would be considered cheating, maybe even outright sinning. To me, it was a date—the second date in one night, if you counted our workout as the first. My prayer was for there to be a third date, one where we just sat and talked. Other than church, I concluded this was the only way I would be able to see her. It was a way to get close to her, but without being physically inappropriate. *God knows, I wanted to be inappropriate.*

As we sat there beneath the stars, enjoying the cool night air and each other's company, I blatantly asked her if I cold leisurely call her. I could not believe I had the courage to be so direct. We linked our devices.

Then she asked me a question I worried was coming.

"Do you always have this entourage with you?" she asked, gesturing at my crew hanging on the opposite side of the track, giving us some space.

"Truthfully, yes," I replied. "Though sometimes just one guy."

She frowned. "But why? What's the point?"

"Protection." I knew we were going to have to deal with the issue eventually. Just because I was accustomed to having people around all the time did not mean she was going to like it. However, I did not see a way to avoid it.

"Okay, then tell me this. Why did you fly back early on Sunday?" she asked.

"Easy. I wanted to see you." *Now I was being excessively honest*, I thought to myself.

"Were you ever going to tell me what you did for a living, and who you were?"

Here, I had no good answer. *Why?* After successfully avoiding her question, we parted ways. I purposefully had two vehicles parked at the track so I could drive home alone, without being insulted and badgered by the guys. They could talk about me all they wanted to behind my back. Tonight they could leave me out of it.

I thought about her while I showered. Afterward, I lay down trying to calm my thoughts. It was impossible. My mind, my heart, and my body were all on fire. I felt both challenged by her and attracted to her, both physically and sexually. There was nothing I could do about it but embrace it--or hurt myself trying to ignore it.

Friday

I left a voice message on her office line, and then followed up with a phone call, at a time I knew she would be at her desk. I asked if we had a date tonight. Her response surprised me.

"Until you respond to my friend request on Facebook, I'm not going on any dates with you."

What friend request? Vickie must have handled it before I ever saw it. I needed to investigate. "I will call you right back," I said. I hastily pulled up my Facebook account, accepted her request, and called her back.

"Done," I said.

"Okay, then. It's a date."

We set the time for eight PM. She gave me two choices of where to dine. I called the first place and made reservations. I was too anxious to come up with some hip new place, and I did not have the courage to ask for anyone's help.

This may strike you as odd, but honestly, Tameka and I never really dated; so all this was new to me. In a way, tonight *would* be my first real date. I was on edge all afternoon. The guys were upset with me because I was not letting them drive me, or even follow me.

Also, for some reason, Danielle insisted we meet at my gym. Was she trying to avoid my finding out where she lived? Too late for that. However, from a single woman's point of view, it definitely made sense.

Since this was a dinner date, I knew I would have to actually eat something more than my usual protein shake. Maybe a dinner date was not such a great idea.

I promised JJ I would take my kit, and test the food for poison. The guys checked out the place before we arrived, and promised to stick close by, unseen but on standby. It was the only way I could go out un-chaperoned. Not to mention, I had to keep my monitor on at all times. I began to see why Tameka hated my profession. Right now, I did too.

Once Danielle arrived at the gym, my anxiety vanished. She looked gorgeous, and the night was filled with good food and wonderful conversation. Everything was perfect until it was time to get her back to her car. Letting her go was almost impossible. Then came the hardest part of the night. How I ached, how I yearned to kiss her--but of course I could not, for reasons both legal and moral. I knew our faces were being captured on every camera and electronic device at the gym; no way could I kiss her here and get away with it. So I kissed her neck--but much more passionately than I intended. How I loved every moment of that kiss.

While I still had her close by, I asked her for a second date; to my delight, she cordially agreed. The plan would be the same--meet at my gym, then go out to eat somewhere. Once she left, I felt intoxicated. Just to burn off some energy, I changed clothes and went for a long, hard run.

Saturday

I could not sleep, so after tossing and turning most of the night, I got up. It was that quiet, peaceful time just before dawn. My adrenaline was still pumping at full speed. I texted Danielle twice. The day was going to be a busy one; I had to keep moving. Instead of responding to my text, to my surprise she called me.

"Hello."

"Hey."

"What are you doing up so early on a Saturday?" I asked.

"Same thing you're doing."

"You can't sleep?"

"I never can. And you?"

"I hardly sleep. Besides, I have a lot on my mind," I said being honest.

"You wanna talk about it?" she offered.

I hesitated. "Would you be offended if I said no?"

"No, I wouldn't." Her voice was warm and kind.

"It's not that I don't want to share personal stuff with you. I do not know where to begin. I do not know what to say or how to say it. Besides, I don't think you have the time—there's so much I would need to explain."

"Well, if you ever do want to talk, I'm here."

"Thanks. Once I get my thoughts together, I will let you in on everything."

"So what are you about to do right now?" she asked.

"Hang out at the gym. Punch some bags, I guess."

"Oh, no, you're not! I'm coming to get you!"

"Huh?"

"I'll meet you in forty minutes at your gym."

"What? You should go back to bed," I scoffed.

"Nope. I'll see you at the gym."

I felt like a teenaged kid. I could have cared less where we went or what we did, as long as I was with her. Exactly forty minutes later, she pulled up in a nice whip, smelling like the perfume counter at Neiman Marcus. Just like me, she was wearing a baseball cap--more proof of how much we were alike. I hopped into her car. It was hard not knowing where we were going; even harder was not being able to reach out and touch her.

She was taking me to meet her best friend. Which caught me off guard all right. *This is payback for having such a big crew,* I thought nervously. *I am about to be sized up.* I suppose that made sense. My crew, Pastor Hunter, and every person in the whole church had been sizing her up, which, to be fair, was partly my doing. For years, the seat I designated as hers was strictly reserved for those on the church payroll; a big RESERVED sign made that clear. The sign remained, but she was the special occupant now. You can bet folks noticed *that.*

It was one thing for a woman to be sized up; it was very different for me to be sized up by Danielle's. We pulled up to a freshly painted quaint bistro tucked away in the heart of Buckhead. In the early light, I saw…not a female, but a *guy,* a dude about Danielle's age. The two of them greeted one another with a kiss on both cheeks.

"Randall, meet Michael Kilpatrick," she sang out. "Mikey, this is Randall." As you imagine, I felt anxious and jealous, all at once. What was I to think? A *guy* was her best friend. I had plenty of questions about their relationship—mainly, how could this dude be just her friend? *Was he insane?* No way could I do that. Yet somehow, during the visit, it became clear they were only friends; there was nothing more between them. This came as a relief.

In her introduction, she told me this Mikey guy truly was an excellent cook. She took it upon herself to order a blended vegetable medley for me.

"A fail-proof cure for hangovers," as Mikey described it.

It was a version of a non-alcoholic Bloody Mary. "I call it a meal for champs," I retorted, wiping my lips with a napkin. "I'll happily come back for any and all hangover cures you blend up. That was terrific." We hung out for an hour or so, chatting. It turned out Mikey was the owner and chef of the restaurant/bar/club. I learned Danielle frequented it regularly--at least every Saturday and Monday, I gathered.

After we left, Danielle drove slowly, much slower than on the way there. What should have taken fifteen minutes or twenty at the max took nearly an hour. She stopped at every yellow light--which seemed oddly out of character. Whatever; even though we have a date tonight, I was loving every extra moment.

As I got out of her car, I thanked her for breakfast. "You know, you can cook a meal for me anytime," I added, hoping she would take the hint. Any fool could see I needed a home-cooked meal; tomorrow being Sunday, I was hoping I would be invited to a family dinner. She outsmarted me.

"How about I bring you a home-cooked meal, packed into some Tupperware, and drop it off at the gym tomorrow?" she asked sweetly.

I did *not* see that coming. Either she was accustomed to game, or mine was pitifully weak.

My plan for the evening was to take her to my restaurant to watch the game. I started the restaurant back when I had more money, literally, than I knew what to do with; my accountant insisted I park some of it somewhere. It turned out to be a real success.

I knew our showing up there would catch everyone by surprise. I have never come by with a woman before; and whenever I did show up, after greeting the customers, I would generally retreat to my office.

For tonight, I decided to invite the crew along, so they would not feel left out again. That meant Danielle would be back under the microscope, surrounded by my guys. It was not safe for me to keep going out without security; and at my own place, the crew could more or less melt into the scenery.

As the day wore on, I started wondering why did she take me to meet her BFF. It meant a lot when a girl wanted you to meet her friends, especially if you were married. It seemed like a good sign. Figuring Danielle and I would probably be spending a lot of time at Mikey's place, I ordered the guys to the check him out, along with his operation as well.

That evening, Danielle showed up at the gym looking great. It was impressive to see the many faces and characters she displayed. Her attire was truly revealing her personality. This was the person I wanted to get to know--not just the modestly dressed praise-and-worship Danielle, but the everyday chick, the girl from around the block.

I hugged her. Our embrace was overwhelming for me. I was forced to make a deal with the guys. They demanded to drive me. They insisted for safety reasons. Not to keep me safe, but to keep her safe, from my desires. I did not have a chance to mention it to her before King pulled the Maybach around. I wanted to ask him to take it back and drive something sensible for the night. Then I decided it was pointless to fret—having nice cars is a part of who I am. Danielle clearly liked them too. Like me, her finances allowed her to indulge her whims. For all I knew, she had a Maybach in her garage as well.

She shook her head at the sight of the car, but she could not stifle a little smile of pleasure. Nor did it seem to trouble her that somehow we acquired a chauffeur in King, with Keith riding shotgun. Sitting beside her in the backseat, I closed my eyes tight, too nervous to look her in the face—trying to keep it low-key.

She leaned in close, indicating not just the guys up front but the car as well, and whispered in my ear, "You are out of control."

"I know. I was hoping you could help me."

Her not making too big a fuss over the situation confirmed my belief that she was neither a gold-digger nor overly impressed--exactly what I needed to see. I suspected it was a relief to King as well. Her perfume was completely intoxicating, and I was having a hard time staying focused. Our conversation was simple. Probably because we had company.

It was obvious it was my place when we pulled in under the building, not to mention the sign, which read Heavy Weights. Before I could exit the car, all the guys were clowning me. *It was always your friends and family that embarrassed you the most,* I thought. Man, did they ever do a good job of it. I steered her through the maze, and began showing her around. I sensed her becoming uneasy.

"Do you come here by yourself, or is this where you bring the groupies?" she asked coolly.

Seriously? That was unfair. I mean, sure, I could have had as many women as I wanted—including the entire female population at church, at least those over age twenty-one, married or single. However, that was not my style.

I felt compelled to open up to her and tell her the truth by answering her underlying questions. I explained I have never brought a female here before. Hence the taunting. Not even Tameka has been here. This was a place I built after she left.

That opened up a floodgate of questions. She was relentless. I attempted to change the conversation. "If this is making you uncomfortable, we do not have to talk about it," I said.

"It doesn't bother me," she assured me. "Actually, it may be important for us to discuss."

"Will this help you in deciding if you should trust me and wait for me to resolve the matter of my divorce?" I asked.

"Maybe."

Being a smarty I said, "If that is the case, then ask as many questions as you want. As a matter of fact, I can get my wife on the phone so you can speak to her as well."

She came back with a remark that struck me. "That won't be necessary. That would result in way more drama than I have the energy for these days."

We kept talking; she was fearless with her questions, so I felt I had to be truthful with my answers. This woman was a truth sermon.

"Anytime I am with you, my heart races," I said. "I get butterflies in my stomach. I cannot think straight. It's more intense than the feelings I get when I am preparing for a fight."

I placed my arm around her neck and we walk down a corridor of metal doors. Photos and memorabilia, along with monitors showing the activity on the other side of the wall, adorned the corridor.

She said softly, "Randall, I feel the same way."

As soon as the metal door opens, I steer her to a reserved table. In the midst of our conversation she asked, what should we call each other?

"Easy for me." I smiled. "How about I just call you 'my love'?" For her, there were plenty of options—Hooks, Deacon Washington, Randall, RW, Randy, or whatever else she chose. I actually preferred her to call me Randall; because *that* was the person I wanted her to get to know. Those other names were just roles I played, characters in my life.

We lightened up with talking about the game. She mentioned TIP again. I saw she really was a big fan. I mean, she gave the guy a lot of love. Could she be a Hooks fan as well? I felt jealous momentarily. Honestly, I liked the brother a lot, and I believed he would grow out of his troublemaking stage, and turn his life around. I wanted nothing more than continued musical success for the brother from Bankhead.

I wanted him to remain the King of the South. Right now, he had something I envied--her interest, maybe even her heart. I needed to get to the place TIP was--and he did not even know he was there. I also understood where the brother was. I have been down that same road myself; luckily, I found a career to keep me busy and out of trouble. Not to mention a best friend, Trevor, who holds me accountable--and who chases after God. Which means I chase after Him, too.

She excused herself to go to the ladies' room. I sent my guy to escort her. Maybe I was anxious, but it seemed like it was taking her a long time. When at last she returned, she said she ran into one of her niece's friends. "I am certain my niece will be here within the hour," she added, laughing with anticipation.

Niece? How old is this niece, I wondered. *She better be over twenty-one.*

Danielle, meanwhile, was making herself right at home with the crowd. She jumped up to dance, tapping Nate on the shoulder to go with her, showing she knew enough to have someone go with her. My worries that she would not get along with the crew were starting to evaporate; she seemed completely cool being here tonight—both girlfriend-cool and homeboy-cool. I could take this woman anywhere, and she would survive.

Her departure gave me a break. The conversation was getting heated and intense. We needed an interruption. Just about the same moment Danielle headed back to the table, here came the niece—busting right through my security as if they were not even there.

"Hi," her niece says gingerly as she approaches us disregarding my team trying to ensure she was safe to enter.

Danielle rolled her eyes in my direction and whispered, "I told you."

I snickered at the resemblance and the identical personalities. "You sure did." I turned to the younger version of Danielle, "Hi, Sade."

"Hey Mr. Hooks," Sade replied and continued aggressively, "what's up?"

"Nothing. We were chilling." Danielle responded in a tone indicating irritability.

I could not stop staring --anyone could see the two were related. They looked so much alike. They could have been mother and daughter, or sisters. It was like looking at a photograph of Danielle taken a few years ago.

The real surprise was this niece's personality—she was like twenty copies of Danielle all rolled into one. I mean, she was more dangerous than all my guys were to the tenth power. Her mouth was a rocket ready to blast off. It was amazing how one person instantly explained another. Suddenly, it all made sense--Danielle's behavior at work, with my guys, and with me. It also explained why Danielle was still single. Like her aunt, Sade was a dangerous, delightful combination of beauty and brains, all wrapped in one combustible package.

Sade observed our food on the table and shouted to Danielle over the noise, "I am going to order real food and drinks. Do you all need anything?"

"Do you have money?"

That was an odd question. As bad as I hated to, I interjected. "What would she need money for?"

"To pay for her food," Danielle stated as if I was an idiot.

"Did you pay?" I asked in disbelief referring to the bottles of water she came back from the dance floor with.

She looked confused, "Yes," she replied.

"You what?" I snapped. Everyone in here should know Danielle is with me. I need to fire somebody right here and now.

"Come with me," I said, tugging at her wrists. "Let's go back to the bar and recapture your money." Sure, I could just as easily have handed Danielle a twenty. But I needed everyone to know that we were together, she was my special guest, and that I was furious.

The game was ending, and as much as I hated the thought, I wanted to have Danielle home by a respectable hour.

"Time to go," I said, whispering into her ear.

She jumped—not because of fright, more like from a tickle in the spine. Somehow, I knew then I had her. Rather, we had each other. She held my hand the entire ride back to her car, something I yearned to do for what seemed like forever. And I had the opportunity to do it in front of all the guys, which of course meant I would have to listen to their mocking for the rest of the week.

"Good night," I said softly. We were standing face-to-face in the parking lot, still holding hands.

"I wish things were different," she said, looking deep into my eyes.

It pleased me but also crushed my heart. I felt the same, of course, but I did not want to mislead or hurt her. No two ways about it—

Tameka would have to give me a divorce. I would make it happen by any means necessary.

Later that night, in the midst of being badgered by the guys and countless calls from the club about what to do with Sade and her friends, I received a text from Danielle, inviting me to a play. I thought to myself, *this is going well, but it is sure going fast—faster than I can get my life and myself together.*

Sunday

This evening my crew and I escorted Danielle and her crew to the play. Afterwards, we all ate at Mikey's. Her crew struck me as a good group of girls—all single, I think, although I could not tell for sure. What I did sense was that they all appreciated my being a male authority figure, a protector. It felt good, knowing Danielle did not need me for gifts any more than I needed them from her; each of us had everything money could buy. What we both lacked was love and companionship, two things money cannot buy. Without them, I knew I would never be whole and complete. I pray she feels the same way.

WEEK 12
Monday

When I called Danielle this morning, she reported that she was having a "rough day". My first impulse was to shower with presents.

"No presents." she said in her next breath, as if reading my mind.

Instead of gifts I met her at the track. Our unofficial meeting spot. The same little fellow running around the track was trying me again. I am saved, and have been for a long time; but I am still hood at heart. I would hate to have to knock someone out in the name of our Lord. But trust me, I would. Realizing I was jealous, there was only one thing left for me to do; formulate a plan.

After my crew ditched us for the night, I went into serious mode. *Time to get this straight*, I thought; I took a deep breath.

"There's something I need to know," I said. "Are you seeing anyone else?"

Her response hit me like a ton of bricks. "What do you mean by *seeing?*"

"I thought it was a simple question." *Is she being difficult, or is she truly asking for clarification?*

A long pause. Then came her reply, "No."

At that point, I did not know what to think. I decided to take her *no* as just that-- a *no.*

Tuesday

I was probably breaching every code, every moral and everyone's trust. I decided to give Danielle a watch like the one I wear. Not just because I want to track her every move, but because I want her to be safe. She leaves home early and comes back late every night, I figure; it is my job to protect her. The last thing I want is for her to be stalked or threatened because of me.

It all has to do with what went down in my career four years ago. I was matched against a tough opponent. The fight was brutal—so brutal for my opponent that it was called by the third round. The guy sustained severe injuries, which caused a lot of ill feelings afterwards. I began to get death threats, hate mail, and other nonsense, all of which went on for a year. Long story short, once my opponent finishes his jail time, he will never fight again on the national stage.

Secretly, my life felt as if it was damaged. I elected not to fight anymore. Tameka decided to leave—citing her own safety, and the safety of our son. To this day, I believe most of the threats were just bluster. In the end, my team, my family and I all had to start living with much tighter security arrangements. To this day, we keep safety first, at the highest level of importance.

All of this is to say that when I gave her the watch, I did not think of it the way she did. To her, it was just another trinket, an expensive gadget. Surprisingly, though, she seemed pleased. Of course, I could not explain why I was giving it to her—that would only frighten her-- but already, I felt better.

Wednesday

I was exhausted, and Danielle could see it.

"Promise me you'll get some sleep tonight," she said, little knowing that she herself was the main reason I could not sleep these days. "You look tired and certainly tanned," she added, smiling. True—I can go a few shades darker in no time.

"Well, that is because I have been doing my workouts outdoors in the hot sun to visit this certain girl. Which makes no sense, considering I own a gym of my own."

"Oh, really? I don't recall having been invited to work out at this gym of yours."

"Fair enough," I said. "From now on, whatever is mine is yours. You do not need an invitation to come work out with me."

She got a twinkle in her eye. "Oh, what's yours is mine, huh? I assume that includes the Maybach and the Phantom."

As bad as I wanted to say yes, I could not. Instead, I offered her a Bentley and a Benz--which meant, of course, someday I would have to make good on my offer. Brilliant move, right?

Thursday

My boy Hunter got me good today. He set up a surprise meeting with me and Danielle, neither one of us knowing the other would be there. As soon as she walked in and spotted me, I could see she was livid; as for me, I was a long way from pleased. But Danielle—wow, this was a side of her I had not met until now. It made me laugh, to be honest. I mean, I fought with my hands; but this woman fought with her mouth. I kept quiet, letting her do the work. She gave Hunter an ear full. *No need to give this woman a monitor,* I thought; *her guard is all the way up. Her defenses are sky-high. She can handle her own.* Hunter, to his credit, was acting polite and courteous; but his approach had been disrespectful. I would not have gotten so pissed if it had been just me sitting there in his office—but why did he have to involve her?

Afterwards, I walked her back to her car, and then stomped back into Hunter's office. He knew I would be back; now, King was with him. Before I was through the door good, I was yelling.

"What the hell was that?" I was up in Hunter's face, shouting. "I do not appreciate what you just did. The least you could have done was be honest. That was real jacked up—you crossed a line here! I do not know if it is the pastor line, or the friendship line, but either way, you were *out of line.*"

King placed his hand on my chest as if to restrain me, then paused to remove it, as if it were some small, weak animal approaching.

"Hunter, hear me now," I said, lowering my voice. "Where, I need your help is with Tameka, not Danielle. In one stroke, you have run off a new church member and maybe even my future wife as well. Was that your plan, Hunter? What would Jesus do?"

"I told you the truth," said Hunter gruffly. "That's what He would have done."

"I will let you know the next time I need your truth. Do not look for me Sunday, because I will be cooling off. In fact, do not call me—I will call you when I am ready. Until then, stay in your lane."

I was too furious with my best friend to blog tonight. We hardly ever fought—and never over a female. I lay before the Lord all night begging Him to order my steps.

Friday

At four this morning, I gave up on sleep and texted King to get ready. I could not call Danielle; I still felt too angry. All day, Hunter tried to reach me, calling, texting, emailing, even posting on Facebook. Then Danielle called. I told King to tell her we were running, which was not a lie--we were. She texted me, saying she urgently needed to talk, and she was heading to my gym after work. I was certain this would be the icing on the cake. Can you call it being dumped if you are not even dating?

The day flew by. Mostly I stayed in my office thinking, waiting, and listening for God. King rang as soon as she stepped out of her car. "Send her in," I told him, not having the simple courage to go out and meet her myself. Expecting the worst, I was shocked when she came in, seated herself, and wordlessly handed me a bag.

"What is this?"

"A thank-you gift."

It was a Louis Vuitton bag. Inside were all sorts of thoughtful and expensive small gifts. As I opened each one, I felt a lump the size of a bowling ball in my throat. People never gave me gifts. It was always the other way around. For a long time I could not speak. I was so moved.

"I did not think you would ever speak to me again after meeting with Pastor yesterday," I said finally. "I know this is as hard for you as it is for me; but promise me you will help me stay on the friend side of the line. I never want to hurt you or disappoint you, Danielle, so I cannot cross that line. You know I want to be so much more than just your friend--but I *must* keep myself in order. If I ever get out of order, will you check me? Can you promise me that?"

Without saying a word, she fell into my arms, weeping. My heart racing, I held her close and gently wiped her tears. After a few minutes, she said she had to go, which seemed like the right idea for now. I felt I was acted ungrateful, but the truth was I needed to be alone; I needed space to let my own tears flow.

As she started to drive off, she halted for a moment at the end of the driveway. It was all I could do not to run to her. I stood there immobile; hands stuffed in my pockets, the tears rolling down my cheeks. I walked back into the gym through the back door to avoid meeting anyone, lay down on the couch in my office, and instantly fell fast asleep.

After what seemed like a few hours, my eyes popped open, my mind racing. *What have I done?* I have better manners and home training than this. Tonight confirmed there was a connection between us. I felt it deep down in my *knowa*.

I grabbed my cell phone and called her. "Throw on some jeans and a tee," I said. "I'm picking you up in twenty minutes." I arrived at her door feeling as if it were the first time I had ever been there—which it was, as far as she knew. What struck me was her security system. Of course—this was Danielle the architect, the builder. Naturally, she had a top-of-the-line security system.

She did not allow me to cross the threshold. That was doubly good, as my coming inside could prove too tempting. Oh, why must she entice me so with her fragrance? I had not had a desire to be intimate with anyone in years. Now I was so desperately fighting the urge to seduce her, to hug her, to touch her. However, each time I shut my eyes, inhaling her sweet scent, I saw Hunter's scolding face. It was as if I was fighting my own flesh, my best friend, and Tameka, all at the same time.

Tonight, I was in the Ferrari. To my pleasant surprise, she mentioned it, in a way which let me know I earned some points. From my stalking, I already knew her favorite casual-dining spot was the Cheesecake Factory, so Vickie called and made reservations.

Simple though it was, it may have been the best dinner of my life. The food, the staff, and of course the cheesecake were all terrific; better yet was how happy all these little things were making both of us. At that moment, I knew I loved her; I knew this would be the first of many dinners we would have together, and that she was the one I would spend the rest of my life with. It would not happen right away, but she would be worth the wait. *I have already waited over thirty years for the woman of my dreams,* I thought. *A little longer will not kill me.*

During our meal, she said something about how people always deferred to my wishes and did what I told them. I explained people did what I *paid* them to do; I have a staff, whom I pay handsomely. Having seen her financial records, I knew my trainer made more than she did. I believe in taking care of those who take care of you. I believe in the tithe and the offering. I also believe in sowing and reaping. If you sow lightly, you will reap lightly. But if you sow richly, so shall you reap richly. And believe me, I have.

The night passed all too fast. It was past closing time; I motioned for the check. The bill was much lower than I anticipated, considering all the staff, and my having the area reserved after hours. Either way, it did not matter. Money was no object. Since the tab was so low, I tipped high, and then slipped an extra bonus to her favorite waiter.

Once we were back in the car, I claimed it. I told her she would marry me one day—and I truly meant it. *Speak those things that are not as though they are.* I invited her and her crew to the photo shoot at the aquarium tomorrow. I wanted her to be there, of course; but even more, I wanted Hunter and the crew to see her for the wonderful person she is.

By now, it was four in the morning, time to take her back home. There was nothing open this time of night other than Mikey's, the Waffle House, and...and legs. *Her legs in my hands, her legs brushing against my legs, her legs wrapped around my body, resting on my shoulders, her feet around my head*...that was the only thing on my mind. *Forgive me, Father, for I have sinned*, I prayed silently.

Hunter was tracking me. I was still not ready to face him. The same swagger he came with to humiliate me was the same swagger he was going to have to come with to apologize and make things right with me. Otherwise, I was going to continue to avoid him. I had not sent my blog or daily inspiration since our meeting. He was concerned and he should have been. In the meantime, he would have to learn to live without my words of inspiration.

Saturday

At the aquarium, I felt on edge—partly because a photo shoot is hard work, partly because Danielle was coming, and partly because Hunter would be there, even though I was avoiding contact with him. Hunter had been trying to get my attention since he arrived; maybe he was ready to make peace and move on. Without saying more than a few words, I sent him to meet Danielle, knowing it was risky. Hunter escorted her to where we were waiting, and then, like always before an any occasion, he prayed us in.

My monitor showed my heartbeat was at the highest level; JJ and King looked at me as if they knew why. It was painfully obvious; Danielle and I were the momentary, uncomfortable center of everyone's attention

Luckily, it did not last long. Today was about me and the fish, not me and Danielle. The camera crew soon put everyone to work,

Danielle included, as we got down to business. After the shoot, we had dinner in the lighted room overlooking the aquarium. The photographers had another assignment, and my crew was exhausted, so soon we found ourselves alone. Right off the bat, she started firing questions at me. First stop was my blog.

"I want to know what you mean in your posts," she said. "What's your motive? Who, exactly, are you talking to?"

I answered as best I could. I said, "My blogs are the only way I can express my feeling for you."

"Uh-*huh*," she snapped. "So you have to express your feelings for me before the entire world?" Her eyes were full of fire. I could not speak. All I wanted was to take her in my arms and kiss her, hold her, take her home, and make love to her. Of course, I did no such thing. At such times, actions really do make liars of words. Maybe that explained why she was getting more pissed by the minute.

"Please, Danielle, don't be angry at me," I said.

"Who says I'm angry?" she snapped.

I knew I was doing exactly what I did not want to do—hurt her. Afterwards, back at my house, I lay myself down on the floor, and waited all night to hear from the Lord. Sometimes He tells you things others may not understand—things that Hunter, King and the rest of the crew could not comprehend. Truthfully, I did not get it either. Just because it does not make sense now does not mean it was not my assignment. Until I heard from Him, I was going to have to shut out everyone else, Danielle included. I needed time to understand where my life was going.

It seemed like I might be right back where I started, with me living the same dismal, solitary life as before. I could not be barefaced about it. It was what it was.

Sunday

I awoke today determined to go to church, and to ignore both Hunter and Danielle. I was still angry at the first; the second was furious with me, even though we were supposed to have dinner with her family tonight. It was too much to handle. Nevertheless, I took my usual seat near her. Several times, we caught ourselves staring at each other. Despite my resolve to keep her at a distance, I could not take my eyes off her—her face, her legs, her feet, her rump, and everything in between. I restrained myself as best I could, knowing I was, as always, on display. Here at the church, I had to be both an example and a role model. I am Hooks Washington, and Pastor Hunter's best friend. Both require attention I would happily do without. As soon as Hunter finished his sermon, I raced out of the sanctuary.

It was at that exact moment He finally spoke.

"Fix your face, son. You have become the master of avoidance. You have avoided my calling to you, Tameka and this ugly divorce. You are tougher than the times you are living in. I know, because I made you tough; I made your hands to be fighting hands, and not just for fighting in the ring. I made you to be mighty in battle--in any battle. You are like David, a man after my own heart. Has there ever been a battle you lost? Nor will there be one. Trust me; you must face the past to get to the future. Envision your purpose. Dream your destiny. Speak your future. Imagine your life. Keep pushing until you see these things."

That changed the whole tone of my day. For dinner, I showed up at Danielle's house with flowers and a non-alcoholic bottle of wine, even though she told me not to bring anything. Dinner was great. The conversation was excellent, and I felt welcomed, especially since Danielle thoughtfully made two meals. One meal for me and one for everyone else. They were a wonderful family, one I wanted to become part of permanently.

WEEK 13

Monday

She showed up to my gym today just as promised. I am sure the rain prompted her arrival. No matter—I would take her anyway I could get her. As she entered the building, I felt an impulse to hide. I remained behind closed doors her entire visit. JJ gave me a disappointed look once she left as if to say, *you invited her; now you need to be a good host and go out and greet her.*

I waited until she finished her workout and was getting into her car, before I checked my monitors. She was sitting in the front seat, looking at her phone--was she going to call me? No; instead, she folded her arms on the steering wheel and lay her head down. Surely, this was my cue. Otherwise, JJ was going to drown me as I sat in the soaking pool. Therefore, I jumped out of the water and raced out into the rain.

"Lord please do not let me get sick," I said as I ran through the building. I do not know what I would have done if she pulled off in the middle of me trying to get there. I wanted to be honest but I could not bring myself to tell her I was purposefully avoiding her. I did not know what else to do. My feelings were increasing. I was going to have to put some distance between us no matter how hard it will be. After being at her house yesterday I felt totally different for her. I could not allow myself to get too close to her. The last thing I wanted to do was hurt her or her family.

We did not speak much, only a simple goodnight. I wanted to say, *Danielle, I love you. I need you. Do not leave me. Become my wife.* However, all the usual obstacles, both legal and moral, remained, so I held my tongue, and simply kissed her cheek. "I will call you," I said. "Please do not turn your locator off."

After she pulled away, I sat on the curb in the pouring rain until JJ came out to get me. I stayed at the gym all night, training. For the first time in years, I gave some real thought to fighting again. I thought about the money that I would need to pay Tameka off and get this divorce finalized. I hate to admit it, but relationships always wind up costing money—especially when they are over.

Tuesday

I woke up thinking *I have to be judicious.* I did not want to make a hasty decision about returning to the ring, because I had a crush on a girl. No point in making a bad decision in haste. When I left fighting four years ago, I was at the peak of my powers, the pinnacle of my career; but I left because I did not want the reputation of having death hands. Truthfully, though, I did. If I wanted a man out, even dead, I could make it happen. Mentally and physically, I was still in top shape. But was it time to start putting in calls? Was this a temporary phase? I needed to put more thought into what I was about
to do.

Saturday

Four days have passed since I last spoke to Danielle in person, even though I have left her a message every morning. After days of not seeing her, I am feeling like an addict who needs his fix. She has me feening.

I keep checking her locator, but she has it turned off. Wednesday night, I skipped Bible Study, trying to stay low-key. In return for my absence, she left me an awful message, which, I admit, I deserved. I was a coward for not facing her, and it was eating me alive. This was a no-win situation, something I was not accustomed to. Finally, I texted her to ask her what she would be wearing Sunday morning; to my delight, she answered. I pushed my luck and texted her again asking if she wanted to do anything later.

Her reply was swift, "No."

I was crushed. Maybe I needed to do better at asking forgiveness. Surely, she gave me the answer I deserved.

Sunday

Today could not come soon enough, because today I would see her—and that, I resolved, would have to be enough. I stood in the back of the sanctuary during service, feeling tormented. Had it really been the Lord speaking to me? Or just my own desires? I planned to remain in the back until the collection was taken, and then make my way to the altar.

Hunter switched it up on me again, making an altar call for people being evicted, so I ended up at the altar earlier than planned. There was no way I could ignore the call; therefore, I took my place among the congregation, as we laid alms and blessed those soon to be without a home. She was up there as well, and when she turned and saw me, her face was glowing and radiant; it was as if a secret understanding passed between us.

Later that night, I lay awake, wrestling with my thoughts. Am I misunderstanding? Is this my flesh speaking to me, or am I hearing from God? I needed Him to bless me and answer me: What was Danielle Rose's purpose in my life?

WEEK 14

Monday

My attorney called with news: Tameka's attorney requested a meeting tomorrow. That was a first; normally, it was my team that initiated meetings, although in four years, all they led to was one angry conference call after another. I know God is a God of order, not the author of confusion--so surely this meant the time has finally come to deal with Tameka.

Per my instruction, Vickie sent Danielle a request to attend the meeting. I could see she accepted and blocked the time on her calendar.

The question was, why did Tameka want to meet? What was she asking for? No matter, it all belonged to me now. All I wanted was to give her what she needed to take proper care of my son. She had the chance to get everything she wanted, but she moved too slowly. Now, her desires are no longer up for discussion.

Tuesday

Today I met with the attorney. I asked Danielle to join us, thinking it would help her to understand better what I have been going through.

Danielle's presence would surely help me to relax. Plus, I needed her input. I did not need any more chaos from Tameka; I needed to stay calm and composed.

Why is divorce so hard? All Tameka and I did twelve years ago was say *I do,* and then exchanged $99 wedding bands. Over the years, the whole business has cost me so much more in grief, headache, and heartache than it ever cost me in money. They say money can fix everything—what a lie. Trevor and I both can confirm it, since both of us have been in the kind of trouble which money could not fix. Trevor caught it coming right out of the gate; being a pastor has its rewards, of course, but it also carries a price tag. I know, because I was there for the journey, not just as his mentor, cheerleader, and best friend, but also as his partner.

Now I have a battle of my own going on. Who knew how this would end? With me once again bruised and broken inside? Of course, I would never hit a woman, but I sorely needed Tameka to be ancient history. The last thing I wanted was for history to repeat itself. Love knocked me down for the last four years, but I was ready to get back up again--ready to experience real love.

Once we arrived at the meeting, I was distracted yet composed. I talked with my legal team beforehand, laying out exactly what I would and would not do. I learned something a long time ago—adrenaline is not your friend. Run purely on adrenaline in the ring, and you will find yourself on the mat before the first bell stops ringing. When I walked into the conference room, I saw at once that Danielle, who is usually so prompt, was not there. Tameka, on the other hand, was present, seated with her lawyers.

Not wanting to seem desperate, I did not ask anyone in the room about Danielle's absence; surely, she would show up. As the meeting was called to order, I stood in back of the room, waiting on Danielle, as if I were a spectator and not the focus of attention. Did she cancel and no one thought it important enough to inform me? Vickie was there, of course, so I started to text her to see what she knew; then out of the corner of my eye, I noticed movement on a projector screen in the front of the room.

I looked up and did a double take. No, I thought, no way was she doing this. This was not the time to play games. She could not possibly be this upset, could she? Because this was hard-core. I have to admit, it made me respect her even more; and it would have been cool if she had not been playing this game at my expense, giving me back what, I have to admit, I myself dished out. However, not today.

I stepped out of the room, and called her cell phone. Her phone went to voice mail. I redialed, stepping back into the room, watching her face onscreen. She did not move an inch as I watched her phone light until it went to voice mail. I addressed the webcam screen.

"Danielle."

"Yes," she replied coolly again.

"I am calling your phone," I said, my voice as stern as I could make it.

"Hi, Mr. Washington," she sang out, as if this was a day just like any other.

What the hell? Since when was I "Mr. Washington"? Why was she clowning me? Now I had two women against me—Danielle and Tameka both. This was a new record for me.

"Step outside the room, please," I said. She could hear me on the webcam speaker just as everyone else in the room could. I got a few looks from others at the table, which meant nothing to me at this moment. I had another problem on my hands which must be dealt with.

She politely excused herself as if nothing was going on between us. "Please excuse me, gentlemen," she said to the audience. "I am so sorry for this interruption."

Once I was back outside the room, neither of us spoke at first. I was struggling to remain composed. "What's with the BS, Danielle?"

"I am not following you," she replied coldly.

"Why are you on a webcam? Why on earth are you not here in person?" Actually, my language was much less polite; I would repent later, I thought angrily. Already I was feeling regretful.

"I'm on a webcam because I was insulted when you asked me via a voice mail to attend your meeting. If I am going to be dealt with like a business partner then I will treat you the same way. If I show up at *your gym*, where you invited me, and you do not have the decency to come out and greet me, then clearly you are no more than my client. Two can play that game...*Mr. Washington*."

"This is not a f***king game!" I yelled. I was furious. Why did she think I invited her? I told her she was being unnecessarily difficult. She counter punched, saying I was the one being rude. The irony was rich-- here I was at my attorney's office, trying to get a divorce, but having my first argument with the one person I loved. Everything was going all wrong.

"You have gone out of your way to avoid me," she said. "You have been incredibly discourteous."

Her accusation was true. The truth hurts. Then to top it off, she hung up. By then, I was so upset and furious that I lost focus. I was unaware of what was going on around me. I stood there gnashing my teeth with my hands in my pockets. I am sure I rubbed the tarnish right off the coins until they shone. I texted her:

> I did not deserve that.

She passed her assistant the phone without looking at it. I interrupted the meeting again.

"Danielle, I am texting you," I took a deep breath. "Look at your phone, please."

She did not respond. I wanted to sling the camera and Polycom across the room. Then flip the table over, and punch holes in the walls until my hands were bloody. My financial future was at stake here. I had to pay attention, or both Tameka and Danielle would get the better of me. There was no way in hell I could let that go down. Tameka's attorneys were complaining about the agreement my team presented. Tameka hated the remarriage clause—if she remarried, she would forfeit the alimony. And why not? Why should I sponsor her marriage to some other person?

She was also to remain permanently under a gag order—no talking to the media, no reality shows, and no tell-all books; nor could she establish a foundation or start a company. Finally yet importantly, I wanted my surname back. Her attorney objected; his client wished to keep my name because of the minor child. I pointed out that the child was born before we wed; the birth certificate and marriage license proved it.

Through it all, Tameka sat there without saying a word, letting her attorneys do the fighting for her. Danielle finally spoke up, her tone all business, effectively shutting the charade down.

"Thanks for the invitation, gentlemen, but I must leave now. Mr. Washington, you may forward all pertinent documents via email or certified mail. Best of luck, and know that you will be in my prayers." She shot a look directly at me. "*Because you surely will need them.*"

"Um hmm," I muttered both hands still in my pockets. This was terrible behavior, completely unnecessary—to make a public spectacle of me, all because she was angry. I left feeling utterly defeated.

Wednesday

I was too angry today to show myself at Bible Study. Once again, I hid. Outside, it was another rainy night in Georgia, which perfectly matched my mood. No way would Danielle come out in this monsoon. Or so I thought.

My radio chirped. "Hey, Deacon."

It was Dexter Hall. "Guess who's here? You coming to escort her inside?"

"No, Dex, I will send King."

She was either as determined as ever to praise Him, or to keep up her attack on me. Or both. Which was it? I had no clue.

King returned dripping wet from escorting her back to her car after service with a disgusted look on his face. He was still angry with me. Was it because I suddenly was interested in a female, or because I was still married, or something to do with my fighting? I tried to get him talking.

"She is different, King--I can feel it. She is not the way you think she is."

"Uh-huh. We can see where you feel it, all right."

"What is that supposed to mean?"

"I see it in your behavior. She has you too scared to come into the sanctuary. In addition, your training—you either miss it, or you show up late. I can see your sleep patterns, and your levels tell me exactly where she touches you the most."

Was he talking about my manhood, my night visions of her? Those were my intimate secrets, not something I wanted to talk about right now. I had too much going on to put up with King and his crudeness. I decided to go home and think. It had been a hard few days. Each time I tried to put my mind in order, it swerved back to her.

Back at the house, deep in thought, something hit me. The balance sheet the lawyers disclosed in the meeting showed my net worth stood close to ten figures. *WTH! When did this happen?* How could I have a billion dollars and not know it? This was a different problem altogether—admittedly a good one to have, but not right now.

Thursday

Late this evening, she called me. I was laid out in the other room and missed her call, having done nothing productive all day. King was right--I was ditching training and making excuses about running. Lately, I was useless. I called her back, knowing she would not answer. Maybe that was a good thing; I was not in the right frame of mind to fight with her. Real men did not waste time battling with words; no, real men wore gloves when they fought.

Friday

I felt bad not leaving Danielle my usual morning message today. After all, I promised her my voice would always be the first she heard; and here I was, going back on my promise.

My run this morning was a drag, more work than relief. I was at the gym, feeling so low I could hardly stand it, when Trevor called. He was coming by; it was going to be a guy day, something we had not done since I met Danielle. It was cool he wanted to chill, but I was not interested in him giving me any more advice. My whole team had years to give me advice, and now that was all anyone wanted to do.

Trevor worked out with me. He threw some hard punches, knowing my routine inside and out. He used to do this with me daily, and trained with me in the ring all those years when I could not afford to pay someone—just like I studied with him long before he had a pastoral staff. Back then, we would fight to scripture. He would say a verse, and I would throw a punch, and vice versa. Those were the days.

After we showered, just as I had suspected, he wanted to talk. To tell the truth, I needed it. Hunter started out trying to scripture-ize me, but as I told him, I already knew the scripture; plus, I already knew how I felt. I was sitting back receiving whatever it was God was laying before me; there was no need for him to test the spirit by the spirit.

In the end, all his lecturing and scripture-izing shifted my perspective—not a lot, but some. I knew I needed to talk to Danielle; I knew I was being rude.

"Why would God send her to me if she was not the right one?" I asked the man of God.

"Are you saying God sent her to you?" he snapped. "Don't be too sure about that."

Saturday

Today, Danielle showed up at my gym, catching me totally off guard. Not only did she show up; she actually brought her own trainer. Who does something so unacceptable? She also knew I could not say anything. I told King to keep quiet or pay a price—namely, I would break his neck if he said so much as a word to her. For all I cared, she could have brought TIP to train her; I was overjoyed she was here.

Suddenly she disappeared. I hurriedly finished what I was doing, showered quickly, and raced to my office. My body was in pain; King beat me nearly to death today. I picked up the phone, put it down, and picked it up again, not sure what to do. Finally, going with my gut, I dialed her number; the phone rang and rang. She picked up right as I was about to hang up.

"Hello," she said dryly.

"How about I meet you at Mikey's?"

"Okay. I suppose," she said hesitantly.

Our visit was not as pleasant as I wished. It was hard but I convinced her we should run by the mall and get a tie for me for tomorrow. I would have preferred to spend more time with her. Right now, I was pleased she was talking to me, period. Before we went our separate ways, my excitement got the best of me and forced me to invite myself to Sunday dinner tomorrow. I was shot down instantly.

"I won't be there," she told me. "I will be at Atlanta Motor Speedway and wanted to know if you'd like to come."

As much as I would have liked to go to the Speedway, there was no way I could have the crew set up the proper security arrangements in less than twenty-four hours. Never having been to a NASCAR race, I knew nothing of the procedures nor of the facility. I could hear King and JJ screaming and fussing now. It broke my heart, but I had to say no.

It was a long, rough night of restless sleep. I awoke almost hourly to a nocturnal emission, repeatedly.

Sunday

I decided on my way to church today that I had to block out all those late-night fantasies about Danielle. My goal seemed a bit easier once I saw her coming into the sanctuary. She had her entire crew with her. Suddenly, she needed all this back-up. It felt like an attack. With all the energy I expended the last few nights, I was already feeling weak. I was also still trying to figure out how I could go to the Speedway with her, something I could not do without my crew. Did she not understand?

It felt like I needed to do something to take charge, so I sent her a text, saying I would be at her house after the race—phrased not as a suggestion, but more like a simple statement. After a long wait, she texted back--she said she was not feeling well, and she would prefer me to come by tomorrow instead. All day, I noticed her levels were spiking, but nothing indicated she did not feel well. So I decided I would meet her whether it suited her or not.

I was waiting at her gate when she arrived. I sat chastely on her front porch while she showered. Once she reappeared, looking cool and refreshed, I tried to explain myself.

"I know my behavior lately has probably seemed strange," I said. "But things have to be done in the right order. Otherwise, I fear I will fall too deep." We were sitting close, on her porch steps. Instead of responding, she reached over and pulled out a magazine from the table, and hastily starting fanning herself.

"Sorry, Randall, I don't mean to ignore you. . .but all of a sudden, I feel so hot. Like I'm burning up. It's weird."

"You're hot? But the weather's perfect tonight, Danielle."

"No, it's like...I don't know, I'm itchy," she replied. "All over. It's crazy."

She stood up. "I'm going to get a Benadryl," she said. The door slammed. In a few moments, she was back, still fanning herself, and invited me into the air. She plopped down on the sofa and let me put my arm around her.

"That stuff will knock you out," I murmured. Next thing I heard was her deep, even breathing—sure enough, she was fast asleep. Quickly I had King and Doc look into it. An hour or so later, she awoke.

"Still here?" she asked drowsily. I could tell she was pleased.

"Look, I better go and let you get some proper sleep," I said. "But if you need me—for anything at all—promise you will call. Okay?"

Little did she know, but I would be meeting her back at my house, just as soon as I closed my eyes—the same way I met her every night.

WEEK 15
Monday

She called me today while I was running. I said I would call her back when I was done. An hour later, I saw her number light up on my phone again.

"Hey, babe. Is everything alright?"

"This is not Danielle, Hooks, it is Leigh."

She sounded upset. "Hey, Leigh. What's up?"

"Dani is sick, that's what's up. How did she look last night when you left her?"

Was this a trick question? "Beautiful, as always. She was feeling a little out of sorts, she took a Benadryl, and she was asleep in no time."

"I will call you back."

Within ten minutes, Danielle's watch was signaling an alarm. I called her phone. Leigh answered and asked me the exact same question again. "How was Danielle when you left her?"

"Why?"

"Her face is swollen three times the normal size. She is extremely incoherent. She can't seem to stay awake. I am on the way to take her to the dermatologist. Did she only take one Benadryl?"

I tried not to panic. I cut my run short, and went back to the gym to change, telling King where I was going. King, of course, did not like it one bit.

"Since when did this girl become your responsibility?" King barked.

I ignored him.

"I knew she was going to ruin you—at this rate, you will never fight again, mark my words!"

I cut him short, balling up my fist, getting right in his face, and gave him a chest-bump. *Hold it, Hooks; you need to pull up.*

"I will handle you later," I said coldly.

At the dermatologist, I found Danielle and Leigh in one of the exam rooms. Leigh was not kidding--Danielle looked terrible. She looked as if she had been in a fight. I felt like taking her in my arms to comfort her. At the same time, I wanted to yell at her. *Why didn't you tell me last night how bad you felt?* Why did she neglect to tell me this morning her whole face was swollen? Leigh was not helping anything with all her attitude. In fact, her attitude troubled me. Did she honestly think I did this? Then something worse occurred to me--had someone else hit her?

Time was moving at a slow crawl, like always at the doctor's office. Finally, her doctor along with my own doctor both saw her at her bedside. They gave her some intravenous meds, then sent her home with strict instructions—no work and no outside activities for at least a week.

I was in charge of taking Danielle home, which meant I was probably in charge of relaying the doctors' orders to her. Once we got half-way down the street, I grabbed her hand on impulse. I pulled it to my face and rubbed it against my cheeks, kissing it repeatedly. This was a cheap shot. I took advantage of the situation, considering she was in my front seat passed out from the pain meds.

I felt so bad because I did not take her to the hospital last night, and just as bad because I did not attend the NASCAR race with her earlier. It was my responsibility to take care of her, even if she sometimes did not see it that way. The first order of business right now, I decided, was to get her home and into bed. The thought felt so right. Why couldn't this be my everyday life? Why couldn't she be my wife? I had to do everything in my power to make it so.

On the way to her place, I stopped at the pharmacy to pick up her prescriptions. Danielle lay slumped in the front seat still out of it. I put my hand on her shoulder and shook her gently.

"Danielle, can you hear me?" She was deep in dreamland. Not wanting to leave her, even for a moment, I hustled into the CVS and dropped off the prescription with Lisa the pharmacist as Leigh instructed. I went back to the car and waited with her. Mostly I stared at her while people walked by staring at me. After twenty minutes I raced back in and picked up the medication and drove her home

I was relieved to find Sade waiting at her door like a parent waiting for a sick child to be delivered home safely. For the second time, Sade addressed me as "Uncle Hooks". I tell you—that did something to me, like when a child calls you daddy for the first time. Or when the woman you love tells you for the first time that she loves you too. Sade's words touched my heart even more than her concern for her aunt.

She led me to Danielle's bedroom, which lay behind a set of stained-glass-ornamented double doors. This was where she slept, I thought in awe as I carried her towards the bed and gently eased her down. I gaped at the room—everything about it was so *Danielle*. The headboard was massive and ornamental; a many-tiered chandelier hung suspended over the bed. The ceilings were coffered with metallic paints in different hues. The walls were faux marble, with specks of glitter, and so glossy they looked wet. The triple-crown molding was, at minimum, thirty-six inches. The exotic South American hardwood floor I was standing on must have cost a small fortune, and the comforter I spread over her was as fluffy and thick as a cloud. There were silken pillows of every shape and color, so many they almost buried her.

Her desk, tucked into a corner, was fitted with a comfortable-looking leather-tufted chair. Magazines and books lay neatly stacked next to a chaise lounge, which was upholstered in a pretty chintz print. On her nightstand, a row of computers sat charging.

French double doors led out to a deck, secluded by yards of pale fabric hung from the ceiling. Her dresser, as tall as she was, held a vase filled with white roses. A floor-length mirror leaning against one wall captured the astonished look on my face; surely, I was standing in the Queen's Chambers. It was like stepping into the pages of *Southern Living* or *Better Homes and Gardens*. Not only does this woman design beautiful architecture, but she creates stunning interiors as well. The room was the very definition of elegance; frankly, I was nervous I might touch something fragile and break it.

Sade was taking her aunt's shoes off gently, as if Danielle herself were so fragile, she might break—true enough, given that she was lying in bed semi-conscious and sick. I felt oddly blessed to see her this way, so vulnerable—not the strong, not the in-charge woman the world was accustomed to seeing. Sade carefully placed her aunt's bag and keys in their respective locations, and plugged her cell phones into their chargers.

"Uncle Hooks," the girl said, interrupting my reverie, "can you help me by hanging up her clothes?"

I walked into what I assumed was Danielle's closet. I was baffled—this was a closet? The space was beyond neat; it was positively anal, especially compared to my own. I stood trying to absorb it all.

Her clothes arranged by color and article. The perfume bottles were lined up by height. Thousands of pairs of shoes lined the shelves, organized, it appeared, by heel height and color. Her sweaters were all precision-folded as if brand-new. There were stacks of hatboxes, all within easy reach, and a rolling library ladder for items up high. More glossy, expensive-looking magazines were heaped in baskets, along with accessories and scarves.

There was too much in this closet for a man to take in. I tried to figure out what she liked the most--shoes, handbags, suits, hats, belts, jewelry or perfume. Who could say? There was so many of each. From all the blue boxes festooned with white bows, and the signature-monogrammed containers corralled neatly on the shelves. Now I know which stores and designers would have the gifts she would love.

Strange to think about buying her gifts, since other than Vickie, my Mom and Lady Gabby, I have not bought any female a gift in over ten years. Tameka simply never asked; if she wanted something, she bought it. Once RJ got big enough to pick out his mom's presents, I would take him to the store, open my wallet, and pay for whatever he picked out. (Now, of course, he has his own debit card and Amex, and thus does not need me to pay.)

Sade interrupted my thoughts again, leading me out of the bedroom and into the family room. I hesitated to leave Danielle's side.

"Don't worry, Uncle Hooks," she said kindly. "Let's leave her in peace. I'll check on her every few minutes." Sade and I proceeded to pound each other on the Wii, me of course letting her win, what with her just being a sweet kid (not to mention the niece of the woman I loved). Afterward, I sent her out to pick us up some lunch. The moment she left, I went back to Danielle's bedroom, just to watch her breathing. To my annoyance, JJ called.

"How's your girl doing, man?" he asked.

JJ was purposefully annoying me, though in a different way than King or Trevor did. They all knew she was only my friend. A legal dispute resulting from an unhealthy decision I made years ago only allowed us to be friends. I knew I was being set up. If I ever confessed to anything more, they would, naturally, crucify me.

I hung up feeling annoyed. Not because JJ called, or because the crew was expressing their concern; and not even because JJ called her "my girl." No, I was pissed because she was *not* my girl, and because I so desperately wanted her to be.

As I stood quietly watching her, I remembered what Sade said about her aunt sometimes playing 'possum; so I leaned closer to reassure myself that yes, she really was sleeping. Sade chose that moment to slip back into the room unheard—I was busted.

By the time Paige and Leigh arrived to relieve Sade and me, Danielle was awake, after another long nap, though still weak and seemingly exhausted by her ordeal.

"Thanks for everything, Randall," she whispered hoarsely to me. "I truly appreciate your being here."

"No problem. I would have been upset if no one called me. I was happy to be here."

"You are very special, Randall 'Hooks' Washington."

"You are too, Danielle Rose. Or should I say, the future Ms. Danielle Rose Washington."

We both smiled. I was standing close to her—maybe a little too close. Oh, how it thrilled me. I tiptoed out and closed the bedroom door, attempting to calm my physical man. All I could do was take a seat on the floor next to her door. My heart was racing; I was out of breath and aroused. I had to regain control.

She allowed me to take them to a quick dinner at Mikey's. On the way back, I stopped by the gym to get some of my things, and to make sure the place was still standing. We headed back to her house, and again they were preparing to leave me alone with her. This was dangerous for me although the medication had her drowsing in the front seat again. I carried her inside gently, and for the second blessed time today, I placed her into her own bed. I left so Paige and Leigh could get her undressed and into her nightclothes. Then they departed, with the understanding that I would stay and keep watch overnight.

I stretched out on the chaise next to the bed, and set to work, trying hard to keep my mind occupied. Each glance at her sleeping brought a surge of ecstasy. Never have I indulged in drugs, but I confess I felt high; parts of my body levitated whenever she moved. When she murmured in her sleep, I throbbed. This was ridiculous--not to mention painful.

I retreated to the family room, where I did pushups, sit-ups, and crunches until I was exhausted--anything to get her off my mind, and to get my erection down. Maybe a glass of warm water would help. No, no—what I *really* needed was her warm body, the only thing that could alleviate my situation. I could not decide which was worse: being home, and waking to the sticky residue of nocturnal emissions; or being here and suffering this epididymal hypertension. I felt like I was about to combust inside; it was agony. How could I survive until daylight?

Trevor texted me once during the long night, checking on Danielle, and asking if I was okay. I texted him back two letters:

> BB

I could see by his response he knew exactly what I meant.

> Haven't heard blue balls in years.

Tuesday

Danielle jumped out of the bed first thing and announced she was going for a run. I started to recite the doctor's discharge instructions—stay inside, rest—but this was the old Danielle again, full of determination and high spirits. No sense in even trying to argue. I decided I would run with her.

It was early, the sun not up yet, but it was already getting hot outside. A short run should suffice. Besides, my body badly needed to burn off some energy, and let the blood flow back to the other areas. I am always up for running. We started out slow, me matching my pace to hers.

"You go on ahead; I'll be fine," she urged.

"Honest, slow is how I like to start off," I said. I was happy to be at her side as long as she would allow it, no matter how slow. Anything was better than the tortures of last night.

After our run, she made us breakfast. We sat on the deck, eating and talking. Our conversation disturbed me. I was led to believe she might not be interested in a relationship. Not right now and maybe not ever. She explained how important her family was important to her. They were already formed. I did not get the impression that starting and producing a family was a high priority on her list.

It disappointed me that she felt this way and had not considered me as a permanent prospect in the way I was considering her. Although she was physically down, yesterday was the happiest day of my life. I could see this as our future. I loved running with her, loved imagining how we would be having breakfast out here on the deck every morning like this, once we were married. It seemed like she did not see it that way. I needed clarification.

Therefore, I asked her why she was not dating.

"You have to be somewhere to meet people," she said, buttering a piece of toast. "Potential boyfriends don't walk into my office, or knock on my door at home. When I am out, I am so preoccupied with work that even if Mr. Right suddenly turned up, I would probably be too busy to notice. It is partially my fault. And as motivated and ambitious as I am, he will have to be the same, or at least okay with me being this way."

For sure, I could relate. Both of us were so ambitious and so disciplined that we scarcely made room in our lives for relationships. I decided to ask her about her ex. "What happened with you and the other guy?" I was dying to know.

"Life, I suppose."

"What does that mean?"

"We grew up, and we grew apart. Or rather I grew up; he grew apart."

"I know the feeling all too well. Tell me more."

At that point, she opened up, and began to pour out her heart, telling me about her hopes and dreams. Wow, I thought—that ex of hers really blew his chance. I guess one man's junk is another man's treasure, right? For sure, I found a treasure; I was at the right place at the right time. I mean, Dexter Hall could have radioed someone else, but he called me. Honestly, I was blessed beyond measure.

Here she was, a beautiful woman with a successful, brilliant career. She owned more than three cars, a home, a big home valued at (I would guess) well over half a million dollars. Me? I had everything a man could ever want; but at that moment, I wanted to give it all to her, on a silver platter from Tiffany's. Yet all she wanted, it sounded like, was the bare minimum. I was not sure if that was good or bad.

There was something else we badly needed to discuss. I asked her how she felt about my returning to the boxing ring. Since she came into my life, I felt great. My skills are at their peak; my soul and spirit are clear. I have tons of pent-up energy. I feel ready. So ready that King booked us all for a flight to Las Vegas to meet with the Boxing Association.

There was also the not-so-small matter of the money. Not that I ever fought for the money—I did it because I loved the sport, and I was good at it. I started thinking about how it would be for us together—doing things, living the life, traveling together, supporting the community, our families, and giving back to the church. Some extra coins could never hurt in that regard.

Her response was so positive and so sincere that I decided it was the right time to explain my crew and team to her. She needed to understand how my team and I worked—how we handled security, my eating habits, and how we trained.

"See, King is my trainer; and JJ is my manager, promoter and trainer," I told her. "I have another set of guys who are my bodyguards." I ran down the list of their names for her, knowing she probably would not remember them all, but wanting to tell her anyway.

"Humph." She sounded a little surprised.

"What does that mean?"

"It means that's a little strange."

"How do you mean, strange?"

"Strange that you would have twelve guys as bodyguards, and that all of them have some form of a Biblical name. Pretty ironic, wouldn't you say?"

Most people did not notice this. Primarily because we did not refer to full names. "So you find it perplexing?"

"Not perplexing, exactly."

"What, then?" I saw a gleam of laughter in her eyes.

"I guess I'd say, *canonical.*"

"Why?"

"You call them the crew. They are more like the twelve disciples."

At that, I laughed long and hard. "It's true," I confessed. "Folks do sometimes call them the disciples." It was incredible that she picked up on this in a matter of seconds. "Technically, there are fourteen guys, not twelve, if you count JJ and King."

"Whose names are also Biblical?"

None of this was what I expected. Sure, they may look like the disciples; sometimes they even act like disciples. All things considered, it was a great compliment to my crew. One thing was for sure—I was a long way from being Jesus Christ. I laughed aloud at the thought.

"What's so funny?"

"By our Biblical analogy, who does this make King?"

She gave me a look. "Peter," she said, at the exact same moment I said, "Simon." We were so in tune with one another.

Then it was her turn. She sprung a question on me.

"Why do you still wear a ring on your ring finger?"

That was easy. It is not a wedding ring, I explained. It is a ring I bought for Tre and me when we both turned thirty—a gift for him, but a cover-up for me, something I wore to avoid unwanted questions and to keep the ladies at a distance. Most of them, anyway.

"I guess it is time for me to take this ring off now," I said, smiling. I know this divorce is going to happen, but the last thing I want is for people to think I got divorced one day, and married another woman the next. People should see this ring gone for a while. However, what they did not see was the four-year separation. So the absence of a ring may cause some heads to turn.

My crew also does a great job of keeping women at bay. At church, I am generally on duty. If I do have to let a woman down, I make it clear I feel uncomfortable being picked up at church. Besides, I am married; and the Word says *he who finds a wife, sisters, let him find you.* Do not chase after him. Make yourself available, so he can find you. As I explained this, she listened quietly.

"Enough talk," she said at length. "Come on." She escorted me down the steps to her backyard. There, I was astonished to see, lay a driving range and three-hole golf course. *What girl had this?* Crystal Fanning?

"How much does drawing pictures of buildings pay, anyway?" I asked.

"Believe me, this stuff" —she indicated the adult playground in her yard—"is not for show. It's purely a stress reliever."

The more we talked, the more I learned. The more I knew, the more I liked; the more I liked, the more I loved about her. *Once I tell JJ and Trevor she has a driving range, they will stop feeling as if she needs to be under surveillance.*

As for golf, honestly, it is not my sport of choice. There is no physical contact. No disrespect to Tiger Woods or Arnold Palmer, but hitting a ball with a metal stick to a location you cannot even see does not impress me. I would rather hit my opponent and see him hit the deck. Fighting—now that is where I let my steam off. "When I am forced to golf, I want to destroy the ball, the flag, the green, and the club," I told her with a wink. "Does that make me a barbarian?" I do love the sound when the club hits the ball; it reminds me of the sound a person makes hitting the mat.

Also, golf is too quiet. My profession is noisy and obnoxious, something I completely block out as I stride down the tunnel to the ring. In a long, quiet round of golf, I find I cannot concentrate. I need to make contact quickly; I cannot waste time examining and measuring where the ball is going. In the ring, I have one simple strategy—to knock the other person down. I deliver my powerful hook, followed by an uppercut; the quicker he goes down, the better. I tell my fans, better not leave your seats until the winner is announced, or you might miss the fight.

Not only did she have a driving range, I saw, but a stinking *digital board* as well. Who was this chick? Short answer: A classy, smart, God-fearing, well-versed woman, so delicate--yet still so hood. I could see how she used this driving range as a way to relieve negative thoughts and emotions. I punched a bag every day for the same reason.

Despite my misgivings about the sport, I showed her how to drive a ball home. The way we were standing, our bodies were in close contact, and I found myself wishing I were driving *something else* home. The closer we got, the stronger was the urge to touch her, to feel her, both inside and out. I began to fear my driver was about to show her a hole in one, she tripped and fell in the grass.

Relieved at the distraction, I helped her up. Quickly, I was back to being purely, innocently happy to be with her, and so relieved to see she felt better. Today, I started again to remind her, the doctor said no working. There could be no argument about it. End of conversation.

"Tell me this," she said, brushing herself off. "If you were writing your life story for the next five years, how would it read?"

I liked the idea. "I wish I *were* a writer," I told her. "Then I could write my story exactly how I want. If I made a mistake, I could erase it. Same with being a builder, like you--if the life you built went sour, you could just tear it down and start again." Which is essentially what I am trying to do right now--tear down my old life, and build a new one with her.

"What about your future in the ministry?" she went on. "Where do you see yourself going?" Only Danielle would ask me a hard question, then follow up with an even harder one.

I tried to be truthful. I first heard the spirit of the Lord years ago; I took the time and the steps to answer my call as best as I could. Once Tameka and I went downhill, I blew the ministry off.

"I still hear the Spirit calling me loud and clear," I added. "But since the split, I have ignored it." A lot of it has to do with Tameka. Just as she hated my fighting, she resented my work in the ministry. She refused to worship at Victory because Hunter did not preach like the ninety-year-old preacher at her church; plus, she was convinced every woman there was after me. Obviously, she would never support my being a pastor. Besides, how could I lead a congregation if I could not shepherd the adult in my own house?

"So I figured all I could do was be a deacon forever. That, or lead a life that would change the heart of my wife," I concluded.

"And the second part obviously failed," she said gently.

Yes—I have to agree with her. It goes without saying a divorce will close off another door; I will never be able to answer the call to be a pastor.

All these questions were making my head spin. On one hand, Danielle barely knew me. At the same time, she knew me so well that I was head-over-heels in love. I loved how she discerned something I heard from God double-digit years ago, even though I was still not ready to act on the call from the Lord. As we kept talking about it, I tried to pretend it did not faze me. In truth, it did.

I was about to leave, and without thinking about it, I started to rattle off instructions for her in my absence. "Remember what the doc said: Do not…" I caught myself mid-sentence, expecting her to tell me to go to you-know-where any second. After all, this was Danielle Rose, not some submissive weak sister that I was talking to. But she was cool. She even agreed to a date later on in the evening.

The hours flew by, and in no time, I was back on her doorstep, ringing her bell. This time, in place of the smiling, agreeable Danielle I left behind earlier, she stood on her front porch staring past me as if I did not exist. She dropped her bag, jumped down the few short steps, and walked directly to the car—the new one Hunter convinced me to buy the other day. Hands on her hips, she walked around it several times.

"What's wrong?" I asked.

She put her index finger up to her lips. "*Shh,*" she hissed. She ran her hand across the car's gleaming hood. I started to walk over, but she held up her hand, motioning me to stay back.

What was going on? Mystified, I sat down on the steps to wait.

"Is everything okay?" I asked gently.

"*No!*" she yelled. "*Not okay!*"

"Why? What is it?"

"*I have had enough of this!*" she shouted.

"Enough of what?" I had no idea what was wrong.

"Of *you.*" She made it sound like a final verdict.

I stepped back a few feet to give her room. That made things worse; she closed in on me, arms folded, face set in a scowl.

"GODLEE BATMAN! WHERE DO YOU GET THESE TOYS?"

"The new car? I swear, I have only a few more at home," I said. I was honestly trying to reassure her.

"A *few* more?"

She yelled at me about the car for the entire ride. Frankly, I was touched she cared what I did with my money. She was no gold-digger, that was for sure; no, here she was acting frugal as a Scotswoman.

"What can I do to make it up to you?" I asked helplessly. "I cannot buy you diamonds." Really, what else was I going to do with my money? I did not have anyone to travel with; I never go anywhere; I hardly eat, never drink, never date. All I could do, I pointed out, was buy exotic cars, futuristic electronics, and custom suits.

Despite her disapproval, I could see by the way she was talking about the car that she knew more about it than Hunter or me. This impressed the heck out of me. She was homeboy cool--yet soft, gentle and feminine.

Once I got her back home, I found I could not leave her. I sat in my car in her driveway like a stalker, watching her look at me through the window, unable to either get the balls to go back to her door or simply to leave. Finally, I remembered I needed to get ready for my upcoming trip to Vegas--I desperately needed the association to approve my request to fight again. I tore myself away, reluctantly headed back to the house, and got my suitcase packed. Afterwards, I blogged.

Wednesday

I woke up determined to get on with the day, to be strictly about business, and not to think about Danielle but I was weak. I had a visceral need to see her before I left--to touch her, smell her, make sure she was all right with my decision to go to Vegas and try to reboot my boxing career. So I did what any fool in love would do. I chartered a chopper and landed it on the roof of her office building. My crew can say whatever they like. It is what it is.

I knocked on her office door. She was shocked to see me standing there, "I told you I wanted to see you and needed to see you before I left." I am so transparent with her sometimes, and today was one of those times. I reached out for a hug, but my heart was pounding, my palms sweating. I was visibly nervous.

She asked me "Why are you nervous?"

I did it again; I told the truth.

"You do that to me."

I knew my helicopter trip to her office to say goodbye was over the top. It was a last minute decision and the quickest means. I do not want to know how much this stunt cost me. The smile on her face was well worth any financial cost. To my crew I am the biggest punk this century. She is the reason I am going back in the ring. My plans and my path are not clear right now, but I know my future includes her. This was truly walking by faith and not by sight.

Once she realized I arrived via helicopter she screamed, "No hell you didn't!"

"Yes, I did. That is how much you mean to me. I detoured my route and landed on the roof of your building to look you in your eyes and say goodbye."

She smiled and sighed. "Randall, may God be with us, both together and apart."

"Amen," I agreed.

I released her, and ran back to the chopper. The helicopter lifted off, the rush of wind flinging her hair like a whirlwind. On the flight to Vegas, the crew ragged me non-stop. I listened to my Beats the entire time, calm as could be. Once we landed, the crew made sure to get Hunter on the phone to tell him about my little detour. It did not matter; I was off in my own world.

"Has it ever occurred to you that you're looking for love in all the wrong places?" asked JJ, laughing.

"You got it all wrong, JJ. I was not looking for love--love found me, and not a moment too soon. This is the Lord's doing, guys. Danielle completes me; she makes me whole again. You may not see it now; but you will. All I ask is that you trust me."

I could tell from the hooting and hollering that they found this highly amusing. "What you saw today was the just the beginning," I told them. Danielle, being an architect, could relate to my thinking. "See, what I am doing now is building a strong foundation. To build high, you need a deep foundation. That is what I am aiming for."

My tongue was unbridled; now, the crew hushed up and was actually paying attention.

"This all means so much to me—my being here, my knowing her, and my knowing you all. It is as if my life is changing before my eyes. See, my soul was formed by the Spirit; my body was built from the DNA of my parents, and later rebuilt by my own hard work. Formed spiritually by Trevor, trained physically by you, my crew, and mentally developed by man."

"Of course God is the original designer. He owns the blueprint, and He assembled me according to His specifications. Now, I am being renovated and redesigned by a woman. She is adding some new parts and pieces and taking the damaged parts away."

"Not that God made a mistake, mind you—He never makes mistakes. It is more as if He is reminding me that it is not all me. It is not all the work that you all do to make me. I depend on Him, on Tre, on my crew, and now on this *wo-man* whom He sent to me. I need her help to complete me, to renovate me and to restore me."

I was not done yet; the words poured out. "For years I have been bound to the altar, and yet I have made a mess of myself, my life, and my career. Not that I lacked for anything, but I never had all I wanted.

I need more--a female companion. God did not make man to be alone. He gave Adam a helpmate. Danielle is my helpmate.

"I have made a covenant with God. I have been in His presence, and He has given me keys and a promise, just as I have given Him sacrifices, and made promises in return. I told Him I would not let him go until He blessed me--with the life I envision. I want to fight again. I want to love again. I want to live again." No one, me least of all, saw all of *that* coming. There was momentary silence.

"Bro," I called out to Trevor. He was still on the phone listening. He cleared his throat. I could sense he was moved.

"Randall, how can we help you?"

"Right now, Pastor, I need you to pray for me. Support me. Help me take one-step at a time. I want to do things in the right order, and the focus this week has to be the association. I will take the next step after I hear their decision."

"And what is that next step?"

"Divorce Tameka. Marry Danielle."

"Man, you are *feeling* this girl." Trevor whistled softly.

I clicked the cell phone speaker off and walked into another room, wanting to talk to Trevor alone. I needed him both ways, as a pastor and as a friend.

I shut the door behind me and spoke quietly. "Tre, fireworks light up the sky when I am with her. I have never felt this way before. Please help me." I was mentally dreading another one of Trevor's diatribes. To my surprise, he did not scold me. Instead, we talked as friends talk, me asking advice, him giving it. This conversation would fuel my soul for days to come; it would ease my mind, and quiet my thoughts of her, so I could focus on my first goal--to fight again.

The rest of the day was back to work--routine after routine, drill after drill, exercise after exercise. The reps from the Boxing Association came and went all day long, saying nothing, only observing. It definitely kept me on my P's and Q's; in fact, I was beyond hyped, running on pure adrenaline. A couple of bananas here and there, a few bottles of water, plus the thought of fighting again, was all I needed to keep going. The crew, on the other hand, was exhausted. Between all the travelling, the training, and dealing with the press, they needed refueling. Sometime after dark, I called time. While the guys ate, I quietly prayed. The boxing association had not given us feedback, nor any clear instructions; that would have been too easy, right? I mean, should I write a dissertation? Run thirty miles? What exactly did they want? It was becoming clear there would be no decision anytime soon. Neither JJ nor King were happy about it; of course, they wanted an answer right away. For my part, I felt I had nothing but time on my hands. I was prepared to stay in Vegas as long as needed. True, I had someone back in Atlanta I was already missing; but in the meantime, I could do without. I rested, trusting God to work things out for the good.

Danielle's reaction gave me such a measure of peace. Her attitude restored my energy; she revived my soul. This was all in God's plan. Knowing she was well again, and that I had her support, helped me put the stress and worry aside.

Much later, after I finished blogging, I lay down to pray, and then called it a night.

Thursday

Since the day she was sick, when I spent twenty-four bliss-filled hours at her house, all of my possessions seem marked by her aroma; my whole room smells of ambrosia. All I want to do is inhale her lovely scent. I have not slept much since the day she went to the NASCAR race. This was boxing, not my first rodeo, so I was not nervous or anxious—just focused on doing my job. When you have confidence in what you do, there is no need to be arrogant. Admit it or not, I would probably be okay if the association turned me down. I have so many other things on my plate to look forward to accomplishing. I could finally start giving boxing lessons, something I have thought about doing for years. There was a laundry list of things I could do at the church and in the community.

King and JJ, meanwhile, were increasingly furious, at the way the hotel lobby was filling with groupies, stalkers, tabloid reporters, women who wanted to be my baby mama, and God only knows who else. None of it distracted me. I did what I needed to do, regardless of the mob in the lobby. In fact, we spent most of the day training, hidden away in the hotel room to avoid them all. When I was not training, I was praying. When I was not praying, I was thinking about training.

I knew I had to pace myself. The divorce was important, but right now, I needed approval to fight again. It was getting harder to stay focused, as thoughts of Danielle began to seep back into the nooks and crannies of my brain. I was never going to be able to shake her. Nor did I want to.

King and JJ were drilling me so hard I had no time to call her, or anyone else for that matter--no texts, no messages, nothing. Practically speaking, I could shut off the world like this because back home, my ambassadors were on duty at the gym, the juice bar and the restaurant; if a problem arose, they knew how to reach King and JJ, who could make executive decisions. Of course, if it was serious, I had to know about it. Barring that, life back home was on hold, letting me focus on the task at hand in Vegas.

Well, not entirely on hold--there was still a certain woman who lay heavy on my psyche, whose mere name stirred me. As I explained earlier, it was like my blueprint was being altered and adjusted, retooled and revolutionized, both inside and out—and all because of a parking spot. Hard to believe such a small thing altered my life. It goes to show--never take the little things for granted. One brief encounter with a girl landed me back in Vegas, would soon thrust me back into the court system, and had me ready and eager to get back to the grind.

For too many years, I was complacent, accepting the notion my life was frozen in place, never to change. In my despair, I often prayed to God for a do-over. Now I realize I was asking God for the wrong thing all those years. He spared me--by *not* giving me a do-over. If so, it could have easily been worse. Tameka and I could have had five babies by now, and our mutual fates linked forever.

But no. Instead of a do-ever, I should have been asking God to reverse things. And so He did, placing me back exactly where I began so many years ago. Here I was, asking the Association for another shot at fighting; and here I was, asking Danielle for another chance at real love. The difference was, now I was wiser, and knew what I was getting into. I was in a far better place. Truly, even if the Association turned me down, the rebirth God sent me was something no one could take away.

King was growing more annoyed by the day. He complained he could not reach me. I was sedated by love, and my love-struck behavior was getting on his nerves. He wanted the old me back. All King really wanted, I decided, was my skills and my talent. To be honest, I was getting almost as anxious as he was.

As part of my training regimen, King strictly prohibited me from making contact with the outside world—no phone calls, no social media, no ESPN or CNN. This was his method; I accepted it. I worked hard, giving him everything I could.

Friday

Another day just like the one before—training, training, and more training. I begin to feel like I was locked up in solitary confinement. I so wished Danielle was here with me. Everywhere I looked, I saw her face, heard her voice, and smelled her sweet, dear scent. Yet in a certain way, my yearning for her kept me focused and on point. I was exhausted, but still I was convinced I could fight anyone when I think of her. I can knock any guy out.

JJ, seeing my stress level rising, asked me what I needed.

"Easy," I told him. "I need my laptop, my phone, and my debit card." Today I wanted to send Danielle gifts. I sent JJ to talk to King, hoping JJ might mollify my hot-tempered trainer. King, to my surprise, sent word that I was permitted three things—to call Hunter, call RJ, and email Danielle. I decided to blog instead of emailing her; my heart was so full, my feelings could not possibly fit into an email. Only in a blog could I show her my whole, true heart.

Saturday

There was still no decision from the Association; everyone was feeling the tension. I *had* to talk to Danielle, I pleaded with JJ. *Yeah, right*, was the look he shot back. We both knew King would never consent, so I decided not to push the issue.

Then King surprised me again. In recognition of all my hard work, he said, I could have my phone back long enough to make a few calls. My first call, of course, was to Danielle. No answer. I texted her; again, no response. I made my other calls, blogged, and re-checked voice messages and emails. I called her once again; still no answer. What was going on? I checked her levels; they were all normal. Maybe she was sleeping.

Later in the day, King gave me another break. I grabbed my phone, heading to the restroom for privacy. Finally, there was a text—not from Danielle, but from Sade. Danielle was feeling neglected and really down, Sade wrote—not something I could properly address at this moment. I was surprised at the news, even hurt. I explained that she needed to be patient, and let the process work itself out. I pleaded with Sade to hold down the fort until I could call back.

By the time I was finally done for the day, it was late. I could not sleep now because I was worried. I emailed Danielle the lyrics of a Brian McKnight song I had been listening to all week, hoping the words would tell her how I felt. To my surprise, Sade texted me back right away. I checked to see where the two of them were.

As I feared, not at home. Why were they out so late? Were they safe? Not the time to act paranoid, I decided, grateful I was communicating with Sade, and not Danielle, who had a bad habit of texting while driving. I felt like I needed some kind of human digital thermometer to check Danielle's emotional temperature--I knew she was feeling some kind of way. It had been three days since I had been in touch. I decided the only thing to do was to call her.

The instant I heard her, I felt terrible—there was so much pain in her voice. How could I explain to her everything I was doing was for our future? How could I say, *Trust me, Danielle, and be patient?* This called for more than just words; I needed to take action, and those actions needed to speak loudly. I did my best to be honest.

"Danielle, I am not supposed to be in contact with anyone. I will face disciplinary actions for calling you." Already, angry voices were yelling at me from the other side of the door.

"We need an understanding," I went on. "I'm trying to start over with so many things right now—with my career as a fighter, and with dating. Sometimes, I hardly know what to do."

"Dating is new to me. I have never really *courted* a woman. Tameka and I were boyfriend/girlfriend, then parents, then husband and wife. We never really dated. I pray the day will come when I will be able to court you. It is scary to have your first date at this age. It is frightening to be your friend and nothing more. I feel as horrible as you may feel about all of this. Right now is the first time in my adult life that I want to, just for a moment, cut myself off from God and do the worldly things my mind and heart have been telling me to do."

I heard her gasp.

"But Danielle, I cannot do that. It is hard to fight against flesh, but twice as hard to fight against God's principles. If you feel the way I do, then we are fighting this together." She said nothing, but I could tell she at least was listening.

"I need you to have patience -- let me finish one thing at a time. Please, Danielle—will you text me when you get home tonight so I will know you are safe? I am sorry I have not called you," I added. "They do not permit me any distractions—I am not allowed to talk to anyone but Pastor."

"Pastor? Oh, yes. I met with *him* yesterday. *Again.*" Her voice trailed off wearily. I was feeling awful about how this conversation was ending. Why did Danielle met with Tre? He mentioned nothing about it to me.

"Hey. Can you at least tell me what you are going wearing to church tomorrow?" I asked. Anything to lighten the mood. It did not help; she blew me off. We said goodbye.

This was an emergency, which called for action. Now was not the time to argue, especially with King. He must have heard the determination in my voice, because he got Vickie on the phone right away. I asked her to make a few calls, and told her I would call back in an hour. By my next phone break, she told me everything was set.

"This is going to cost a lot of money," she warned. I told her I could care less about the money.

Not wanting to press my luck with King, I went over the details of my new plan with him and JJ. They both looked at me as if I had completely lost my mind. I tried hard to relax. We got back to training, then my phone chirped. I desperately wanted to see the phone, but I knew better than to ask King, especially after he laid out his own expectations for the next few days.

Sunday

When I awoke, it was still night in Vegas--but early morning in Atlanta. As everyone began to stir, I tried to convince myself I was still feeling confident about the plan Vickie and I put together. JJ and King were more convinced than ever that I was sprung. There was no way I could avoid taking a beating over this. What I was doing was totally out of character, and as far as my crew was concerned, not cool at all.

In silence, except for the dull roar of the plane engine, we traveled through the velvety darkness over the desert. Soon the sky brightened, and the sun was shining fiercely by the time we reached the smoggy outskirts of Atlanta. Everyone on board made it clear they thought I was completely insane.

True, this was something new for me. *Eyes had not seen nor ears heard the things in my mind.* There at the landing strip was the helicopter Vickie chartered. Soon after we climbed in, the chopper touched down atop the church. I knew King would never let me live this down, and Hunter—well, he was surely going to lay hands on me, and not to bless me, but more likely to kill me.

We took the stairwell down as I sent one of the guys to pull Danielle out of the sanctuary. I was standing on the other end of the corridor when she and Sade came out, both looking confused and annoyed. Danielle's face lit up when she saw me. She was nowhere near as happy as I was to see her. Her smile was worth all the money in the world, no matter what this trip cost. She and Sade were speechless. That was a first.

"I did not fly all night from Vegas to Atlanta and then land on the roof of the church in this chopper to be a show-off," I told her. "I did it because of how I feel about you." I apologized for interrupting her during service. "What I mean to tell you is that this is how much you mean to me, Danielle. Never forget it."

She still had not spoken. "Say something," I begged. Had this all been a huge mistake? She answered my question.

"Oh, Randall," she cried, seizing me in her arms—a hug so hard it almost knocked me off balance. Not that she was stronger than I was, but because my body was weak from training hard. I mean, my knees were like licorice, my legs like spaghetti, and my arms like melted chocolate. My abs felt pierced by millions of needles; my internal organs seemed to have been forcibly shifted to a new location. I was, in a word, beat.

Still holding me close, she whispered, "Randall, why? Why are you doing this?"

I told her the truth. "The same way you sometimes have to do crazy things at work to gain your clients' trust, I am trying to win your trust in me. I want you to know no matter where I am, or what I am doing, you are always my first priority. I want your trust and your confidence, Danielle. When the time is right, I want you to be my wife."

"You didn't have to do all this," she whispered, shaking her head.

"Truthfully, it isn't enough," I replied. "We had a bad conversation last night. I had to see you face to face to get this resolved." Right or wrong, everything was straight from my heart.

"Oh, Randall, you need to be worried about yourself right now, not about me."

"No. Don't you get it? You *are* my worry. My main interest. My biggest concern."

"But you can't just hop on a jet and land a helicopter on a roof whenever we have a conversation you don't like," she said.

Clearly, she must not know me, I thought. I can do whatever I want, whenever I want.

"Besides, where do they think you are?" she asked, meaning the Association back in Vegas.

"Where am I?" I answered her with a question.

"At church."

"There you have it."

"You told them you were going to church?"

"Am I not at church?"

"Well, technically, yes. But two thousand miles away!"

"I didn't tell them *what* church I was going to. Maybe I left out a few details." I could see she was about to give me a scolding.

"Omission is also a lie," she reminded me.

Right now, I was not worried about sins of omission. Rather, I needed her to understand what was going on between us at this moment. I had done so much to be here right now. I had no idea how much my little antic cost me, but surely, King was hard at work calculating. I am sure I will hear about it a lot over the coming days.

Of course, I would have to work extra hard not to make any mistakes, and never admit I was tired, or show any signs of weakness or exhaustion. King will say flying cross-country on a whim is what was making others unhappy with me. I assumed Trevor would soon be among them.

"You worry about Hooks," she said in parting. "Take care of yourself." I loved it when she sometimes called me Hooks; it showed she knew I was divided into three different people, almost like multiple personalities.

In a way, I was. Hooks, Deacon Washington, and Randall never seemed to collide with one another; they co-existed peaceably most of the time. Yet none of them alone made up a complete person. Hooks was a totally different breed from Randall. Thank God. Deacon Washington was his own person, a busy and capable servant. Nevertheless, Randall was the man Danielle knew best.

Did these three people need to become one? Was it right that they were separate? This was something I would ponder a lot in the coming weeks, trying to understand these three who dwell inside of me. The way Danielle made me stop and think about such things was one of the ways she ministered to my soul, something I truly needed right now. There surely was a purpose for her in my life, a purpose I began to discern the very moment I met her.

She inspired me to land a helicopter on the roof of her office building, and then on top of the church—something I would have never done before. In four brief months, she encouraged me to take steps toward getting the divorce I should have gotten four years ago.

Sometimes we fail to move on to the next step until we have no other choice; in a way, Danielle blocked all the other exits. With her, it was piss or get off the pot—a powerful epiphany. For that, I would be forever grateful to her, despite the monetary cost, despite all the sleepless nights, and despite the beat-down I was sure to receive.

She touched my face, interrupting my thoughts.

"Are you okay?"

I nodded yes. She was like truth serum to me. Every time I opened my mouth, I could do nothing but speak my true feelings. She picked the next moment to ask the million-dollar question, the one I could not yet answer--the one I could not call Vickie and get her to fix.

"So," she asked, "what do we do now?"

"Well," I said, trying to make light of the subject, "right now I jump back into this helicopter. I fly back to Vegas to resume training. I listen to my crew dog me about this for the remainder of my natural life, while I pray something happens to take the attention off me. I pray God has favor upon me, and Trevor does not find out I landed a helicopter on his house of worship. Because I am sure I will never live this down."

"No, I don't think you will," she laughed. "I actually think they taped the landing, from the conversation I can hear."

My crew was standing close by, laughing and talking among themselves. She could hear them? I could not, although I was not listening to them because I was so engulfed in her presence.

Part of me understood what my guys felt. Danielle *was* a distraction, not just from my training but also from my sense of right and wrong. For the time being, I would always need someone to watch me when I was with her.

King pointed to his wrist, again indicating it was time to go. I told Danielle to get Sade; they would ride back to the airport with us, just so I could be with Danielle a few minutes longer.

We raced back up the stairs to the roof. Sade's presence helped me to get back on track and regain control. I told Danielle I expected to be gone another week. Just then, my phone rang; Sade answered it.

"I have no clue who *you are,* young lady, but I do know there was a helicopter on the roof of my church." That was Trevor's voice on speaker. "Randall DeWayne Washington, land it on my roof again," he urged me. Then he did what he always does, what any father would do--a spiritual father, a biological father, even God. He encouraged me: "Run it. Make us proud. Redeem yourself for landing on my roof."

That was just the kind of encouragement I needed. Now I have received it, and from the two people I loved the most—Trev and Danielle. Missing the two of them was exactly why I had to make this crazy trip.

On the way back to Vegas, the crew kindly gave me half the flight in silence before they started ragging me. That gave me time to think, and to digest what just happened. I made a big statement, for sure. However, that was not the point. I wanted to prove something to Danielle. Hopefully, showing up on the roof again changed the game. Life had me up against the ropes, but not knocked out. There was still lots of fight left in me.

Also, there was someone else I could tag in at any time. He was always there, waiting on me to ask for His help. I had not done so before, not until recently. Instead, I rode it out in the ring alone. Now I was asking His help. I needed my third man in the ring. What if people have forgotten about me? What if people were upset I returned to the ring? It was an upset in the making for many people. Right now, my crew and Trevor were the ones upset. They all had been with me through this tragedy, but no one ever told me it was over, because it was not. They forgot to tell Randall, Hooks and Deacon Washington the fight was over. For the three of us the game was just beginning. Not that I considered this a game - more like a challenge.

I have so many challenges before me with the Association, my crew, King's bad temper, Trevor's righteous anger--and of course the beautiful conundrum which is Danielle Rose. Overnight, I changed and the game changed as well.

First, I had to start over with myself. I felt like an eagle, ready to soar. If you know anything about eagles, you know their lifespan is seventy years. Once the eagle reaches age thirty, its talons and beak become weak and bent; then the bird can no longer survive, because it cannot catch prey. At this point, the creature must make a decision.

There are two options—either die, or go through a painful, five-month-long rebirthing process. If the bird picks the second choice, it flies to a mountaintop. There it knocks its beak off and waits for it to grow back. Once the beak grows back, it plucks out its own talons and all its feathers, one by one. After one hundred-and-fifty days, the bird's beak, talons, and feathers will have grown back. Now it can live for another thirty years.

This rebirth process all sounded familiar. At thirty, I was faced with having to make a decision. Nor did I have a long list to choose from, there were only two choices. In a way, I had already died. I could stay stuck in a life without meaning or purpose; or I could fly to the mountaintop and begin the work of change.

Right now, my mountain is the MGM Grand in Las Vegas. I have been knocking my beak out for the last few days, killing myself working out. Now, it is time to start plucking feathers and talons. I need this transformation; I have to be reborn. Danielle was the wind beneath my wings.

For the eagle, they call this the "flight of rebirth;" for Hooks, they will term it "a comeback". Deacon Washington will refer to it as "being reborn".

And Randall, the part of me who needs this the most, will call it "getting his life back."

WEEK 16
Monday

Pastor Trevor Hunter arrived this morning in Vegas, amid much publicity. Every reporter in town was crammed into the lobby of the MGM Grand. Women were lined up as if for a casting call. The size of the crowd was shocking. Hunter, a man fully at ease with addressing a crowd, had to admit he was relieved to be here to address one particular person, not the hundreds lined up in the lobby.

Hunter was here to support his friend and to chasten him.

He was glad Randall remained focused and humble over the years. Until now, he never had to chasten him about women before. However, being his best friend and of the cloth, Hunter had no other choice but to help get his friend pointed back in the right direction.

The two men greeted each other joyfully. Hunter realized Hooks was at the church yesterday but he did not get a chance to see him. Today, he saw, Hooks looked exhausted. He could tell he had been going hard at it the past few days. By the looks of things, the grueling schedule was not about to let up anytime soon. Hunter watched his friend closely throughout the long day, until he found the right tone and the proper time to begin the conversation he felt the two of them must have.

Hooks wearily sat back and simply listened. Hunter accused him of being overzealous and selfish of trying too hard to impress. Hooks had no desire to try to win this debate.

"Get your head on straight, RW. You are losing it," Hunter said. "You should be worried about fighting, and nothing more. You have lost your focus." Clearly, Hunter was not happy with any of Hooks' actions. Hooks was moving too fast; he was completely out of line. He needed to get back in his own lane. He was being obsessive, behaving like a stalker. (That word again.) He was being far too possessive, pursuing Danielle as if she were a fancy car, or some other kind of prized item to be added to his collection. The last accusation stung; still, Hooks held his tongue.

"Hooks, you are going about this all wrong. You are trying to secure one deal before you break ties with the previous one. Not only do you risk failing; you risk hurting Danielle. Things could spiral out of control, resulting in an even a bigger mess in court. Stop putting the cart before the horse. All things must be done in decency and in order. You know how I am about order," declared the Hunter. "I am not going to change. The Word never changes, nor will I. Hooks, you are doing things on your own, not in accordance with His will." Hunter added he spoke with Danielle earlier in the week, reminding her she was available and Hooks was not. She should remove herself from the situation until Hooks' situation changed, he instructed her. Otherwise, she would be making a fool of herself. "She is not that kind of person, Hooks," Hunter concluded. "Neither are you!"

What did he just say? Was he serious? Suddenly, Hooks was furious. Now his friend was totally out of line. How dare the man speak such things to Danielle? For all his mounting fury, Hooks held his tongue. He knew his friend was not done with him yet.

Sure enough, Hunter proceeded to bring up the helicopter landing on the church's roof. At that point, things went downhill swiftly. Hunter said words his friend was sure were *not* Christ-like, going on and on. At least, Hooks thought bitterly, he was not being humiliated in front of his crew. At the end of the long harangue, Hunter finally bestowed some praise on his friend's disciplined approach to fighting, and all his hard work—although it was not enough in Hooks' mind to compensate for the tongue-lashing he received.

After Hunter departed, Hooks sat alone, recalling all the unkind words his best friend said. In despondency, he threw himself facedown--not to praise God, but to weep. Hunter's words hurt; the truth usually did.

Perhaps, Hooks reflected, he *was* out of control. The helicopter stunt was over the top. Who lands a helicopter on someone's roof— not once, but twice in a single week? Something was wrong. Hooks doubted he could change; he could neither turn his emotions off nor even tamp them down. All he could do was roll with it.

He must try to behave more reasonably. He could not promise anything, though; his body, mind and heart had been completely taken over.

At the same time, he reflected, was it not Danielle herself who restored to him the will to fight again? The trouble was he was too fervent about this woman. There were thousands of desirable women downstairs in the lobby, but Hooks had eyes for none of them. Each time he was forced to pass them by, he pulled down his hoodie and donned shades to avoid them as much as possible. Right now, all that mattered were three things: God, getting back to the ring, and Danielle Rose. Nothing more, nothing less.

Gradually, the black cloud hanging over his spirits lifted. He splashed cold water on his face in the bathroom, and looked at himself in the mirror. He smiled. *If everyone felt so strongly about the helicopter and flight back to Atlanta, wait until they see what he had planned next,* he thought. It would cause a fine ruckus; Hunter would be angry with him for a month of Sundays. That night, he broke the rules again. He called Danielle, and the two of them talked all night.

Wednesday

After a long, bumpy flight, I was finally back in Atlanta. I tried to call her all day today to let her know I would be coming to Bible Study. She was not answering. Even though I was not on Deacon Duty, I arrived at the church early, and spotted her in the sanctuary. I had to disturb her; no way could I hold out until after the service to see her. I motioned for her to meet me in the lobby.

Her fashion sense and style were, once again, impeccable. As usual, she looked completely put-together in a way that was perfect, yet seemed effortless. What was not effortless was me, trying with all my might not to do what I really wanted to do. Luckily, I was too exhausted to do more than take her gently in my arms.

After the service, I went home and crashed, visions of Danielle running through my head as I dozed on and off to sleep. I tried to understand what I saw tonight. Did she really have something mounted in her car for her iPads? That was ridiculous. Something had to be done about her and the notion to work while driving. And to think, she told me I was out of control! I had a plan no one would like, especially not Ms. Rose.

Thursday

Today was a big day: I was finally getting the answer from the Boxing Association. I could not believe I asked for this to be a semipublic moment. Normally, I would have hidden away in my man-cave, to deal in private with whatever verdict might be handed down. But today I wanted to receive the news with her. I knew the only way I could do so was along with the crowd.

The day dragged by at a snail's pace. All day I contemplated cancelling the small gathering. Why didn't I arrange to pass the evening alone in my dark bedroom, just King and JJ pacing the floor?

My heart would not allow me to cancel. I kept with the original plan. This was very short notice, with everyone involved doing a great job to put this elaborate gathering together. It turned into party and not a business meeting as I suggested.

Fed up with watching the clock, I finally gathered my key players, and we headed to my office. In no time, I was laid out on the floor.

A few minutes before eight, JJ got me up. Suddenly, this gathering seemed like a terrible idea. I paced; Danielle was sitting at my desk, her back to everyone else in the room. No one spoke a word. Right on time, the phone rang. JJ quieted everyone in the room and those hanging around outside the door patiently waiting on the news. I was deathly nervous.

You could have heard a pin drop. I could scarcely breathe. I looked around the crowded room, suddenly wanting desperately to take the call in private. Too late. It would be rude if I asked everyone to leave; therefore, I turned my back, and took a deep breath as JJ handed me the phone.

It was a short conversation, brief and to the point, with no chance for me to say much. At the end, I thanked the person on the other end of the line, and set the phone down. I knelt on the floor and lay my head in Danielle's lap, unable to speak.

"Randall, look at me," she said softly.

I struggled to my feet, raising her up as well and placing my forehead against hers, and whispered, "I love you so much. I do not know where you have been all my life, but I am glad you are here now. I need a moment to get myself together."

No one moved or spoke, although cameras were flashing incessantly. It seemed I was weeping; then Danielle too began to sob, with deep, jagged breaths. I knew everyone in the room was staring at us, but I did not care.

"Why are *you* crying?" I asked her.

"Because you are. Because you will not talk to me, or look at me."

It felt like the right moment.

"Danielle, I love you," I said, my voice loud and clear.

She responded without a moment's hesitation. "Randall, I love you, too."

The words burned my throat and touched my heart all at the same time. For some reason, I could not open my eyes or speak. All I could do was take this time and give thanks. I needed a minute to myself although I knew everyone was waiting on me. I did not want to be rude. However, right now it was all about me. I needed to digest all of this. I had a lot to take in and a very short time to do so.

Once I could move, I lifted her off her feet and swung her like a parent swings a kid at the playground, her feet knocking everything off my desk.

"I'm fighting!" I yelled at the top of my voice. *"They said yes! I'm fighting again!"*

JJ flung open the door, a big grin on his face, and announced to the crowd waiting outside, "Hooks Washington will be putting his gloves back on, people. He's been cleared to fight again."

I have never seen JJ this excited before. Camera flashes greeting the news. I gave everyone a few moments to settle down, and then I politely kicked the crew out of my office—I needed a few moments with Danielle, all to myself. I lay down on the floor as she lay beside me. Before I knew it, she climbed on top of me.

"I am so proud of you," she said, her beautiful face smiling down at me.

"This means so much to me."

"I know," she replied.

"No, you really do not," I laughed. "And what's more, you are lying on top of me. If you do not get off, something serious is going to happen. We will miss our party. Plus, you know how upset Tre would be." She giggled, struggling to get off. At that point, the inevitable happened; to be truthful, I was not embarrassed about it. I was trying hard to be a gentleman, but I was still a man. Sure, some might say that was lame of me, asking her to get off, right when I had the opportunity to take advantage of her. After all, we were two consenting adults, our two bodies completely in tune with one other. I needed to go out and greet my guests. Besides, I needed to do things in the proper order.

Therefore, difficult as it was, we stood up, straightened our clothes, laughed, and allowed ourselves to enjoy the moment. "Randall, sweetie, tell me how you're feeling right now," she said, tugging at her blouse.

"Like all of my dreams are coming true. I have never felt this good in my life," I replied, caressing her cheek.

That was the honest truth. The first time I made it big, it was almost as if success was handed to me on a platter. I was just a dumb kid, an un-caged fighter, who got a lot more than what he bargained for. I was a man now, a skilled athlete, as well as a father, a successful business owner, and a man of God. This time, I was ready.

"What about our future?" she asked. "Where do we go from here?" Those were valid questions; I took my time answering, gently reminding her again of how I wished to do everything in the right order. After much more talk, with me still having trouble controlling myself, we prepared to go out to greet our guests.

"Your shirt is wrinkled," Leigh told me as we made ready to emerge from our hideaway, a knowing look in her eye. "Oh my goodness, look at Danielle's shoes." They were ruined; neither of us cared. I changed shirts and promised Danielle a new pair of shoes—an entire shoe store, if she liked.

For one brief moment, I thought about announcing our engagement to the gathered crowd.

God spoke to me, saying, "Slow down. One thing at a time."

"To whom much is given, much is required," I mumbled to myself. "Speak, Lord; your servant listens."

Outside my office, the guests awaited. Everyone had words of congratulation and encouragement. I listened intently to each person, even though my gaze stayed locked on Danielle. Soon it was time for dinner. When dinner was served, someone placed a burger in front of me, along with fries. Unfortunately, Danielle was serious about the burger and champagne I previously agreed to. However, I managed to talk my way out of the fries. Then, it was toast time. Danielle, seated beside me, never shy in public situations, caught me off guard when she stood and held up her champagne flute, pausing until the noisy room settled down.

"To my dearest Randall," she began her voice strong and sure. She half-turned so she was facing me as well as the crowd, the glass still held high in her hand. "I hope from this day and forever more that all your dreams become a reality. I hope you walk away from each fight, whole, unharmed and the winner. I pray for your health, strength and safety in all that you do. I pray the protection of God continually surrounds you to comfort and keep you on a daily basis. There is nothing impossible for you. I hope you continue to remain the humble, nice, caring, considerate, and fun loving person you are. I look forward to your growth and maturity in your walk with God. I see big and great things for you. I have faith in you. I pray you are blessed and covered from the crown of your head to the soles of your feet. I pray that the paths you tread are filled with abundance. That rings you battle and the pathways of your daily journey are covered and illuminated by the light of God. This is only the beginning. You have yet to see. Eyes have not seen, ears have not heard nor has it crossed the hearts of boxers what you are about to show this world. Your cup shall be filled with plenty and prepared before the presence of your enemies." She paused for emphasis; now her voice was brimming with excitement and joy. *"Get ready. Get ready. Get ready. It's time to rumble!"*

I was astonished. Before I could recover myself, Danielle astounded me further by presenting me with gifts-- boxing shorts and a beautiful robe, along with a tastefully framed collage of dozens of photographs of me. To loud cheers, I held up the robe for all to see.

"I will certainly be wearing this for the first fight," I said, shaking my head in wonder. How did she have time to do all this? I was overcome.

"I want to take you home," I whispered to her. All I want right now is to be alone with her, if only for a little while.

On the ride back, she asked permission to eat the slice of cake she brought along with her. "Of course," I said. I glanced at her fondly, as she had already fallen asleep, the tiny slice of cake balanced carefully in her hand. I could not resist taking a picture of her lovely, sleeping face; but the sound of the phone awakened her. She invited me inside, once we arrived at her house, and it took every ounce of my willpower to decline her invitation.

I got back in my car and pulled off, getting as far as the gate before I paused. I turned the car back around, ran to her porch, and rang her doorbell. As soon as she opened the door, I poured out my heart. "Danielle, you are so special. What am I going to do with you? I was rude to just say good-bye and leave, especially after all the work you put into making tonight so perfect."

I was rethinking her invitation to come in, when who should call but Trevor. I explained to him that I could not talk; whatever chastening he had in mind would have to wait until later.

His call broke the spell, and I knew what I had to do. "I have to leave now, Danielle," I said. We hugged passionately, and I turned and walked away as she shut the front door. I heard the bolt slide into the lock. I was so annoyed with Trevor for interrupting that it felt easier to leave this time. On my ride home, I thought of everything I wanted to say to him.

I am sure he thought he was doing his job, but tonight was my night. *Please let me have one day. Surely, after all the hard times, the difficult days and nights that have come before, I have earned it.*

I called Trevor when I pulled up to the house. He did not answer. Now it seemed *he* was being a coward. I yearned to call Danielle, just to say good night. Instead, I texted her.

> Good night and thank you.

Friday

I awoke to the sound of rain still feeling angry with Trevor. When I got to the gym, I remembered I gave King the day off. I was left to train alone to let off some steam. I decided to run, despite the fact it was pouring. Thunder rumbled, and lightning flashed on the horizon. In no time, I was soaked to the skin. The sensation refocused my thoughts, away from my anger at Tre; suddenly, nothing was troubling me. The rain felt good.

A car pulled up: Danielle. I was impressed. Being herself, she made a huge fuss about me running in the rain, and dragged me back to the gym. Truly, it was a monsoon out there. As I toweled off and put on a dry T-shirt, I offered to drive her to work, wanting to make sure she was safe, and not driving around in such weather. I mean, Danielle was dangerous behind the wheel of a car on a sunny day; she was hell on wheels in the rain. I did not want her texting, emailing or working while driving in this mess. But why kid myself? I also wanted to spend more time with her.

We were just leaving the gym when Hunter, of all people, showed up. I knew he would not leave until we finished exchanging words, so in the end, Danielle's and my plan was aborted, and she drove herself to work. Trevor managed to ruin my day once again.

I got so frustrated with him, I began to jump rope to relieve the tension. As if by magic, King showed up as well. Some snitch (not Danielle, I was sure of that) must have called him, and told him I was running in the pouring rain.

King and Tre decided they were going to tag-team me for the rest of the day. I was in no mood to fight with them. On a whim, I called RJ; my son always helped me get back to my happy place. I arranged with Tameka to pick up my child this afternoon, thinking I would let Tre, his godfather, tag along. It would be good for Tre to observe my relationship with Tameka close-up. This way he would be reminded what I was enduring with this woman.

After I got off the phone with RJ, I realized I did not consult with Danielle about her weekend plans; I needed to call her and make sure it was okay with her. Not that I needed permission to pick up my own child, but I did not want to neglect her needs either. It was also imperative for her to understand RJ was a part of my life. We are a packaged deal.

"Hi, sweetie," Danielle said in greeting. She totally blew my focus. She kills me with her sweetness. It melts my heart every time she refers to me with a term of endearment.

After I finished talking with Danielle, Trevor and King both started in criticizing me. My instinct was to blast Trevor, but I stayed cool, waiting for a more opportune moment. It was an uncomfortable situation-- Tre and I hardly ever fight about anything, and when we do, it is never fun. I hated having tension between us, especially since this spat was essentially over a female. Worse, a female I could not have right now. Instead of fighting with me, I needed my friend to encourage me, and remind me that maybe one day, she would be a part of my life.

Once I let the two of them have their say, the mood lightened a little. Tre and I talked about going out for a ride, maybe getting a haircut. I pointed out that could wait until tomorrow, since I would have RJ with me; and, that way, we would be fresh for Sunday. It was still a bit tense between us, when Trevor spoke up.

"Hooks. Let's go check out some whips."

I was delighted at the thought. "Man, I thought you would never ask," I replied. "Not only are you a whip down, but I need to treat myself to a present for being allowed to fight again." I needed a pick-me-up, a celebratory gift to myself, one to commemorate my going back to the ring. I also wanted to celebrate my renewed relationship with Danielle. I wanted a toy. Toys distracted me. It was not as if I could spend my money on Danielle; I never knew what to buy her. Besides, she already has everything she wants. The things I wanted to buy her, like her own personal island, would imply a lot more than friendship.

In high spirits, I decided to call her. Really, I had nothing to say; I just dialed her number. Our conversation was so pleasant and so easy. Her magic kicked right in, and once again, I simply told her the truth. "I do not really know what I wanted to say or why I called," I admitted. "I just wanted to hear your voice." After Tre's interrupting us this morning, I felt like I needed to spend some time with her one-on-one. I wanted to get her true feelings and thoughts about me fighting again, now that it was finally official. It was one thing for her to say she felt okay about it, back when it was just a theoretical matter, but how did she really feel now? Everything was happening so fast; I was feeling unprepared. I arranged for us to talk on Sunday.

Then I remembered I owed her a pair of shoes. I told her to come pick up an envelope from the front desk of the gym to replace the pair I ruined. She sounded completely uninterested.

"Don't bother. I think I will get them polished next week."

"Not 'til next week?"

"I want to look at the scuffs today. Battle scars. Or shall I say the beginning."

"The beginning of what?" I asked

"Whatever you want to call it," she replied.

"I am not sure I follow you."

"The beginning of the millions of times you will tell me you love me."

"Oh. That." Suddenly, I was embarrassed.

"What's the matter? Were you not being sincere?"

I respected her asking, but this was just not a topic I wanted to cover right now. I was planning to have a real talk on Sunday; it sounded as if she could not wait until then. Yes, I did tell her I loved her on Wednesday, something I meant with all my heart. The trouble was I did not mean to tell her yet; I suppose I was not ready for the aftermath.

Either way, the cat was out of the bag. Nor had I let the cat out slowly and deliberately. I opened the bag, and out flew the cat. I needed to man up and face facts. Not only was it game time, it was fight time and face-time. Maybe it was better I was having to deal with all this over the phone, rather than on Sunday in person.

"Would you prefer to retract the statement?" Now she was playing it cool, all the sweetness in her voice having evaporated.

I could not retract for two reasons. One, I said it more than once; and two; I cannot retract it because it is true. Everyone knows you cannot un-say something in an effort to save it for later. I would lose every shred of credibility.

"No way do I want to retract," I told her. "Although I do wish I had done it differently. I would have preferred to say those words over a nice dinner alone. When I say alone, I mean me being alone without legal attachments. However, I said it when my heart was full and overflowing. Saying it made one of the most important nights of my life complete, by telling you exactly how I feel. Even so, I wish I had not said it to you while I was under a boat load of tears."

"Oh, Randall, you cry every week at church. You know you do."

That was even more embarrassing. Besides, shedding tears in church does not count as crying; that is what called *being full*. I switched it up on her.

"So, Danielle, what about you? Did you mean what you said? If not, you can tell me; it will not hurt my feelings."

She shut me down. "I want to talk about this face-to-face," she said. "It can wait until Sunday."

Really Danielle, come on. Why didn't she answer the question? She was not playing fair. I bared my soul, and now she refused to reciprocate. This would be hanging over my head all day long. All weekend, actually.

She must have sensed my distress, because mercifully, she relented. "Randall, of course I meant what I said and I said what I meant."

"Thank God." I held the phone to my chest. If Tre knocked on that door one more time, he was going to kick it down. I told Danielle I had to run, but I still wanted her to pick up a pair of new shoes at my expense. I am sure her shoes were going to cost more like a grand than a bill. Not that it mattered--she could have whatever she liked. I promised to leave an envelope at the front desk since I was the reason her shoes were scuffed when her feet kicked everything off my desk. Speaking of which, I thought, I should probably make sure everything still works in the office. After much thought, I placed two grand in an envelope and wrote her name on the outside. A note would have been overkill.

Tre and I headed out. Once we began to walk the car lots, our frustrations with each other evaporated. Car hunting was like make-up sex for us; we both forgot why we were angry. We went from one lot to the next, scoping out McLaren, Koenigsegg, Saleen S7 Twin-Turbo, Leblanc Mirabeau, Pagani Zonda, Bugatti Veyron and Porsche Carrera GT.

Trevor confessed he did not have approval from First Lady. I could not relate to what he was saying, but I respected it. In fact, I looked forward to having the same constraint myself someday. Obviously, I could have bought him a car right then and there, or at least offered to split the cost with him, but that would have been interfering. If he did not have approval to come home with a new whip, I knew enough to stay out of it. What's more, I did not want him or my crew to think I was trying to buy his approval of Danielle. I knew him well enough to know a car would not change his mind.

As for me, I desperately wanted the Bugatti. Since Tre was not buying anything, I decided to take it down to a reasonable notch. I needed my divorce to be final before I dropped a mil on a car. My thoughts drifted back to the McLaren. I did not have a Porsche, and Danielle seemed fond of them, so I took my time and looked over the Carrera.

Then I heard her scolding voice in my head, saying, *"Randall, you are out of control."* Therefore, I took the price tag down again, until Trevor began calling me hen-pecked. No matter, I did not feel insulted. This seemed to move him to a little confession.

"I am sure I will regret saying this, Hooks, but honestly I do like Danielle. I never said I did not. All I said to you was you needed to pull up. I am hanging with you all weekend to make sure you do. This weekend is a good weekend for you two to slip up. She is everything you need. You cannot keep your hands off her. Believe me, I can understand why," he smiled. "She is so smart, and to top it off, she is a genuinely beautiful person. I see what you see; we all see it. However, I want you to acknowledge the brick wall which still stands between you two, the one named Tameka. Until it is removed, I will keep after you." He winked. "You better hurry up and handle your business before she is taken."

I laughed. "That would be my luck. She has been single for four years, and now that I am interested, she will suddenly become unavailable. That scares me, Tre. It is why I am going hard in the paint. I need to make a statement. I need some leverage in case the next man comes around."

That reminded me how Tre actually encouraged Danielle to date other guys. I wanted to punch him in the face for that. However, I appreciated his continual reminder that I had to handle my business.

"You know what, Hooks? You are shameless. Telling her you love her in front of an audience." He was having fun now.

"I was overwhelmed, Tre, I was emotional. I plan on taking it back," I said, knowing I was lying. "Tre, they say you only live once. However, I feel like somehow I am starting life number two. The first one is dead and gone, and I am determined to make the best of this new one."

"Hooks, if I wasn't riding you so hard right now, you know full well you would be enjoying the luscious fruits of her labor. Your emotional state is pulling you toward physical intimacy. Tell the truth," Trevor urged me.

I confessed—yes, it had been a hard struggle for me last night. How desperately I needed her and wanted her. My body ached for her body.

Some kind of way, Tre and I went from my confession to praising the Lord for His goodness and mercy.

Then Trevor changed gears again. He gave me some lessons; I gave him back some truth. I had been patient with Tameka, but at heart, I was a fighter, and she started a war, I told him. I tried to battle nicely, but there was nothing nice about her anymore. I was ready for combat, and Danielle Rose was my prize at the end of the struggle. If it meant an ugly legal brawl for me and Tameka, then so be it. The time for her holding out on signing expired. I played it civilized up until now. At this point, it was every man for himself, blow for blow, pound for pound, and round for round. Anyway I looked at it, Tameka had to go.

Then we talked for a while about my calling. "I have three things I want you to take away from today," Tre said. "One, you are missing a calling. I know you have heard the voice of the Lord tell you to take it to the next level. You heard it a long time ago. Why are you not being obedient?"

I knew I had a calling on my life and so did he. However, I could not address it right now. Tre confessed he needed my help in the ministry. But right now, I needed his help. Then he did what Tre always does. He laid it out there.

"So, do you love her?"

My first thought was, *love who?* I knew he was not referring to Tameka; even so, I almost came to a complete stop on I-285. What did I say last night that was so unconvincing that everyone has to ask me to say it all over again? I am certain it was loud enough for everyone to hear me.

"Trevor, I have never felt like this before in my life," I told him, straightening the wheel, as other cars honked their displeasure. "I want this feeling to last forever. I never want it to go away. She makes me happy; all I want is to make her happy in return. She believes in me. She encourages me. She inspires me. She trusts me. She listens. She is smart. She is beautiful. She has her own, and she can hold her own. She is a woman of God. I need her, Trevor. I do not think I can live without her. Where has she been my entire life? I want to give her the world."

"Don't worry," said Tre. "When you find the right person, the feeling will truly last forever."

Later, he went with me to pick up Randall Junior. Tameka acted just as I knew she would--dismissive, sullen, and angry all at once.

Tre was sympathetic. "Hooks, I see you are correct. Your point is taken," he said referring to Tameka's behavior.

Back at the house, I realized I had not spoken to Danielle since early this morning, and by now, I was in serious withdrawal. I was not sure if I said something earlier to upset her, so I called. During our conversation, she asked how my day had been, and if Trevor and I enjoyed ourselves.

"Are things better with you guys?" she asked.

"Tre finally simmered down," I replied. "But only after he told me exactly how he felt."

Unexpectedly, she asked me what had I been doing for the last four years. I was shocked; I assumed she meant sexually. "Nothing," I said. It was the truth. I could tell she did not believe me. Being Danielle, she asked the same question, even more directly this time.

"Randall, what I mean is, what have you done *physically?*"

This girl had no fear. She went hard in the paint every chance she got. I better get used to it. I realized she was talking to me exactly how she spoke to her colleagues--direct and fierce. Now, I supposed she was testing to see if I would say the same thing, or be caught in a lie. I answered as best I could. I realized how strange it sounded, but I told her again I had not been with anyone intimately other than Tameka, not for the last four years, and truthfully, not for my entire life. Was she expecting me to expound further?

She sounded chastened. "I apologize for asking an inappropriate question."

Tre entered the room listening closely, of course, so I decided to take it down a little. "For the record," I continued, "there has not been another woman in my life. Not a friend, not a girlfriend, not a boo. Not even a friend who is a girl." Then, reminding myself what year it was, I added, "Nor a man, either, for that matter."

We agreed to continue the conversation Sunday. Clearly, we had a lot to discuss. By now, it was dark outside, and I knew she was out with her girls. I always worried about her safety. "Can I send someone to drive you all where you need to go?" I asked.

Of course, she refused the offer. I always hated it, though I cannot say whether my resentment arose from my always wanting to be in control, or from my wanting her to need me. Either way, I had to accept it.

"Don't worry—you can locate us any time you like," she said breezily.

She added jokingly, I could check her locator to see what her blood-alcohol levels were. Yeah I could. But only her levels, not those of the others in the car. That right there was the problem. I had no way to know who was driving, and I had to trust that no one would be drinking and driving. If so, hopefully she would call me for a ride. So much was riding on faith.

I felt the need to at least get her opinion. I was not looking for her approval, exactly; maybe I was hoping to get it. All of this was so new to me. Never before have I asked anyone for permission to do or buy something; normally, I buy what I want. I am not sure what I was expecting, but I knew I wanted her to trust me. In order for her to do so, I would have to adjust my routine.

So here I was asking a woman who is preparing to go salsa dancing if I could take my earnings and buy the car that I wanted. I sent her two photographs.

Her response, strong and loud, was an immediate: "Oh, *hell* naw!"

Like a disappointed child, I heard myself ask, "But why not?"

"Where is Hunter?" Clearly, she was done talking with me.

"Tre," I called out. He walked in, and I put my phone on speaker.

"My answer is no," her voice rang out. "The last time you two were out together, he came back with an Aston. You are sitting over there so worried about what he is doing with me, but not paying attention to what you are doing with him. I am checking you, Pastor. My final answer is HELL NO. Did you two hear me loud and clear?"

I think we both jumped. She was even harsher than Gabby was--and she was not my wife--not even, officially speaking, my girlfriend. Why was she so fired up about me and my love of cars? A sense of stewardship, maybe? Regardless, the man in me would not let me let it rest. I pressed her. "Will you think at least about it?"

That fired her up even more, and I had to take her off speaker, with her already having let loose one bad word—if another came out, Trevor might ban me from seeing her forever.

Given that she was out on the town with her girls, I decided I best let her get back to her fun. I ended the conversation with an "I love you," of course--not to score points toward getting my car, but because I meant it. There was no longer any shame in saying it.

It thrilled me when she reciprocated. "I love you, too, sweetie, and I need you." At that moment, I could have cared less about a Lamborghini.

Even so, I was fretful for the better part of the night. Not because I thought she was with another guy, but because this dating business was all so new to me. I refrained from calling her, but kept checking her levels and locations. If this was stalking, arrest me now. Finally, I sent Trevor home, and commanded RJ to take a shower. It was two AM. I finally gave in and texted her, to make sure they were all safe and headed home. "Yes, and yes," she texted back at once.

With that, I let out a sigh of relief, and walked outside onto the deck. It was a beautiful night sky, filled with stars--a night made for love.

I was settling down while RJ flipped the remote control, when my phone rang. It was Danielle, calling at three AM to let me know she was home. I was relieved to hear it, but utterly exhausted--either because of Trevor and all his chastisement, or from worrying about her. Probably a toss-up, I figured. We spoke briefly, and said our good nights. Before RJ and I went to bed, I made sure to blog.

Saturday

I sent out my daily inspiration. As I would soon discover, everyone was disturbed by my tone, especially Trevor. It seemed like a normal blog to me; apparently not.

I put in a call to Danielle, who was still sleeping.

"Rough night?" I asked.

"No, it's all good," she murmured. "I'm sleeping in. After all, it is Saturday."

"Here's why I'm calling. Today, you are going to be chauffeured wherever you want to go," I said.

"Randall, for heaven's sake. You don't need to do that," she protested.

"Look," I explained. "I miss you so much. I have to spend the day with Trevor, which means my day may not go all that well. It will make me happy to know *you* are having a great day. Please let me do this."

She agreed. I could hear sounds in the background, sounds of silky sheets and fluffy comforters being flung aside. It was far too early for my mind to be wondering, but instantly, visions of Danielle sent me to Wonderland. As always, she excited my mind, my body, and my soul. *Time to end this call.* After we hung up, I proceeded to wake my son.

I was already dressed. Like any kid his age, RJ was getting it together slowly. In my dining room, I discovered Trevor, King and Tony were already assembled at the table. Apparently, they were having a conversation about me before I got there. I could tell Hunter had an agenda, and from the look on his face, it did not look as if I was going to enjoy hearing about it.

"Randall, may I speak with you in your office for a moment," Tre said. It was an order, not a request. "King, Tony, join us please," he added.

This is going to be serious, I thought to myself. If so, let them wait for me, I thought angrily. After a few minutes of stalling, I met them in my office; tension was thick in the air.

"Tre, what's up?"

"I'm not sure, RW. Why don't you tell me?"

"What are you talking about?"

"Let's start with your blog."

"What about it?"

"It was, shall we say, a little disheartening."

"I wrote exactly what I was feeling, Trevor."

"It felt like an attack directly aimed at me."

"No, not directly at you, Tre."

"At the very least, RW, this morning's daily inspiration was not what I would call *inspiring*."

"So expressing myself honestly is not an inspiration to you?"

"Do we need to talk about this, RW? What's going on?"

"No, Tre--we do *not* need to talk about it. I think you have been very clear on how you feel; so have I. And I know precisely what your expectations of me are."

"That's where you're wrong, RW--they are not *my* expectations; they are mandates set by God. It is my duty as a friend and as your pastor to keep you on track with His mandates."

"If you think so."

"I detect hostility here, RW. What's really going on?"

I did not speak. Trevor knew what was going on.

"If we have a problem, Hooks, let's air it out."

"Trevor, the things you have said to me this week have been obnoxious and unnecessary. Should I be insulted? Should I feel privileged to have you as a friend? What I would really like is for you to be happy for me. But lately, you seem incapable of that."

King and Tony looked at each other and stirred uneasily. Hunter ignored them and addressed me sternly.

"Hooks, I have always been happy for you; you have done nothing to make me unhappy. However, my job as your friend and pastor is to keep you on track and to keep you focused. Challenges in life are going to happen, but they are not necessarily the workings of the enemy. All I am trying to do is to equip you to handle these challenges."

"Tre, right now all you are doing is adding to the drama. I don't do drama."

The room went silent. King's eyebrows were raised, Tony was pacing the floor, and Hunter was scanning his phone. I am sure I was giving everyone the death-stare.

Finally, Hunter burst into laughter. No one but me spoke. "I'm glad you find this amusing."

"My child," said Hunter, still chuckling. "Be patient with me. I speak to you as your pastor but also as your mentor. No one's life is, as you put it, *drama-free*. For it is written, you will have drama in your life. Nevertheless, if you live by the Word, your life will be *drama-proof*. The drama you seem to be encountering is by design. Your dilemma is tailor-made for you. The blueprint of your story has already been engraved—signed, sealed, and delivered long before you were ever born. Just as God designed your life, He can cancel or change it, though you yourself cannot.

"But RW, know that God hears your cries; He sees your faithfulness, and will reward you in due season. He desires not that you feel pain; rather, He wants to see how strong you are, and to test you in battle. Do not waste time and energy battling with yourself, me, Him or the crew. Now is the time for you to disarm and devise a new plan of battle. This test is giving you a testimony. Trust me, friend, He will pull you through this. I have prayed for you. Do not let your faith fail you now. God is waiting until the eleventh hour—the eleventh round, we might say. Trust me when I say He will come, but on His own time. You have to trust Him."

My day had not officially begun yet, but in the midst of all this, Keith—whom I assigned to watch over Danielle--was texting me minute-by-minute updates. I was not expecting her to be in touch, when to my surprise she texted me to let me know she and her girls were all at the spa. I needed the sunshine, given the lousy start of my day. Minutes later, she texted again, to let me know there would be no cute guy performing her spa services this time—unknown to her, I arranged for a woman to perform her services. Call me insecure if you want; to me, I was playing it safe. I could tell from the tone of her text she was not happy with my decision, but what other choice did she have? Keith would intercede on my behalf if she attempted to change masseuse.

The next call I received was from Keith or so I thought. Instead, it was from the girls. As soon as I said hello, they all sang "Hooooooks! Thaaaaank youuuuuuu!"

They were my little angels, looking after Danielle, entertaining her while I put up with my boys. The better I got to know her friends and family, the more I liked them.

If only my situation were different, I thought for the millionth time, all of this would have been so easy. Why, oh why, had I not met this woman fifteen years ago?

Meanwhile, my day with my fellows began to pick up. I was dying to swing by and check out those Lambos one more time, but why frustrate myself? Besides, we had a packed day. After we managed to get back onto the right track with each other, Trevor left to go prepare his sermon.

I decided to take RJ to dinner at the restaurant, since Keith informed me they would be there later. I tried to call a few times to find out if it was okay with her for me and RJ to come, but I got no answer. At the restaurant, I left RJ in my office to order dinner for himself, while I went out to the dining area.

I spotted her right away, out on the dance floor. I walked up behind her, gently placing my hand on her lower back, leading her out to the hall where we could talk. It felt like I was on a date. If RJ had not been with me, I would have happily stayed with her all night. Kids are sometimes your greatest blessing and sometimes your biggest curse. Right now, RJ was being a true blessing, by keeping me away from temptation and sin. The curse was that I was still tethered to the person who carried my son in her womb, and who would not let me go. However, this was not the end. Instead, fortified by Hunter's reassurance, I had to believe it was just the beginning.

As we stood there talking in the hallway, I was getting updates on her heart rate. I could see it was up, as was mine. I asked her which color, lemon or lime? Instead of answering, she demanded I get my accountant on the line. I was touched she cared enough to want to keep my finances in order. They spoke briefly; when she hung up, I could tell the answer was still a resounding "no."

I finally had no choice but to say good night. I met Keith outside the restaurant, and was shocked when he handed me a bag full of shirts and ties. More gifts? This girl was amazing. I went back to my office to get RJ and got caught up watching her on the monitors. Sure, it was stalking—but I could not help myself.

I prolonged staying as long as I could. RJ did not have a problem with it but I knew I had to go. It would not be right for him to stay at the club all night, and we both had to be at church early the next day. Besides, I do not hang out at my place all that much, certainly not to eat or drink. Obviously, I was only there to see her.

I got RJ in the car, still wanting to say good night to Danielle one last time, to hold her and kiss her. Instead, RJ and I headed home, having a good conversation the entire ride, not a word of which I could remember afterwards. She called to inform me I left the shirt she bought for me to wear tomorrow. I told her I would come for it in the morning.

I was not worried about them being out late. I knew she was safe with Keith, who was even stricter and tougher than King, though less boisterous. Keith did not speak much. I guess you could say he was G style, hitting first, asking questions later. With King, you saw him and heard him coming for you. He was more like a freight train, noisy and unstoppable. Keith, on the other hand, was like a thief in the night. You heard nothing and you saw nothing. All you knew was damage was done and a lot of it. Keith's job tonight was simply to treat her as if she were my most precious possession, ranking right up there with RJ. Tomorrow, I would see her again—once for service, and again with her family for dinner. The day seemed great before it even started. I lay there sleepless but filled with joy, thinking of her.

Sunday

Picking up my shirt provided me with a reason to arrive at her house early. Better to have been waking up there--but hey, this was the best I could do. I did not stay long, just long enough to drop off breakfast. I had already awakened to morning wood, no point in enhancing the problem.

I did do one thing as I was leaving, and then called her to let her know what I did.

"Hey, I left the Maybach in your driveway," I said. "The keys are inside."

There was no doubt, something had taken over me. Hell, I barely let the guys drive that car, and here I was leaving it in the hands of a girl. On the face of it, it made no sense. She teasingly asked me for the car once before; today I was granting her wish. Looks as if I was really pulling out all of the stops for this girl.

"What?" she yelled. "No sir! Come back here and get this car."

"You wanted it. Now you have it."

"Come get this car, Randall. And no, this doesn't mean you can get a Lamborghini."

"Hey, come on. Drive the car to church. Tell me what you think."

"No, I can't. I need a lesson before I drive it."

"Fine," I said disappointed. "Turn around," I instructed King. I had to admit, she was right; it was a good call on her part.

Instead, I wound up leaving her my Benz. I was not convinced she would agree to drive it either, given that she had her own garage full of luxury cars. All I was trying to do was give her what she asked.

At church, I was radioed when she pulled up to the lot. Seconds later, I got word Pastor was pulling in as well. *Nice.* This would give him something else to ride me about. I had nothing to hide. Besides, Tre and I kept no secrets from each other.

I strode out to the parking lot, and stood patiently waiting for her to exit the car. Tre, pulling into his own specially marked space, gave me a look which seemed to say a whole lot of different things, none of which I could clearly discern. She was sitting still in the front seat emailing and texting.

My patience was wearing thin. "Who are you texting," I asked jokingly, "your boyfriend?"

"Why? Are you jealous?" She smiled.

"Absolutely not. Unless you want me to break his neck into a thousand pieces."

At that, she quickly shut me down, reminding me I still had a wife. Ouch. That was a technical knock-out right there, I thought, feeling deflated. Normally, I would have struck back. However, not today.

No, today I was the perfect gentleman. "May I help you out of your car?" I asked politely although it was my car. I opened the car door, and took her arm; with a graceful swivel of her legs and hips, she was up and standing next to me.

Beautiful did not come close; no, she surpassed the word without even trying. The crazy part was she had been out all night; almost all weekend, in fact. Beauty, it seemed, just happened to her, like smart happened to people who never studied or went to class, but still got high marks. Danielle Rose was getting extremely high marks in my book.

"You look sexy and handsome, Deacon Washington."

She had a thing about referring to me as sexy. I have no idea why, but it made me blush every time. I consider myself an average person, nothing impressive, whereas she makes me feel spectacular. That was another thing she was good at, turning it on and off, the way I was "Randall" yesterday, and today I am "Deacon Washington."

Trevor, standing nearby doing his best to look like a drill sergeant, seemed to reach the end of his endurance. Instead of greeting his parishioners in his T-shirt, he should have been in his office by now. However, it would not have been Trevor if he did not embarrass me.

"Good morning, you two," he said, finally acknowledging us. "Very nice coordinating attire."

I could tell Danielle did not realize I was being subtly chastised, and on three accounts—first, because I was outside, not inside where I belonged; second because she and I were dressed alike again; and third, because she arrived in my ride.

I could have melted into the pavement; no thirteen-year-old could have been more embarrassed. I vowed right then never to humiliate my child in front of his peers. I shot Trevor the look of death. It made me feel good to see a flicker of fear in his eyes as he walked away.

Inside, as I escorted Danielle to her seat, she caught me off guard with an unexpected remark of her own: "Don't let me catch you out there flirting, Deacon Washington."

What? Does she think I am a flirt? Maybe I need to be more circumspect in my behavior. The last thing I want to be called is "the flirting deacon." Truly, I have never held an inappropriate conversation with anyone here. Note to self: this is one more thing I need to discuss with her later today.

I raced to my office and put my jacket on. Gave a quick prayer with the other Deacons, and then jetted to Hunter's office to jump in while they were covering him. I needed no nonsense from him right now. As soon as I arrived back at my seat in the sanctuary, I made eye contact with Danielle. I was sitting up on my knees like always, trying hard not to stare; but it was not working. Even when I focused hard on something else, my eyes and my thoughts swung right back to her. I admit it, women are not my forte—not because I am not interested, but because I have been tied down with a ball and chain for most of my adult life.

A few weeks ago, I had no idea I would end up here, in the middle of service, trying to avoid eye contact with a woman, trying not to inhale her fragrance, which was overpowering--but in the best way possible.

Up front, Pastor did everything in his power to get my attention. I was determinedly ignoring his antics, when before I knew it, I looked up and saw him standing in the aisle between us. He placed his hands on each of our shoulders, shifting his weight from side to side. *This was low down,* I thought furiously; *why drag her into it?* His beef was with me; we men could handle this outside of the sanctuary. I could not believe Trevor sunk to such a childish level.

I gave it right back to him during the sermon, making sarcastic remarks like, "Really, Pastor?" I felt close to clipping him up, and started kicking my leg out, obstructing his path--no harm intended. As he was wrapping his sermon up, I looked around, and realized that to the rest of the congregation, this was business as usual. Whereas to me, it was a shaping up to be a fight. Tre played dirty this morning, hitting way below the belt.

When Pastor instructed us to grab our neighbor's hand, before I knew it I was knocking over King and Keith, reaching across the aisle to seize Danielle's hand. Her hand felt so fragile, and I was squeezing it so hard, I feared I might be hurting her, but I could not let go. My crew did not know what to do, and I could tell they were feeling awkward, but I did not care. During the benediction, Tre did something he has never done before—he walked down to where Danielle and I were, and wrenched our hands apart. He took each of our hands and squeezed both of them so hard it hurt. It was all I do not to punch him.

As soon as service was over, Tre sent Jon-Jon to summon me to his office. No need to tell me, I snapped; I am on my way right this second. Hunter was off the chain today. *If he were not a pastor*, I thought. I hated to think what this meeting was about to be like.

As soon as I walked in, I saw Danielle sitting there as well. "Let's go," I said to her, feeling a fresh surge of anger. Right as we were leaving, Tre walked in. It felt like I was being robbed. *Man, your beef is with me, do not mess with women and children*, I telegraphed him with my eyes. He ignored me, even though he knew the look, having seen it many times before. He was the first to define it, and right now, he was defying it. "Man," I said before he cut me off.

"Sit down, you two," Tre said calmly. "I want to talk to her."

Why? For what? To grill her? To make her feel as if she has sinned? To make her feel lower than a harlot? He has no right to judge her. We have all sinned, including him. Though a pastor, Tre has been touched by the same infirmities that touch us all. Why is he acting so brand new?

I told him the truth, and added, "There's nothing going on between us."

"Well, then, why can't I talk to her?" he smirked.

Danielle, her eyes smoldering, spoke up angrily. "Excuse me, but you all seem to have forgotten that I am right here. I am a little confused—is this a pastoral conversation, or a let's embarrass RW and Dani meeting?"

Her anger only seemed to amuse Trevor.

"You may go, RW," he said, not looking at me.

"Not today, my friend," I snapped. "I am not leaving her alone with you. You want to chastise someone; you talk to both of us."

"Okay. Let's start with the color-coordinated outfits." *If he were so observant and brilliant, he would have noticed that weeks ago*, I thought.

"Man, stop it," I said.

"I just want to let you two know how it looks."

"How does it look, Trevor?" My voice rose.

"IN-AP-PRO-PRI-ATE."

"So you can enunciate. The praise team was also dressed alike, and no one seemed to care," I shot back.

"I don't like your tone, RW."

"I don't like your accusations, Tre." The truth is, I was cool with what he was saying. I just wanted him to say it behind closed doors with the two of us. "Hold your horses, Tre. I get where you are coming from, but your attitude has gotten a little fetid towards Danielle and me. Can you take it down a few notches?" I was struggling hard to be nice.

Tre laughed. "Man, you all are dressed alike. You cannot do that-- it sends the wrong message. Absolute wrong message. Unacceptable."

He strode out of the office. We looked at each other in confusion. Seconds later, he was back, carrying two plates of fresh fruit. One plate he passed to Danielle, which she ignored; the other he held out in my direction. I took a handful of grapes.

"Look, I am not accusing anyone of anything. However, you two are dressed alike, and what is more, if I am not mistaken, that was your ride she pulled up in this morning. RW, it seems pretty cut and dry if you ask me."

"Tre, if I was not your boy, you would never pay any attention to this. I—we—appreciate your advisory. However, know we are still in order. Let it ride."

Danielle spoke up. "Pastor, it looks like you two Boy Scouts have this under control. If you do not need me for anything more, I have my crew waiting on me." I said nothing. Trevor, being a married man, likewise should have had the sense to keep quiet.

Alas, he did not. "Make sure I get the memo next week on the color scheme," he said, smiling nastily. The look she gave him, though out of line, was just what he deserved. I mean, if looks could kill, he was stinking in the grave.

"You lose," I whispered to him.

Danielle did not stop with a look. She proceeded to rip Trevor so bad it was almost funny. How I loved her spunk. She gave Trevor exactly what he gave her, and showed no more respect to him than she had to King.

"I will call you later," I told her, trying to get my thoughts together, before deciding there was no point in letting Trevor's presence inhibit me. "Wait, Danielle, let me walk you to the car. How rude of me not to have offered."

"Your car," Trevor mumbled.

To Trevor, I added, "I will be back."

I could see RJ waiting at the other end of the hall. I wanted to introduce him to Danielle, but figured that might constitute an overload on a day like this one. We made our way over to her girls, and I asked, "Ladies, any requests for dinner?"

"Yes. Solid food," Sade shot back.

"Is fish good?"

"That'll work. Although it does not require much chewing. Not all that solid," Leigh laughed. I confirmed dinner arrangements before walking them to my car. Then, true to my word, I headed back to the torture chamber.

Tre gave me a look. "Hen-pecked," he said, shaking his head.

"No, I am not. Not yet anyway."

"You got your hands full, son. This is going to be interesting—you have truly met your match. She is not going to lie down and take it from you."

I laughed aloud. "I am glad you say so. Fact is, I would love for her to just lie down…and give it to me." That was wrong for me to say, and I knew it. I blushed. Trevor was not only my pastor; he was also my friend, and this is how friends talk to each other. Perhaps for that reason, he seemed to have a change of heart.

"I am not sure how to respond."

"Tre, lay hands on me."

He stopped dead in his tracks. Removed his glasses. Took his towel from JJ and wiped his head. "Lay hands? I could rub all the oil in Canada on you. I could take my Alabaster, yours, Danielle's and Mary's. I could grease you until we fry could chicken off your forehead and it still would not be enough. You need to be immersed. Over and over and over again."

I looked at him, and all I could do was laugh. He was probably right. Either way, my remark was a good icebreaker, and we ended our meeting on peaceful terms.

As I was rode back to the house, Danielle lay heavy on my mind. I tried calling her, but she did not answer. Finally, I called her landline; Leigh answered, and reported that Danielle had gone to the track. I knew why--she was walking off her anger at the conversation with Trevor.

RJ was with me, so I had to make a quick decision. I did not mind my son meeting her; but I was not sure she was ready to meet him.

One thing I was knew was I did not want Trevor, my best friend, to become a wedge between us. I decided all of us—RJ, King, and myself--would head for the track. There was not much time; I was to be at Danielle's home for dinner by five, but I felt like the two of us needed to wipe the slate clean and start the day fresh.

Before I knew it, King and RJ were out of the car, horsing around. I ordered them to get back in and quiet down. Danielle saw us pull up, and stood quietly waiting for me on the other side of track.

I lifted her sunglasses, and saw the redness around her eyes. "Danielle, please. Do not do this right now. I cannot be weak; I have my child with me. Give me a few hours, and you can cry as much as you want, yell as much as you want, curse me as much as you want. Please help me, Lord." Next thing I knew, she threw herself down and was lying on the ground. This was killing me--all of it, every part of it. From beginning to end. "King," I yelled, "I will catch you and RJ down the street." I bent over to touch her. "Danielle, get up. Please let me take you home." Perhaps she heard my mounting desperation; for whatever reason, she agreed to go home and get some rest.

By the time I showed up at her house for dinner she was still sound asleep, passed out on the sofa. I could not believe how this rebellious, hardheaded, self-sufficient woman followed my instructions for once. The thought made me smile. She was a hard, sugar-cone shell on the outside; but inside, she could be as soft as ice cream melting on a hot summer's day.

I started the grill with the ladies helping. After we got everything going, I sat on the end of the sofa and lay Danielle's feet gently in my lap as I stared at her. She murmured in her sleep. Outside, the girls were making a lot of noise, and my first instinct was to tell them to take it down. Then I decided I was the guest; therefore, I stayed quiet. Whatever was going on, I was sure they could handle it. Danielle, slowly waking up, struggled to move, and then realized I was holding her feet down. She looked at me and smiled peacefully. I went out to check the food, and by the time I returned she was sitting up.

"You might want to check in the kitchen," I told her. "There's something in there for you." It had to do with something she mentioned the night before. She and her girls had a conversation, which ended up with me being sopped up "like a biscuit and syrup." I have to admit I was embarrassed at the time--but it was quite a compliment.

Therefore, I had to flush her back. She took it back Georgia G style, so I did what only a G would do—I provided some biscuits and Karo syrup. It was my way of saying that not only did I adore her, but also I felt the same way about her. Honestly, I did not need biscuits and syrup for what I planned to do to her one day—syrup could prove a little too messy. I had enough saliva of my own to saturate what I needed to moisten. No, make that "drench." *Enough Hooks!* I smacked myself across my own cheek, embarrassed at my thoughts.

During dinner, I was struck once again by the conversation around the table. I could not decide if it was more like hanging out with the Golden Girls, Charlie's Angels, the crew from Facts of Life, or Destiny's Child. They sure kept it real, and it was fun being with them—better, I thought, than being with my own crew.

Seven o'clock drew near. I loved these girls, and hated to be the bad guy, but I still needed to talk to Danielle alone. I politely asked them to give us some space. They took my request semi-well, wasting as much time as possible before leaving us. We stood outside and watched them go as if we were seeing our kids off to college.

Now that it was just the two of us, my old problem was back; I had to touch her. I loved putting my hand around her waist and lower back. It seemed like the perfect resting place for a boxer's hands. We wasted as much time standing on the front porch as we could. I had to get up the courage to move us back inside the house.

First, we cleaned up the kitchen. She sat on the counter as I dried the last dish. For some reason, watching her in the kitchen was turning me on. God was really trying and testing me. Reluctantly, I suggested we go outside. It was a beautiful night; I was with a beautiful woman. What more could I ask? Besides, I knew I would be safe outside.

Sitting on her front porch under a canopy of stars, I got up my courage. "Danielle," I asked, "is something bothering you?"

She did not answer.

"Do not do this, Danielle." She was silent. I sat up and turned to face her, but she refused to look in my direction.

"Talk to me," I whispered. "Danielle."

"Yes."

"Please tell me what is bothering you. I cannot fix it if I do not know what is broken."

"I don't know where to start."

"Anywhere." I was not prepared for what came next.

"I do not think I can do this," she said, still not looking at me.

I swallowed hard. Before I could reply, she spoke again.

"I have worked so hard and so long to avoid being hurt."

"Danielle, I have no intention of hurting you," I protested. Truly, I did not. Why did she think I did? This stabbed me like a dagger in my heart.

"Randall, the situation is overwhelming," she continued.

"Overwhelming? How?"

"I wasn't expecting for anyone to show up in my life and turn it upside down, all topsy-turvy like this."

"Topsy-turvy? Is that good...or bad?"

She did not hesitate. "Option two."

My heart was pounding. I slid my fingers under my watch to try to hold it up away from my wrist; the last thing I needed now was a call from King about my levels.

"Come on, Randall, let's be real."

This was going downhill fast. Had sleep changed her thought process? Was this all because of Trevor? I was lost. She seemed to be telling me that she cared a lot about me, but it was a bad thing, not a good thing. I needed a time-out; in the boxing world, I needed the bell to ring. I needed help from The Father, The Son, and The Holy Spirit; but right now, I would take JJ, King and Trevor. I needed coaching; I had no clue of what I had gotten myself into.

"If I could make this divorce happen today, would we be having this conversation?"

She was not backing down.

"I can't say it isn't an issue, Randall. I like to live a simple life."

She did not stop there.

"Randall, you know me--I work hard, and I play hard. Drama has no place or purpose in my life. I like it that way, and that is how I want to keep it. I do not need all this BS. I got Pastor riding me like a jockey in the Kentucky Derby. My heart is racing as if I am in the Indy 500. And all this because of a guy who may one day be available--or who may not."

Her response got me a little pissed. "What is this really about? Me? You? Tameka? Or Trevor?" I was trying to remain calm. With each question I asked, she came back harder.

"You don't understand. I do not want to get caught up."

What was she being caught up in? What did I need to do to show her I was serious? She bounced around words like *mess, drama* and *BS,* until I could not keep up--it was blow, jab, uppercut, and then hook after hook, back to back to back. At last, she came at me with the worst of all: *pull up*.

I sat back in my seat struggling for composure. "What do you mean by pull up? I do not see that happening, Danielle." Now she was bringing out the "I quit you" words. Did she honestly think we could rewind what we had done? Having pushed all my buttons, having poured gasoline all over my soul, she proceeded to light the match. Yes, she said; she wished we could go back to the first day when she pulled into the church parking lot.

I put my finger to her lips.

"Danielle, please, let me speak. Hush. I love you. I love you right now, just as we are, more than I have ever loved anyone in my life. I cannot let you go. It would destroy me. Earlier today, you called me the church flirt. I have never ever had a conversation other than normal church business with anyone there. You are the first and last woman at the church I have spoken to outside of those walls. I promise, I will never talk to anyone again if it makes you feel better. Just say the word."

I rubbed my aching head. She and Trevor drained me today. I could have fought five guys today and feel less exhausted than I feel right now. All I could say was *f**k*. I rarely speak bad words; that is not my style. She shifted gears, and the next thing I knew I was yelling.

"What in the hell am I supposed to do, Danielle?" I yelled. Instantly, I felt terrible. "I am so sorry. Forgive me for yelling. That was rude and inappropriate."

Before I knew it, I was yanking her chair closer to me. Sometimes I forget how strong I am; anger makes me stronger.

"Let me tell you this, Deacon Washington," she yelled. "I wish I had gone with my first mind and turned around that day at the church."

That felt like a slap; it was as if she spit in my face. I quickly went from Randall to Deacon Washington. She took my hands, looking at me steady again. "Please don't misunderstand me. I do love you, Randall; but I do not want to get hurt. I do not want to disappoint God. I want your good name to remain unblemished. Nor do I ever want to deal with your groupies. If I don't back out now, it will be too late."

"Oh, Danielle. What am I going to do?" I could only think of one question. "Do you not want to see me anymore?"

"I want to see you every day. From the rising of the sun until the going down of the same. But I can't."

I could tell she spoke from the heart. I could see it in her eyes and hear it in her voice. She remained unemotional. I knew she was sincere, but struggling with this conversation just as I was. However, I respected the fact that she attempted to shake it off. That was an important gesture. There would be numerous situations and occurrences where she would be required to shake the dust off. The main place would be at church. I tried to act and pretend as if I was not aware of the female attention I received, but I was clearly aware of it. I learned over the years to expect it and ignore it. Most people you ignore finally give up and go away. Hopefully, she would learn to ignore them also. Right now that seemed increasingly unlikely.

"Can we take it day by day?" I asked. "I respect what you are saying. I get how you feel. But I will never be able to walk away from you. I have so many things planned for us, Danielle. Do you want to spend the rest of your life with me?"

I took it old school, and wrote on a piece of paper: *Do you want to spend your life me? Check the box.* She ignored my "yes" and "no" boxes, and wrote *maybe*. At least it was not a "no." Eventually, we wore ourselves out talking, and sat in silence. I could have sat there with her until the sun came up, but I knew it would not help. "I should leave," I said at last. We said a quick goodbye, and I walked to my car.

Sure enough, a neighbor was standing outside watching us.

"Hi," she called gaily, waving her hand.

I looked closer. I threw my hand up with hesitation. The paparazzi was the last thing I needed Trevor or Tameka's attorney to see. "Have a good night," I said as pleasantly as I could manage. I wanted to get in my car and ease my mind before I pulled off. However, Benita Butrell was not taking no for an answer.

She addressed me loudly. "You doing okay this evening?"

"I sure am. Thank you for asking. And you?"

"I am doing wonderful."

"Great. Have a good night."

"Say, is Dani home?"

"Yes. She is."

"How is she doing?"

"She is great. I will tell her you asked about her."

"I don't see her much these days, now that you two have started dating," the nosey neighbor added.

What was going on here? I did not want to say, no, we are not dating—that would have put Danielle in an awkward position. I needed to be careful; after all, I was still married. The best I could manage was, "I wish I was that lucky. She has not agreed to date me yet."

"Oh, Mr. Hooks. She would love to date you--every woman in the world would."

I laughed. "Thanks. That is very generous of you."

"Do I need talk to her?"

I laughed again. "No, thank you, I think I have it under control," I lied.

"Well, when is the wedding?"

Talk about hard in the paint. "I do not think that will be necessary. Thank you kindly for the offer."

"If you need my help, just let me know."

"I sure will."

"Tell Dani I said hello."

"Will do. I will call her as soon I get home." I purposefully said *home* so she would know we lived in separate places. From the way it sounded, I did not have to stress it. Benita Butrell was already aware.

"We should all have dinner together sometime."

"I will have Danielle make arrangements."

"Great. I would love for you to meet my husband."

This was turning into a fiasco. I sat in my car for a minute, rubbing my aching head, when a light went on; now, Miss Nosey Neighbor was back in her open doorway next to a sleepy-looking older man, presumably her husband.

Was no one going to let me have a moment of peace today? I threw my hands up, and pulled out. All of this was so new to me. Now I was "dating," or so her neighbor thought. I cranked up the radio—it was Trey Songz, singing, *I bet the neighbors know my name.* They sure did. I burst out laughing, feeling a little better.

I got home and expressed myself the only way I could: I blogged.

WEEK 17

Monday

I started the day the same way I had ended my night, blogging.

I am cool by myself, but so much better when are together. Like hot and cold, neither of us is great alone, but we work well when mixed together. You take me higher. You bring out the best in me. Give me time. Before long, I will change your life. They will call

181

you the Deacon's wife.

I was still feeling low about our conversation the night before. Undeniably, I was still married. I decided we needed to talk; it was too early to call, but I hoped she would be awake.

She answered on the first ring. "Our conversation troubled me last night," I said. "I hope I did not anger you. Good luck with your presentation," I added before I hung up. "You know you are a winner."

"Why, thanks for the encouragement, champ. Between us two, really you are the winner. So why not keep it simple, and just call me the Deacon's wife?"

I blushed. Her saying it gave me hope that someday it would come true. If she did not want it or did not believe in it, why else say it?

Around eleven PM, I found myself back at her door. No special reason—I wanted to say goodnight. I nearly thought better of it, and started to turn around and leave, until I remembered who would likely be watching—her nosey neighbor, Mrs. Benita Butrell and her surveillance system. Leaving so soon might look suspicious and stalker-ish. I had better stick with my original plan.

After we greeted, hugged and chatted briefly, then we said our good nights. I went back to the house, sat down, and shot some thoughts into cyberspace. Often it helped me sort things out to write them down.

> If I had known this was coming, I would have been prepared. My status would have changed long ago. I was blindsided—but in the best imaginable way possible. BY LOVE!

Tonight, I was having trouble finding the right words to describe my present relationship with Danielle. So I composed a series of missives addressed to my Heavenly Father, Pastor Hunter, King, JJ, Keith, myself--and of course Danielle. I desperately wanted everyone to understand the big picture, not just the present moment. I wanted them to see, as I could, beyond today with all its difficulties and into the future. If I had to, I could wait four more months—even four more years. The point was that I was not going to give up.

If the worst came to pass, and after the waiting Danielle were no longer available, well—I would wait some more. It was only fitting that I would have to take my own turn at waiting, since that was what I was asking her to do right now. I would never, ever stop waiting for this woman; she was that dear to me.

Between writing these personal letters, I kept blogging. Everything seemed to require more words to explain than I anticipated. One thing I carefully avoided mentioning were the failings and infractions of those to whom I wrote. I brought up no details, neither happy nor sad, of their own personal tribulations. I wrote only about how I felt; and I asked my friends for mercy and understanding. I asked for their forgiveness. Mainly, I asked for their blessings.

Tuesday

No one other than Trevor knew what today would bring. Last night, I received a call. To my shock and disbelief, it was one of the lawyers representing Tameka; their client agreed to meet my team today. Tameka decided she was ready to sign the divorce papers.

I did not sleep a wink the night before. All morning I tried not to get my hopes up; there was no telling which of my wife's crazy antics might be awaiting me. For the exact same reason, I did not share the news with Danielle. Tameka pulled stunts like this before, which never turned out happily. The woman was completely unpredictable.

As I dressed, it felt like the old days--as if I were preparing for a fight. King and I arrived at the law office early. Once the proceedings began, the preliminary procedures seemed to drag on forever. It was starting to look as if what should have been a simple agreement between two reasonable people would turn into another all-day, Tameka-style train wreck. As the hours dragged on, my phone must have lit up a hundred times with a text or a call from Danielle and JJ who waited anxiously at the gym for an update. Obviously, I could not talk to Danielle; involving her at this point would have been impossible, not to mention mentally exhausting. All I could do was try to stay focused—and pray.

I was almost at my wits end, and ready to let loose with a stream of obscenities, when Tameka finally relented. After a whispered conference between her and the head of her legal team, it was announced she accepted the terms of the negotiation.

In shocked disbelief, I watched her reach into her designer bag, pull out my Mont Blanc fountain pen, and make ready to sign her name. She wrote hastily, scratching out her signature in what I imagined was her worst possible penmanship. I could have cared less how she signed the piece of paper. *She signed*--that was all that mattered.

I reached over, snatched the Mount Blanc pen from her hand, and signed my name in the biggest letters that would fit in the space allotted. Then I picked up the paper and kissed it. I felt beaten up, bruised, and bloody—but finally, I won!

I shook Tameka's attorney hand, buttoned my jacket, and thanked my attorney. King was on his feet, shooting an angry look at the person who was, finally, my *ex-wife*. I walked out feeling victorious; who cares how much it cost me? The bill would come soon enough. All I knew was I finally had what I wanted. I was single and free. I made it to the elevator before I realized King was not with me. I doubled back to find him and Tameka facing each other, engaged in a shouting match. I burst out laughing; knowing the two of them could go like this for days.

"King," I called to him, "I'll be in the car. Don't be too long."

I crawled into the back seat and laid my head on the seat rest. Suddenly exhausted, I burst into tears. I gave thanks to my Heavenly Father, thanking Him for the good and the bad alike, then praising Him for what was to come. I heard the car door open and shut. Then the engine purred as King started the ignition.

"Home, please."

"Yes, boss."

We rode in silence. Once we pulled in, I wiped my face, straightened my tie, and read the texts from Danielle. "Let JJ know I will be here for the next few days," I told King. "Please do not disturb me unless it is an emergency."

"Yes, sir."

"Thank you."

"Hooks, do you need anything?"

"Thanks, I am fine. But if I do need anything, I will call you."

"Congratulations."

"Much appreciated."

Before I got out of the car, I hit send on the brief text I composed to Danielle. All it said was, *"It's final. She signed."*

I let myself in; everything in my house suddenly seemed different. It was as if I had never been here before. I changed into a pair of jeans and a T-shirt, went out onto the deck, and sat there with my eyes closed. I prayed to God for guidance on the next part of my journey.

My phone rang. Of course, it was Danielle. "Hello."

"Can you open the gate?"

"Where are you?" I ran to the monitor to check, as I hit the code to open the gate and raced outside.

"Congratulations," she cried.

"What are you doing here?"

"Am I not invited?"

"You never need an invitation."

"I came to celebrate. Is that okay?"

I was not expecting a celebration. My plan was to sit on the deck, alone in the darkness, until the sun finally came up. Then maybe just sit some more, until the sun went down. Then came up again. I was that exhausted.

Danielle's sudden sweet presence showed how wrong all that was. This was a moment to savor. I felt boundless energy course through my body and spirit, lifting me up.

"This wonderful. I am so happy you are here," I said, meaning every word.

She pulled from her bag a bottle of nonalcoholic champagne.

"You are so thoughtful," I told her. "But I propose today, this once, we drink alcohol. This has been a long time coming, Danielle."

Realizing we were still standing in front of the house, I walked her inside, still feeling dazed. Was this really happening? One woman walked out of my life and another walked right in. Had my long nightmare finally turned into a dream come true?

Perhaps sensing my bewilderment, Danielle cried, "Let's celebrate!"

"I'll get dressed," I said, heading toward my bedroom to change.

"Wait."

She pulled something out of her bag and held it up.

"What in the hell is that?"

"A swim suit, silly man."

"Says who?"

"Shut up! Says Victoria Secret. We are going swimming, Randall. Change your clothes," she instructed.

"Why should I?" I asked. I walked through the kitchen doors onto the deck, and jumped into the pool, fully clothed. Without a second's hesitation, she jumped in after me. When we both bobbed up from under the water gasping, we were floating face to face. I leaned my forehead against hers. Our lips almost touched.

I felt the need to make a formal request.

"Danielle, may I kiss you?"

"Do you have to ask?" she said as we kissed for the first time.

Finale

For almost my entire life, I have been a fighter. I can conquer any enemy, overcome any obstacle, do battle in any war. I can stand before huge crowds and disrobe without shame. I can speak to millions without a moment's hesitation.

Yet knowing the day has come when I must finally share my love to the world has me terrified. I am weak; my hands are shaking; my palms are sweating, and my knees are knocking. I am, to put it bluntly, a complete basket case, all because of a girl. A certain girl who has turned my world completely upside-down. I will never be the same after today.

Luckily, all of my fighter's training and conditioning has paid off—all the years spent running, jumping rope, doing cardio; all the weight training, strength training, shadowboxing, and bag training. With all of these disciplines, I see now, I was not just training my body; I was also conditioning my mind, my thoughts, my heart, my emotions, my soul, my habits, my routine, my spirit, my faith, and my flesh.

All of this hard work was to prepare for her, for my new life, and for the journey I am about to begin. I have been cut down and built back up. After years of pruning and purging, I am finally prepared.

It has been a hard task. Yet the long-awaited moment is finally here, and I am ready. The time has come. I am hyped! After a long silence, I speak to the man in the mirror. **"LET'S GET READY TO RUMBLE!"**

www.ingramcontent.com/pod-product-compliance
Lightning Source LLC
Chambersburg PA
CBHW022113170626
46808CB00002B/717